TROVE

TROVE

Peter Smalley

W · W · NORTON & COMPANY · INC ·

NEW YORK

Library of Congress Cataloging in Publication Data
Smalley, Peter, 1943–
    Trove.
    I. Title.
PZ4.S6383Tr   1978   [PR9619.3.S537]   823   78–13654
ISBN 0–393–08835–9
1 2 3 4 5 6 7 8 9 0

'Seek, and ye shall find.'

Matthew 7:7

to Clytie

Contents

This book was written with the help of a literary fellowship from the Literature Board of the Australia Council.

TROVE

Prologue

A traced pink line stretched across the sky in the afterglow of sunset. The jet, flying north at thirty-five thousand feet, was invisible in the luminous expanse; only the contrail, fading even as it appeared, bore witness to its high, rushing flight. Storton House lay quietly in the gathering gloom below.

Daley woke and reached for the light on the small wooden locker by his bed. The light was not there. The locker was not there. Blindly, in instant panic, he flailed about him. His left arm hit a light shade above his head. Punching at it with his fingers, he managed to locate the switch. Brilliance shattered the darkness, and hurt his eyes. For a moment he saw nothing, and sat up, a quaking figure bathed in white light. The locker was on the wrong side of the bed. It was the wrong shape, and was made of metal, The bedstead, to which the light was attached, was also metal. There were too many pillows. Everything was white, even – he stared across the room – the floor.

"What?" he said aloud. Then he found the buzzer, a teat on a long cord. Frowning, he pressed it. A muffled buzz beyond the white door made him blink and stare. Still he could not understand where all this was going on. When the door opened and a middle-aged female nurse appeared, he knew that he was not dreaming.

"You're awake, Mr Daley," she said superfluously, but her voice was pleasant.

"My do how you name?" said Daley. "Know?"

He was aware that the words had not come out in the right order, but felt an urgency only to understand what was happening to him. Surely the woman could put them in the right order for herself.

"Mmmm?" he said, turning his head to hear what she said; she had not replied.

"It's all right," she said. "Slowly does it." She moved forward and straightened the covers, and picked up a fallen pillow.

"Um . . ." said Daley. "No . . . What I wanted to here is say why? Understand?"

"Oh, I see," said the nurse. "You don't remember coming here."

"I didn't," said Daley emphatically. "I didn't come here." He shook his head. "How the hell did I get here?"

"In an ambulance," said the nurse. "You had quite a time of it."

"Time of what?" demanded Daley, irritation rising up in his stomach. "Why don't you just straight answer."

"You've been drying out," said the nurse. "You slipped crossing a street, and fell, and cracked three ribs for yourself. Then you went into DTs, and you were brought here."

"What are you talking about DTs?" said Daley with scorn. "I must have hit my head."

"You did. You had a severe concussion. That, combined with the blood alcohol level, nearly finished you off."

Daley sat up further, and glared at the nurse. He felt exhausted and weak. He sighed involuntarily.

"Stop," he said. "Stop. I want to leave in the morning. Understand?"

"You might want to do a lot of things," said the nurse with a smile. "But you won't be able to do them tomorrow."

"You mean, you're keeping me here, no matter what I say? I've got rights, you know!" Daley sank back, panting, feeling dizzy. "Bloody rights, bloody rights . . . bloody . . ." Tears formed in his eyes.

"I'll give you a tablet to swallow," said the nurse gently. "It'll help you to sleep."

"I don't want to sleep, you bloody white-uniformed bitch!" said Daley in a passionate, drained voice. He felt that his face was white, that his entire body was pure white, all blood gone; his life was as white as the room he lay in.

The nurse went away and returned, as she had promised, with a tablet and a glass of water. Firmly, with friendly little movements, she helped Daley to sit up and take the tablet. He was too weak to resist, or complain. A few minutes later, when the nurse had gone, he sank below the surface of the white ocean and knew nothing. But not for long.

Electric tiddleywinks flew in tight, swift arcs through a silent barrage of red, green, purple, yellow, and blue flashes. Monstrous birds, topheavy, slowly tumbled upside down and flew on absurdly small wings, twittering. A huge black fish rose from behind a rock and swallowed a multi-coloured umbrella. Sirens moaned sadistically as great steel engines chugged and spat, drivebelts hissing and snapping. A man carrying a stone jug appeared on top of a rise, and poured water over a dry rock face. The water sluiced down the rock, then was abruptly absorbed, leaving no trace of moisture.

A gargoyle, its face set in a hideous grimace, vomited orange, fizzing fluid. A spaceship sent a ray and pulverized it, leaving only an oily patch which steamed slightly. The sun became very hot, and burned a line of smocks hanging in mid-air. Smoke drifted in a canyon, and was turned to grey sleet in a sudden blizzard.

On the fourth morning after his memory returned, Daley said to the doctor who came at eleven o'clock, on his rounds: "Listen, can you arrange with the matron or the nurse, or whoever it is, for me to have something to drink with my meals?"

"No," said the doctor. "No alcohol is permitted here. The nurses have explained that to you."

"But listen, it's OK," said Daley. Almost as he said it, he realized that his voice had a wheedling tone. Briefly, he despised himself; he began to cry.

"It's all right," said the doctor. "You're still pretty weak."

"But why? Why?" wept Daley, when the doctor left him alone. "Why am I so weak?" He lay quietly for an hour, dozing off every few minutes, and waking each time with a start, as if an electrical charge had passed through his body. "Why am I so bloody weak?" he muttered, over and over.

"You must try and rest, Mr Daley," said the nurse who came to check his pulse every hour. "You're still very weak."

"Look, I know I'm weak," Daley told her cuttingly. "The question is, why?"

"Open your mouth, please."

"Go to hell."

"Your temperature can't take itself, Mr Daley."

"I'll do it," said Daley, holding out his hand. "I'm not helpless." But when the nurse gave him the thermometer, it slipped from his fingers and smashed on the hard white floor.

"Listen, I need a drink," he told her. He did not know that he sounded desperate.

"Not in here, love."

Daley lay alone in his small, sterile room, staring at the ceiling. "Oh, Jesus. Oh, Jesus. Oh, Christ. Why?" he said. No one answered.

During the fourth week of his stay at the house Daley discovered that it lay in Wiltshire, and had been until 1949 the home of the Storton family. It had lain empty for a number of years, then in 1960 a Miss Gorm had bought it cheap and turned it into a private nursing home. Part of the original

library was intact; Daley spent an afternoon turning the pages
of heavy, dusty volumes – a kind of estate diary – which he
found on a high shelf in the north annexe. The house had been
built in 1726, with a striking façade; the whole of the building
achieved that delicate blend of grace and symmetry which
gives houses of that period their distinctive style and makes
them so pleasing to the eye. Daley, still shaky and prone to
palpitations and sweating, made an effort and began to explore.
The therapy worked.

The stables, linked to the rear of the house by a long stone
wall ornamented with urns, were built by the grandson of the
original owner in 1757, after he'd won a large sum at cards.
They were in the shape of a squared U, with a cobbled yard,
and were now in a derelict condition. Miss Gorm had debated
pulling them down, then left them standing in case of a need
to expand; later, they had simply been forgotten altogether.

Daley stood in the stable yard, getting his breath. A climb
over a pile of rubble, along the wall from the house, had
sapped his strength. He coughed, and jackdaws clattered up
from the chimneys, their black wings shining in the June sun.
At length Daley moved to a heavy door let into the east wing
of the building, and gave it a tentative kick. It swung open, a
semi-circular brass handle rattling. He went inside to the stale
smell of straw, manure and dust. An iron ladder rose to a trap-
door to the right of the entrance. Without quite knowing why,
Daley immediately began to climb, his shoes ringing on the
thin metal rungs. The sound echoed along the rotting stalls that
ran the length of the wing. Sunlight streamed through four
dirt-blurred windows, giving the long room a faintly sepul-
chral appearance. Daley smiled to himself at this notion, made
a sign of the cross, and nearly lost his footing. He paused,
waited until his breathing was again steady, and went on up,
pushing up the trap-door with arm and shoulder, and thrusting
himself – with a great heave – into the dim, airless loft.

Despite the warmth of the sun outside, the loft was chill;

Daley found himself shivering. Chinks of light showed in many places where slates had slipped or cracked. The ceiling, angled to the slope of the roof, was bare to the slate over at least half of its surface, where plaster had come away with damp. Towards the outside of the building, where the roof sloped down to meet the floor, a pile of straw lay next to a tangled mass of old furniture, curtains, mattresses and cushions, all festooned with webs and thick with dust. There was a faintly menacing air about everything, as if the chaos of decay had been commenced on purpose, to ward off intruders. Undeterred, Daley reached forward in the half-light and took hold of an upturned chair by one of its legs. He gave a sharp tug, and the leg came away in his hand. A thick cloud of dust flew into his face, setting off his cough. This, combined with the oppressive air, drove him down and out into the yard, a handkerchief to his streaming eyes.

He sat on an upturned bucket for a few minutes, then took off his jacket and went in again, and up to the loft. An absurd curiosity had established itself within him. He felt driven to go back to the pile of broken furniture and pull it apart. He wanted to wrench some response from the inanimate, brooding mass.

I'm probably going bananas, he thought as he emerged into the forbidding atmosphere of the loft, this time letting the trapdoor fall shut behind him. He approached the ramshackle heap, and an old silly tune came into his head. He hummed it lightly: "Yes, we have no bananas." Then, savagely, he kicked the broken chair aside and scrabbled at a small table under a vast, sagging cushion. The table was stuck; again the dust assailed him. He drew back cursing, his eyes gritty, his nose clogging. He fumbled in his pockets, found the grimy handkerchief and tied it across his nose and mouth. Screwing up his eyes, he lurched forward, tossing things aside, pushing, pulling, shoving. What was he after, what the devil was he trying to find?

"You are mad, Daley," he muttered to himself. "And you haven't even had a drink."

He worked furiously at the pile of rubbish. Eliot's bleak line about stony rubbish repeated itself in his head. It made him angrier, and he swore, pulling at a heavy folded gaming table with fury. Suddenly, with a muffled crack, a great chunk of plaster detached itself from the ceiling above his head. It hung by a thread for an instant, then fell with a thudding crash. He had time only to fling himself backwards, sprawling down, before he was blinded by the dust.

Choking, gasping, he lurched to where he thought the trap-door was, felt for it, and found it. He jerked it up, and leaned down. Even the old, horse-dung smell of the air below seemed fresh and sweet. He sucked it in with relief, crouching over the square opening. His feeling that some alien presence was trying to drive him out returned strongly, and he had to fight back a desire to plunge down the quivering iron ladder and dash into the sun-dazzled yard.

"Dammit, I'm going to pull that pile of crap apart," he said aloud. "Until I know there isn't anything there worth looking for."

With renewed enthusiasm he attacked the pile yet again. He saw the box almost at once. Caught beween a broken chest of drawers and a rolled horsehair mattress, it lay on its side, half hidden on the solid old boards of the loft floor. Daley knew at once that he had to have it. Oblong, roughly the size of a small suitcase, it was made of oak, with a stout, brass hasp and a heavy padlock of an old-fashioned design. It was firmly wedged in place, and it took him several minutes to pull it free. The chest of drawers fell on his arm, and he gashed his ankle on an iron bed frame, but he got the box out, and took it down to the yard in triumph.

Dishevelled, filthy, and out of breath, he ought to have been feeling close to collapse. Instead, he felt happier and healthier – or so it seemed to him – than he had ever felt in his life. He put the box down on the mossy cobbles, sat on the upturned bucket, and wondered how he was going to break the large, rusty padlock. He wandered in and out of doors all round the building, until he found an old pick-axe in the corner of the tack-room, beneath a row of rotting saddles perched on wooden pegs along one wall. Returning to the box, he gripped the pick-axe firmly, swung it over his head and brought it down hard on the padlocked hasp. The padlock broke in a scatter of rust flakes, and skidded away across the cobbles. Dropping the pick-axe, Daley squatted on his heels, took hold of the box and pulled open the lid.

Daley sat in his new room in the convalescent wing, took an oblong oilcloth packet from the box and put it beside a small pile of silver coins on the writing desk in front of him. The coins gleamed faintly in the light from the reading lamp. Before opening the packet, Daley again examined the coins. On the obverse side of each was a coat of arms and the word "PHILIPPVS"; on the reverse, the word "HISPANIA" and the figure 8. Again he felt a thrill of excitement, and pushing the coins aside, he picked up the packet and began to untie the pale, frayed tapes which secured it. He worked very carefully, anxious not to damage the packet in any way. Gingerly he pulled the last piece of tape away, and opened the folds of oil-cloth. They were stiff with age. A dry, fusty smell of vellum rose to his nostrils as he spread the packet out. What he saw was to change his life for ever.

The packet was full of documents. Daley glanced rapidly through them, his fingers trembling slightly. There were some loose sheets – three or four – and one large bundle of several dozen sheets bound together; these were covered in a fine copperplate hand. All the sheets were of vellum, in a fair state of preservation. Daley saw that the loose sheets appeared to be diagrams or charts of some kind. His heart thumped alarmingly for a moment, then steadied to a normal beat. Daley knew that he was getting well. The sweating had stopped, and the dizziness, and he was able to concentrate for longer and longer periods. Resisting the impulse to look first at the charts, he turned his attention to the bound pages, and began to read.

A man, William Carter, having today come to the premises in Bristol of my employer, Mr James Mathers (late apprenticed of Thomas Kitchen, master mapmaker, of Holborn Hill, London), with certain documents or sketches which he desires rendered permanently, in ink, by a skilled hand, my employer agreed and retired, and I sat by Carter and took particulars of his sketches, and heard an accompanying account of a voyage so extraordinary that I prevailed upon my employer to hear it for himself from Carter, and I am now appointed to transcribe the entire account, at the earnest request of Carter and my employer both, so that it may be as permanent as the three documents, and it follows, as near as I am able, verbatim, while allowing for certain simplification of seafaring langauge, which affects the import not at all.

"My name is William Carter, of the county of Devonshire, retired seaman, now a stablehand, but with a little ready money put aside for such a purpose as this. Everything related here is the truth, and done at my request, since I cannot write with any skill, or would have set it down long since. It is not a tale I am proud to tell, but these events described are twenty years gone, and nothing to be done.

"We sailed from Bristol in March of 1760 in the brig *Gothic Maid* bound for Jamaica with a cargo of glassware and other goods for trade. This was given out in the port at least as the purpose of the cruise, but was not the whole truth, since our Captain, William

Prologue

Gough, held Letters of Marque granted by the Admiralty to his
Owners, to take enemy shipping as a privateer, England being at
war with the French and the Spaniards.

"I remember clearly most of the voyage, from the earliest stage,
and what took place, most particularly acts of cruelty. Not long out
of Bristol we encountered a westerly gale, which struck with great
ferocity, and all of us were ordered aloft to hand the sails, save the
foretopsail, that was reefed, and we lost a man overboard in the
blow, which took us badly off course, having to run before it, or
heave to for several days, else be dismasted.

"This early setback was to mark the voyage, as will be seen. Even
after the great blasts of the gale had passed over, we had to beat into
the wind, boarding short, and hard work with a constant rain
driving, all hands turned to and the Captain very severe, and in my
opinion not the sailor his Owners might have supposed, but a seaman has no opinion once he ships and dare not speak out. From this
uneasy start it was plain we were in for a harsh stretch, for the
Captain put a man in irons for throwing up his guts over the chains
and hanging in the rats when ordered aloft by the first mate, who
was nothing but a savage dog and no friend to any living creature.
So there we were, less than two weeks at sea, a man lost, and another
in irons below while sick, and no man in any doubt as to the
Captain's ideas of discipline, which were no help in rough weather."

Daley stood up and walked to the window. The evening
light was beginning to fade. In the distance, he could just make
out the clump of trees which marked the gate at the edge of
Storton Park. Beyond lay the village of Storton Devrill. He
would walk there one day soon, when he was feeling a little
stronger . . . when he had discovered all there was to discover
in the vellum sheets on his desk. He felt suddenly frightened
of what they might reveal, of having to commit himself
irrevocably to something. He shivered, then braced himself
on the window-sill. For a moment he wanted a drink very
badly, then he turned and went back to the writing desk.

He read for some time, occasionally frowning when he came
across words and phrases he couldn't understand, to do with

21

the day-to-day business of sailing a ship. William Carter's account was both thorough and precise; almost dignified. After the gale and the initial severity of the captain and the mate, both the weather and the atmosphere aboard had improved. They bore south and west, into the trade winds, and had a fair passage to Kingston, without further incident.

Daley began to warm to the story, and the occasional ironic asides of the narrator. Carter had evidently been a man of considerable sensibility and intelligence. Daley particularly noted a passage that ran:

"I have often, during the cold hours of the midnight watch, sat for'ard in the knees, and set my feet against the motion of the ship, and stared aft and aloft. On such a night the sky, if it were clear, had a great brilliance, and against the stars the sails drawing full were dark and strange, not at all as they seemed under the sun. Beneath me the sea rushed, dark and glittering, at once intimate and immense, and after perhaps the quarter of an hour I could believe myself a human god, free and powerful, flying alongside, sweeping across the ship, heading it into the wind at will, bringing forth the wind itself. My head would burn like a cold white star, and I perceive myself with doublets of silver thread in the blackness. In such moments of exaltation a seaman may lose himself, and forget the true bitterness of his life, which has no freedom in it save what he may dream."

And further on, another:

"I have said that the mate was a savage dog, but he was, too, a plausible orator – the men believed him to be their champion, despite his cruelties from time to time – and was thought well of in the fo'c's'le. He would pretend that he was one of us, and his harshness would be forgiven, for in the way that a thief among his cronies, if he speaks out of injustice, is soon accorded the status of Robin Hood and like heroic fellows, the mate (John Barnes by name) gained favour."

Daley paced up and down his room. For the first time, it
occurred to him that he had no idea who was paying for all
this. He caught sight of himself in the mirror standing on the
chest of drawers by the window. Who would bother to pay
for the resurrection of Michael Ward Daley, alcoholic pilot?
Pilot wasn't the word; he hadn't flown – except as a passenger,
stupefied in the tourist cabin – for over eight years. His face
was lined, there was grey through all of his hair, not just at the
temples. He was thirty-eight years old, and he looked nearly
fifty. Who would pay for that? Irritably he swung away from
the mirror. "I'm getting better," he told himself, and forced
his mind back to the account he was reading.

It was beginning to worry him; something wasn't quite
right with it. For one thing, Carter had clearly had some
schooling, since he could not otherwise have expressed himself
with such stylish clarity. Therefore, why had he pretended that
he could not write? Why had he told his story to the mapmaker's assistant at all? Despite his intention to read the account
through before looking at the loose charts, Daley felt obliged
to shake them from the packet and examine them at once.

The first depicted an island in the North Pacific, with an
anchorage and soundings marked. The latitude and longitude
were also given; Daley checked them against an old atlas he
found by looking through the bookcase in the corridor outside his room; he concluded immediately that they were
spurious. The second chart was headed "Part of the Island", and
showed in detail the easterly shore, a point, trees, rocks, and
soundings, and three lines connecting three marked stones and
a cross. Below a compass rose were scrawled the words:
"Strike due N of it. Thrum under the sand." These in turn
were initialled: "L.C." The third sheet was a diagram, and
bore the title: "The Excavation." It was a side elevation of a
shaft, set in a clearing, and carried intricate details of the
contents of the shaft, which had been filled with a variety of
substances, and sealed twice with pitch. In the bottom right

corner, in the scrawling hand, were the words: "Look to the
tablet. L.C." Daley looked again at the shaft, and saw that
there was indeed a tablet marked, at a level of fifty feet.

More puzzled and intrigued than ever, he was about to call
it a night and go to bed when he noticed, at the bottom of the
packet – caught under a loose fold – a fourth sheet of vellum.
Trembling, he snatched it up, and read:

> All heerin declared true
> before God Novembir 1781.

> Only the dates was altered
> and names and bearings to
> preteckt it from spies and
> enimies.

> 14.10.S. – 127.34 W.(G)

> The ship was the *Severn Gull*
> of Bristol and sailed 1762
> with 63 soulls. My true
> name is heer

> Lawrence Cogswell
> His seel 1781.

Daley sat down slowly and forced himself – with some
difficulty – to be calm. Carter/Cogswell hadn't been pretending he couldn't express himself well. What had happened was
that having heard the account, the mapmaker's anonymous
clerk had been so impressed that he'd embellished it with his
own style. Carter/Cogswell, while having some rough gift of
words, was nearly illiterate, and *had* needed someone to write
out his story for him. Which in turn meant that he'd intended
to pass it on, either to a friend or a relation. However, on seeing

the excitement of the mapmaker and his clerk, he cannily
covered his tracks with a false identity, false dates and false
bearings. Then, before he could pass on his extraordinary
legacy, he had died, leaving it to moulder in the stable loft for
nearly two hundred years. He'd had it all planned, down to the
hoarding of the money to pay for the maps and the transcrib-
ing of the story. The possibility that death might call early had
simply not occurred to him.

Satisfied that he'd pieced together the probable chain of
events, Daley felt ready to return to the account itself, and to
the explanation of the charts it undoubtedly contained. All
thought of an early night had left him. He could not even be
bothered to go down and collect his bedtime mug of cocoa, a
ritual Miss Gorm had insisted on. Daley realized, with pleasure,
that he loathed the stuff. He lit a cigarette, and resumed reading. In the woods a pair of owls struck up a ghostly dialogue.
Daley shivered slightly, oblivious, absorbed.

"At Kingston we unloaded in the normal way, but rather than
the customary shore leave for all save the anchor watch, Captain
Gough confined every man to the vessel and set us to work on the
rigging, and staying up the mainmast, and replacing the main royal
and main topgallant yards, which he maintained were sprung, but
were sound. In all the great activity over the ship we were aware all
the while that we lay not a quarter of a league from the pleasures of
the town, and the mood grew restless, and ere long resentful. It is
not natural to most captains to torment seamen in this way, yet to
Gough, under whom I had not sailed before, it was as drawing
breath to make men suffer.

"We sailed after only five days, unloading and victalling included
– plus the repairs – north-east from Kingston through the Windward Passage. It was early in the month of August, and here it is
timely to relate an incident that occurred during the discharge of
our cargo, involving Gough, who went ashore in the agent's pin-
nace, and there learned something which contributed to our hurried
departure. Upon his return he was greatly excited and could scarce

contain himself, for he stalked about the deck muttering, and slapping the bulwarks with a rope's end, and his eyes on fire. So seized with enthusiasm was he for putting straightway to sea again that the mate Barnes had to plead with him above an hour in his cabin before he would relent and allow the taking in of victuals and water on the morrow. And on the morrow, as described above, he put us to work at a furious pace, carrying out both real and imagined repairs.

"On the fourth morning out of Kingston, Gough at last revealed what he was about; he assembled all hands in the waist and told us that he held Letters of Marque, and that we must now consider ourselves under the jurisdiction of the Admiralty, and any man who so much as coughed in protest would be clapped in irons directly, and any man who did not rouse about his duties would be flogged. It was plain now why we had not been allowed ashore, but there was nothing for it but to accept the position and think of ourselves as His Majesty's tars – which we were, after a fashion – since to do otherwise meant crossing Gough.

"We ran before a light wind through the forenoon watch, then the Captain ordered the ship about, to head west-north-west. A dreadful accident then occurred. The ship was coming around to the new heading when a shipmate of mine, Harry L——, aloft on the fore topgallant yard, lost his footing, clung briefly by one hand to the footrope, then tumbled into the sea. At once the cry went up: 'Man overboard!' Since this was the second time we had heard it on the voyage, there was an instant response. However, the Captain was more intent on bringing his ship up to the wind on the new course, and bellowed from the quarterdeck that no man should leave his place, even as poor Harry sank beneath the waves astern, and not for the quarter of an hour would the Captain unbend, and by that time we had sailed half a league. The Captain, seeing that his crew was appalled by such callous disregard for a sailor's life, endeavoured to make amends by saying that L—— could not swim, and was drowned as soon as he fell, and that heaving to would have availed naught, that 'twould have been a waste of time, what with lowering a boat and pulling in circles and so forth. This guilty discourse did little to appease us, and men for'ard were beginning to mutter blackly, when from the maintop came a ringing shout that was heard all over the ship. L——'s crony, Joseph Bell, was leaning down from the futtock shrouds, clinging by one hand, and pointing with the other at the Captain. He shouted again: 'You'll hang for that, Gough, you bastard!' And taking a better purchase on the rats, Bell sent his knife singing at the Captain's head, missing him by inches. By now we were all staring aloft in wonder, already fearful for Bell, as he would have to pay severely for what he had done, which was mutiny.

"The inevitable resulted. The mate Barnes went aloft with the second mate Farley, and three hands, and brought Bell down and put him in irons. The Captain, twitching with anger, ordered him freed from the irons, and had him spread on the main shroud lanyards, and Barnes – his face set in righteous furrows – flogged him, with Gough bellowing encouragement, until the hapless fellow's back was cut and flayed like an ill-butchered sheep, and he hung by his wrists unconscious. After a short while he was cut down and chained up in the bilges, still in a faint, and the Captain again assembled us and ranted and raved at us, and swore that this was to be the voyage of his life and no man would ruin it for him, on pain of the harshest punishment. We began to think him mad, and it must have been then that the first stirrings of possible concerted action were felt, of which more later.

"We bore north-west two days, out of sight of the coast of Cuba to the south, until we were under the Cancer Tropic, and now it was clear the Captain planned to attack Spanish shipping from Havana, which I thought a risky affair, since we were but a brig, lightly armed – we could muster all told only fourteen guns, including a pair of light swivels mounted aft. But we had one advantage, which was that of surprise, and when this was coupled with the fair pace we could make, under crowded masts, things did not look so black, merely a deep shade of grey.

"On the seventh day, in the first dogwatch, we sighted a ship well to the north, in the Florida Strait, and followed until night closed in. I, in the starboard watch, which turned to at four in the morning of the eighth day, was for'ard at six bells when the lookout sighted the ship we had chased the day before, sailing close in to the Florida coast, which lay low on the horizon to the north-west. The Captain came on deck directly, and taking his glass peered at the ship long and hard, and pronounced her Spanish.

"All hands were turned to, topgallants and royals set, and we came near to flying; in fact, Gough would have welcomed it. In an hour or two, we were well up on the Spaniard's windward quarter, and could see that here indeed was a fat ship, for she was low in the water and although carrying more sail than was wise, unable to outrun us. Nor, for a sizeable three-master, was she heavily armed; 'tho ported considerably, there were few cannon protruding, and Gough surmised aloud that she had been laden in haste with as much as she might carry, and the cannon run out of her and left behind at Havana.

"We soon came up on her, close on her windward quarter, and suffered only a broadside of muskets for our pains, of which the balls went wide, and fell harmless into the sea. We could see her captain on the poop, feverish, and yelling to his crew, and they, some of them dressed rather fancy for seamen, seemed unable to know what was in their captain's mind from one minute to the next, so that Gough swiftly gave out of his intention to board the enemy and subdue him at once.

"This was achieved with great alacrity, and to Gough's credit, with seamanship of a passing high order; he manoeuvred aft of the Spaniard, then slipped by him to leeward and at exactly the right moment shivered the wind from our sails and lay up alongside. The grapnels were ready and we had them thrown up and hooked into her before the Spaniard could make his counter, which was to have been to put his courses aback and lose way abruptly, while we shot ahead. But we were over his rail before it could be done, and fighting hand to hand. Now we had our greatest surprise, for the Spanish crew put up little resistance, beyond an initial token flurry of swordsmanship and the odd pistol shot. Very rapidly they fell back, threw down their arms and surrendered, and the ship was ours. Gough was in a great way of excitement, and strode on to the Spaniard's poop, very arrogant, waving his cutlass about, and pretty red in the face, while we tended to the business of furling sail, and heaving to. Presently, after a brief delay to save his honour, the Spanish captain gave up his sword.

"Just at that moment, Barnes gave a shout to the rest of us, and on

28

going to where he stood just aft of the foremast, by an empty gun port. we were apprehended of the reason for the Spaniards' peculiar made of dress which would not have looked amiss in the streets of Madrid so careful was it of fashion rather than of utility. For Barnes had captive a member of the enemy crew, and had turned up his palms for us to examine; they were soft and white, unsullied by the callouses and cracks which characterize the hands of every seaman from his first cruise. Some of us caught hold of the wrists of several others of the Spaniards, and found their hands similarly unscarred, but manicured and soft, like those of women or fops. No wonder these fellows had put up no fight! They were not seamen at all, but landlubbers, and pampered at that. Gough came for'ard to see what the commotion was about, and on learning of our discovery, ordered the main hatch opened, to see what other surprises might be in store for us below.

"With the enemy crew, if that is what they could be called, huddled on the quarterdeck, and their captain confined in his cabin aft, we waited on Barnes and two or three men to bring us a sample of the cargo. Barnes was long about it, and our Captain went to the Spanish master's quarters, to strut no doubt, and throw his weight about and drink some of his captive's brandy. At last Barnes came on deck, and we had never seen him look so strange; his face was as white as fresh linen, his hands trembled, and his eye was bright like a consumptive's. He would say nothing to our questions, but brushed us aside and went in search of Gough, whom he met at the aft companion, and the two straightway went into a huddle. All this while, the boarding party grew more and more curious, for not only was Barnes playing the secretive game, but the men he'd taken below with him had not reappeared. We began to fear for their safety, and Gordon B——, one of our number, went to Barnes and the Captain and asked leave to go below and bring our shipmates on deck. But Barnes ordered him back amongst us, and went himself below and brought the men up, and made them stand apart from us, near himself and Gough.

"After upwards of twenty minutes, Gough gave orders to these men to lower the longboat and pull around under the stern. This was done, and the Spanish crew was ordered into the longboat, and slid and fumbled their way into it by ropes, or as best they could, and the jollyboat was lowered alongside of them, and the Spanish captain, full of protest, placed aboard it with his few officers. In all their whole numbers was not above fifty men, and it was a miracle they had cleared Havana, leave aside negotiating the swirling currents of the Gulf Stream, and risking the erratic winds under a doldrums spread of sail.

"So they were set adrift, but not wholly helpless, since they had oars and a supply of water and biscuit, and were not a great distance from the coast of Florida, and out of the Stream, so in no danger of being swept to certain ruin in the broad Atlantic. When they were well clear, Gough came for'ard and stood before us, staring into our faces as if he had not perceived them before that day, and muttering to himself. At length he gave a great sigh, and said that he had something to tell us. There was prize money for every man of us, he began, then broke off, and continued in a hushed tone to the effect that we would all shortly be rich men. Then he laughed oddly, and we saw that he was drunk, having taken too freely of the Spaniard's cognac, and he lurched a little against the riding of the ship, and suddenly raised his voice to a thunderous bellow, and swore that he'd hang any man that dared cross him. Then once again his tone became hushed and wheedling, and he promised us fine houses and all manner of luxury, and ten whores to a bed and so forth, if only we would serve him in his purpose.

"Naturally, we had surmised by now that the contents of the ship's hold was rich booty indeed, and to a man we assured the Captain that we were with him, and had never been otherwise, whereupon he grew affable and called us stout fellows, hearty seamen, honest, true, brave Englishmen and such, until we could scarce believe our ears, for not only was his demeanour most particularly unusual, but the very scene itself, for a ship's master does not have such intercourse with his men even at the best of times, lest his authority should seem too little, and he lose their respect.

"He then left us and went below with Barnes, taking the men who had first gone below with the mate. A brief squall heralded heavier weather, and Gough came on deck again, more in possession of himself, and ordered all of us save the man at the helm and one or two others, at the ropes, to go below. When we got into her hold, we saw amidst a mass of stuffs, roughly stowed and secured, and amongst casks and all manner of sacks, four great chests, all broken open and their lids thrown back, that were filled with the most prodigious number of doubloons, silver eights and other coins, and in one chest there were tiers of gold ingots, with markings imprinted on them, numbering in hundreds as I remember the sight. I know that I was struck dumb by such massive riches, but several of the boarding party about me gasped and made exclamations and repeated, 'Oh!' and 'By God!' over and again until Barnes demanded silence.

"The ship was beginning to shift in the uneasy sea, and no doubt so was our own ship, and Gough knew that we could not risk being caught in foul weather in these unpredictable latitudes, with the two vessels grappled together. The loading boom was rigged, blocks and tackles rove up, and the chests heaved, in an increasing treacherous sea, precariously across the gap between the two ships, and from the decks of our brig into the smaller space of her hold, and lashed and stowed in the stead of stone ballast, which went over the side even as the chests were swinging aboard, lest we set our vessel to heeling and be unable to right her.

"When the chests were all safely and securely stowed, and the sea now running nasty, it was dangerous to remain close to the Spanish ship any longer, and Gough ordered the grapnels cut free at the same time as sending a man into the bilges of the empty ship to open the cocks. The man taken off, we put our helm down, and under much shortened sail, beat into the weather away from the coast, which could not have been a moment too soon, for the other ship, although settling in the water, was driven in rapidly to the lee shore. Then rain began to fall suddenly, and the doomed ship, a lonely creature, faded from sight like a ghost in the curtains that fell over her, and over us and all the surrounding sea.

"The weather grew worse, and the wind increased until we thought that we must surely be caught in a hurricane. But we were not, only tossed about and blown this way and that by a tropical storm of considerable ferocity. Many ships have been lost in storms of this character, which, while not of the same dire strength as a hurricane, can for a short time assume certain features of that most terrible of nature's assaults. Within an hour we had reduced sail to the barest necessity to keep her head up, and had in truth suffered a topsail torn to shreds before it could be furled, and by then no man, not even the nimblest, could stay aloft but would risk his life, for the footropes were as whips in the shrieking tempest.

"We hove to as night fell and the wind died. Next morning, the sky having cleared, the Captain was able to get a fix on the sun with his sextant, and calculate our position. We had been blown into the Stream, and were being carried north-east into the Atlantic. This suited Gough well enough, since he gave out that England was our destination, where we should deliver up the chests of coins and gold bars to the High Court of the Admiralty and receive our share, which would be considerable, given the sheer weight of the booty we had taken. Now in the storm we had suffered considerable damage. The main topgallant mast was sprung, the backstays slackened, and everywhere was evidence of rigging needing attention, and sails with bowlines torn away from bolt-ropes and the like, and it was plain that a voyage clear across the Atlantic, with summer storms almost a certainty, was a risky business, and with what we had aboard – so much to gain for every man jack – a foolhardy business.

"Gough broached a cask of grog and gave every man a double tot, in honour of the victory over the Spaniard and the taking of the wondrous prize, which we had not had the opportunity of celebrating until that moment, and also in honour of our seamanlike conduct in riding the storm with as little damage as could be hoped for, getting in canvas even as we were clearing the other ship and so forth, and making all secure as possible before the fury broke. Then, and you may measure the wisdom of this who read it, whether or no it was to his credit, Gough told us that on consulting with his officers, there was a feeling among them that a return to England was unwise because of the condition of the ship, and that a return to Kingston was the safest course. There was, he said, a Prize Court at Kingston, to which the chests could be turned over, and every man given a paper describing his share, which would be honoured on our return to England. This raised a cheer, and the ship was brought about and set on a course south-east that would take us north of all the Bahamas to the Turks Isles, thence south-west through the Windward Passage to Kingston, a distance of some three hundred and fifty leagues. With any luck, such a passage should likely be accomplished in about twelve days or a fortnight of sailing.

"But luck was not with us. Squalls and storms plagued us for more than a week, until more than half the ship's company were down with terrible seasickness, and during which time Captain Gough found it impossible to get a proper fix on the sun or stars, and our position became a thing of conjecture and opinion. Always mindful of our precious cargo, Gough spent scarce any time below, excepting when he took his meals and lay down thereafter in his cabin for brief spells of sleep, which never lasted above thirty or forty minutes, and which were constantly interrupted by the lurching of our small vessel, which was never intended for weather so continuous foul and ugly, but was built for the lighter work of coastal waters nearer home. In truth, I do not know how Gough persuaded the Owners to allow him to set out as a privateer at all, in so relatively frail a ship, for while allowing there is no better than a brigantine for the business of dart-and-fetch, or dart-and-steal, as the case may be, there is no such case to be made for her as a ship for oceans and storms and long, hard voyages. At least, that is my opinion, and it is a view held only after much bitter experience."

1

Scurvy

Here Daley paused again. The sounds of the night were fewer and slighter; he did not look at his watch, in fact he had removed it some time ago; he had no desire to be disturbed or distracted by questions of time and sleep. For more than a page Carter/Cogswell explored in extraordinary detail in which seas and under which conditions a brig handled best, and worst, giving examples of other vessels he had sailed in. Daley began to grow irritated, until he realized that it was just this kind of detail which made the account itself stand up. The man who had written all this down – dictated it, rather – had cared for the life of the sea, despite his protestations about the appalling conditions, the cruelty and the rest.

"When waring her," he read, "the greatest diligence must be employed in keeping her from broaching to, for even with so simple a rig, the running gear being quite the neatest of any square-rigger, not the greatest sailor in all the nations' fleets can prevent a catastrophe if so much as a squall, or a sudden gust, should set the sea into a flurry of uneven swells and troughs."

There followed a highly technical dissertation on the relatively poor skills of Captain Gough in the business of tricky manœuvres at sea, although Carter/Cogswell appeared ready enough to praise his admirable technique in laying alongside and boarding. All that the narrator was doing here, decided Daley, was exercising the right of an old man to digress on a subject he knew better than most. He ploughed through it all, and was rewarded. Carter/Cogswell, in making his points on the handling of the ship by Gough, had been leading up to the drama that followed.

"I cannot recall on which day it was that we sighted an island to the south-west at a distance of some five or six leagues, in clearing weather, but Gough determined to make a landing, and we closed the island, reaching it well before nightfall, and finding a relatively easy passage through a reef into a tolerably sheltered natural harbour. Again I do not know if this were an island of the Caicos group, or one of the smaller and most northerly of the Turks, for events were to overtake us so rapidly that the name of our landfall became of small importance to us.

"Gough lowered the longboat and a party went ashore to seek water and wood. Trees abounded on the island, inshore from wide and brilliant beaches, and since the little bay was quite deep enough for us to anchor in, the boat had but a short journey to the shore, and we were able to observe the party beach her and move off amongst the trees. Presently they returned, and took the casks off, and the axes and adzes. Altogether, as I recall, there were twenty men ashore, including Barnes, and the third mate, and the party had with them a dozen or so of the muskets. Naturally, the arms chest had been unlocked to provide the crew of the boat with these fire-arms, and it lay open on the lower deck beneath the main hatch. In it were a further three dozen muskets and twenty pistols, with powder and ballshot in pouches and flasks.

"Whilst the boat was ashore, Gough ordered the main topgallant mast and the yards struck, and the running rigging most in need of attention was looked to. After an hour, we heard a number of shots ashore, some way inland. Thinking that the landing party were shooting birds or beasts, since the shots were not great in number, we on board did not remark them overly. Since Stigwood, the carpenter, was one of the shore party, we made more of this amongst ourselves – in that we could do little without him – than we did of a few reports from the shore party's muskets.

"However, we were to remark these sounds soon enough, for not above a quarter of an hour later, Barnes came staggering down on to the sands from the trees, and fell at the water's edge. Presently, two more men came running at a furious rate, followed by half a dozen more. The second group were all of them armed, and fired a volley at the fleeing pair, who pitched forward and lay still. Gough now came on deck, having been brought the news of the alarming situation on the beach. The armed men were now joined by a further four men, also carrying pieces, and this smaller group pushed before them Skerrow, the third mate, and Stigwood, the carpenter. All twelve men now made their way to the longboat, and put off for the ship. They were within hailing distance almost at once, and Gough bellowed at them to know what the devil was their business. Getting no reply, Gough ordered one of the three-pounder swivels, and two of the twelve-pounders, loaded and primed. The swivel was loaded with shot, and the long guns with balls. As the longboat drew nearer, we saw that the leader of the party appeared to be James Argent, a heavy set fellow from Liverpool, whom I had never liked, since he was always surly and quick to pick a fight. He stood up in the bow, and shouted suddenly: 'Surrender, Gough, for the ship is taken!'

"Now, this was a signal more than anything, for just as suddenly as Argent had risen in the approaching boat and shouted, those of us on the port rail became aware of a commotion on the lower deck. Then up the for'ard companion streamed fifteen or twenty of our shipmates, who had somehow contrived to get below as Gough came on deck, and remove the remainder of the arms from the chest. They were led by Gilbert Downs, another Liverpudlian, and Argent's greatest crony in the fo'c's'le. There were some two dozen of us who were without the slightest knowledge of what these two had been plotting between them, and now as Downs and his party advanced aft, armed to the teeth, I felt the mightiest fear. We were well outnumbered by Downs's and Argent's parties combined, and we had no weapons, save the knives that we habitually carried.

"I must say that Gough acted with some courage being thus confronted. Straightway, he turned to the gunner and ordered the longboat blown out of the water, notwithstanding she carried one of his officers, and the ship's carpenter. Before Downs could prevent it, one of the twelves had been touched off, and the ball passed through the starboard gunwale, beneath Argent's feet, shattering the whole of the starboard side, and throwing Argent into the water. The boat sank instantly, and since the ball had struck at such close range, and had made sharp splinters of the boat's timbers, most of those on board were grievously injured, and went down with her. One or two rose briefly in the mass of wood that was floating on the surface, but they sank again and that was their end.

"All of this took not above five or ten seconds, and caught Downs and his group by surprise, since they by their absence below at the arms chest had failed to see the cannon loaded. However, Downs recovered from this first setback almost instantly, and when Gough gave the order for the swivel to be trained for'ard at the mutineers, raised his musket and fired, bringing down the two men manning the swivel, one being killed outright and falling heavily against the other, clutching at his belt, so they both slumped to the deck. Downs called for another musket, which he aimed direct at Gough, and said: 'By God, you'll surrender now, or I'll spread your brains over the taffrail.'

"Gough saw that it was hopeless to resist and replied that he would come to terms. Those of us who might be called neutral, standing abaft the main mast on the quarterdeck, stood where we were, afraid to move lest one of Downs's mob should mistake this for resistance, and fire among us.

"'There'll be no terms, Gough, save what I give out,' said Downs, 'and I tell you that I think you are a bastard, and you had best call upon your Maker to show mercy, for I have none to give you.'

"Gough then attempted to placate Downs, a foolish effort it was plain, for Downs was in the humour of a man who takes fierce pleasure in making corpses, and gave vent to his feelings in a passionate outburst against Gough's tyranny, poor seamanship, base motives and contempt for his fellow human creatures. There was indeed some truth in what he said, but the manner in which he delivered this speech was so violent and savage that it rendered the import of the words hardly more meaningful than the snarl of a wild beast. Gough was by now very pale, for he sensed that at best he had but a few minutes more of life. Downs paused to draw

breath, then, speaking in a calmer tone, said: 'If I did not want
something of you, you would be a dead man already. You must
come aft with me now,' and Downs advanced towards the Captain,
still with his musket trained at his breast, 'and go below to your
cabin, and write me a letter saying that we have been attacked by a
Spanish frigate, and that due to great loss of life aboard, all the
officers killed, and yourself sinking from a terrible wound, due to
these calamities, you are putting me in command to make a run for
it and return to England as best we can.'

" 'I'll never agree to it,' said Gough with some dignity, and he
turned and walked towards the aft companion. Downs hesitated
only an instant, then tightened his grip on the musket and pulled the
trigger. The sound of that final shot aboard the ship was awful, and
the sight of the Captain, half of his skull blown away by the double
load of ball shot, struck a chord in all of us, I think, including the
mutineers. He fell in a sprawl on the deck, the muck of his brains
spilling over the planking, and there was a horrible silence. Even
Downs must have realized at that instant what a terrible act he had
done.

"For a minute nothing happened, then Downs turned to those of
us who were unarmed and at his – by his own statement, doubtful –
mercy, and ordered us to surrender any weapons we might have.
Having nothing but our knives, we gave these up, and Downs
asked us, in a fairly civil way, whether we would like to help him
sail the ship, or be put over the side then and there. It will come as
no surprise to those whose eyes follow this account that not a single
man of us chose the latter course, but I think it true to say that a
majority of us – and remember, we were twenty or more – felt the
gravest misgivings at having to sail under so ruthless a man as
Downs, who might well prove to be far worse even then Gough.
Again, none of us knew what had become of the remainder of the
shore party who had not been in the doomed longboat, nor what
fate might lie before us, if Downs came round to the idea that he
might handle the brig tolerably well with his own followers alone.
However, we had little time to dwell on such thoughts, for Downs
soon had us at work, preparing the jolly-boat, so that a second party
might go ashore on the morrow, at sunrise, to complete the business
of the first – that is, the legitimate business – and to bury the dead.

"At sunrise of the next day, I was among those lowered in the jolly-boat, manning an oar. The corpses of our Captain and the luckless swivel gunner lay at our feet, sewn in canvas shrouds, along with the shovels that would bury them, and those others who lay murdered on the beach; and, as Downs revealed before we were lowered in the boat, those of the shore party whom we had not seen after the longboat went ashore: they too lay dead in the trees, shot by Argent's gang. With us in the boat were three of Downs's followers, each armed with a musket and a brace of pistols. We at the oars were six. Downs had allowed his core of supporters at the grog Gough had had brought up a week or so before, and since the cask had been nearly full, these fellows were now mightily in drink, and in unpredictable temper. Had we been less intimidated by the number of dead at the hands of the mutineers, I suppose we might have attempted to overpower our guards when we got ashore, but the work of burial is sombre and unencouraging of rebellion, and we simply did as we were bidden."

Daley stretched, yawning. The fine script was beginning to tire his eyes. He rubbed them, then went to the handbasin and dashed cold water over his face. Immediately he felt awake and alert, and knew that he was able to go on reading; would go on, in fact, until he had read right through the account. He wiped his face over with a towel, breathed deeply several times, and feeling greatly refreshed sat down again and turned another page. The account continued in the same style, with meticulous attention to detail, but with occasional gaps in the continuity – obviously where the ageing Carter/Cogswell's memory had failed him.

The ship had evidently remained at the unnamed island for only a brief period, probably not more than a week or ten days, which was the minimum time Downs would have required to make the vessel at least reasonably seaworthy. The main top-gallant mast had to be replaced, and several yards, plus a great deal of the running rigging. Downs was fortunate in that the rope lockers appeared to have been properly stocked, and although the carpenter had been killed, the carpenter's mate had not; he was found lying dead drunk in the fo'c's'le. The ship was made ready for the open sea as soon as the work was done. Some wild fruit and coconuts were taken aboard with as many barrels of fresh water as they could manage, then Downs, evidently a man of impatient character, put to sea without attempting to careen the ship in the calm waters of the bay, and scrape her clean.

"Now we were forty-one, and put to sea under Downs as Captain. The neutral members of the original crew were in one watch, and Downs and his followers made up the other. All went very well for that first day we were at sea again, until Downs made a statement as the island fell below the horizon astern. He would continue south, he said, once we had been bearing east long enough to clear all islands bordering the Caribbean Sea, and by so doing would make good time to the Horn, which we could double at about Christmas, sail on up the coast of Chile, as Drake and Anson had done before us, and then sail west for Canton across the Pacific. There was no difficulty, he assured us, in forging the letter Gough had refused to write, and with this we should be able to dispose of the gold at Canton.

"Breek, one of his own, made the objection that we might equally sail boldly into Kingston with the same forged letter, collect our share of the prize, and save ourselves the appalling journey Downs proposed. Downs, who was still in drink himself, saw that his feeble story held no water, and resolved to give us the truth of his intentions.

" 'Very well, my lads,' he continued, 'we'll have no more falsehood and back-and-fill and so forth, but I'll give you the plan straight. We cannot risk Kingston, for the company agent would not believe us, I'm convinced, and it is he and his like we'd have to face there, and they'd have us in irons an hour after we'd dropped anchor, and all we'd see of the riches a man might hold in his palm and see naught but flesh, and that in a prison cell, with the gallows for a future. Nay, shipmates, Canton it is, if we're to have any chance at all. Who is to know us in Canton? Who knows Gough there?

Who knows our ship there? In Canton, for all they may know, I am Captain Downs and this be my vessel . . . of any name you care to say . . . *Caroline*, or *Rosemary*, or *The Admiral's Whore*. And if all this be the case, then in Christ's name, lads, the whole of the gold belongs to us, and who is to say how we acquired it?'

"This, of course, raised a mighty cheer from Downs's mob, which we of the neutral watch (if I may call it that) echoed with a deal less enthusiasm, and more out of a sense of self-preservation than anything. We were, after all, in no way able to defy Downs, on whose whim we remained alive. Yet there was among us a glimmer of hope, for if Downs was mad enough to try to carry through his scheme, then he would need every seaman aboard, not only to double the Horn, but to sail the wide Pacific beyond.

"This added to my own private hopes of at length being able to overthrow Downs and his watch, when conditions had deteriorated along with the humour of all, at some time of great stress – for example, after a storm, or when water and food might run low on the run south. However, these thoughts and the hopes that went with them, were soon shattered by Downs's announcement of a policy of risking the ship as little as possible during the next few months, and that he knew a place on the South American coast, north of Rio de Janeiro, where we might go ashore without risk, and take in meat and water, and other provisions that the Indians of the region would supply for money, since they had no cause to love the Spanish. Any scheme of revolt against Downs would have to wait, I knew then, until after we had rounded the dreaded Cape Horn, since there would be no real chance for it before.

"We bore south now many weeks, increasing short of all provisions, despite our reduced number, and by the middle of the month of October we were beginning to be wasted. At one time several sail were sighted, making up a squadron, and Downs crowded on canvas and outran them, but he never informed us that in doing so he had left the anchorage where we were to have taken in our supplies far to the north. Thus we sailed a deal further south than we of the neutral corner – as it were – knew, nor were the others of Downs's own party aware of it, I think, for Downs kept the business of navigating and conning and the like strictly to himself and a small number of his followers, never allowing anyone else to take the wheel, or to be near when he took sightings and consulted his charts. So that if Downs knew every minute what our position was, we did not, believing that fresh provisions lay close at hand, and only a few days' sailing ahead. Downs encouraged this belief, even among his own men, until it was discovered by one of them that Downs was keeping back the better rations for himself and a few of his closest allies, to keep up strength and vigour. The terrible commotion and wrath that this discovery provoked, chiefly in his own ranks, caused Downs in a moment of retreat to admit our genuine position, which was nearer to Puerto San Julian in Patagonia than anywhere else. He placated his own men by informing them that we would put in at San Julian, or thereabouts, and take in fresh food and water, and the long run south had been of the greatest necessity in order to avoid either Spanish or British ships, and to thus protect our precious cargo.

"This device secured him the peace, but only for a brief while, for now began to appear the dreaded and unmistakable signs of the seaman's blight, that is to say, the scurvy. No man who has not seen scurvy should make light of it, or scoff at it as a mild ague, and no man who has seen it will allow such talk, for it is a horrible disease, and worse than many other, for it can take a man who believes himself well merely if he rises from where he lies to go on deck for a little wind in his face.

"The disease struck both Downs's followers and our own watch without discrimination, and within a week of its first showing ten men were ailing so wretchedly that they were unable to carry out even their lightest duties. As I have said, scurvy is a most horrible disease, and it is made the more so not merely for its sufferers but for those who must needs inhabit the same quarters by the frightful stench which manifests itself in the mouths of the diseased, and in their armpits, groins and behind the knees, where great wens and ulcers erupt and putrefy. Added to these symptoms were a general lassitude of the spirits, and a seizing up of the bowels, which seemed to produce the most terrible breathlessness and fear of loud noises or sudden movement of any kind.

"Downs at first paid little heed to the mounting consternation of everyone aboard, and pretended that the scurvy was merely some tropical fever which we had taken aboard in the Caribbean islands, late in emerging among us, and due to our meagre food and weakened morale.

"A fortnight passed, during which we made good progress southwards, but more men fell ill, as had been feared by the old hands among us, and three died, two without leaving their hammocks and the third upon endeavouring to go on deck, saying that he was sound as any man and would not give in to a passing cold. He managed half a dozen steps up the companion, then fell back and was found to be dead, scarce thirty seconds after his last brave speech.

"These deaths would, I think, have convinced Downs to put in anywhere along the coast where a reasonable anchorage could be found, whether or no it were inhabited by civilized people, but for the untimely arrival of half a dozen sail on the horizon. Anxious, as ever, to avoid contact with either Spanish or English men-of-war, Downs again crowded on sail and ran further to the south, and declared that we stood no chance at all if we were to be taken at sea, and that we must now make the best of things and brace ourselves for the doubling of Cape Horn.

"I was standing near Downs on the quarterdeck when he made this announcement of his intentions, and I took care to mark the reactions of the crew in general. Like my own, these were a mixture of surprise, and disbelief, and apprehension. I had been observing the men – particularly of Downs's watch – for some days, and thought I could see signs that they grew increasing sceptical of their Captain's abilities. This, in the midst of my fear – both of the scurvy and of rounding the Horn in a frail brig – gave me renewed hope, for I felt sure that I could persuade some of my shipmates in the neutral camp of the need to overthrow Downs before he drove us all to our deaths.

"I whispered this scheme to a few of my cronies as we lay in our hammocks amidst the loathsome stink of our sick and dying fellows, and was gratified to learn of their approval and agreement. Except for one man – my friend Thomas Crigg – they eagerly seconded my proposal. Tom kept silence, and I puzzled at this. It was now mid-November, and Downs clearly believed that our passage round the Horn would be made easier by virtue of the fact that south of the

Equator summer was approaching. This made our tackling of Downs all the more urgent, for there is no safe season in the seas of the Cape, and Nature vents her greatest wraths upon those who are foolish enough to think contrariwise.

"When we turned to, to take the midnight watch, Tom Crigg suddenly turned on us as we came on deck, and said he was not with us. When I asked him why that was, he asked us to follow him and went aft to the mainmast. When we came up on him, he drew a belaying pin from the fife-rail, and turned on us in a sudden passion.

" 'This is all we have,' he said, waving the pin. 'This and nothing else. No pistols, or cutlasses, or muskets. You are all mad. You will have every man in this watch dead in a minute if you go on with this three-legged scheme.'

"All the while he spoke he did not once raise his voice, but kept it low and forceful, a-quiver with conviction. I made to protest our case, but he would have none of it, and went on in the same vein as before. In truth, he said he would split the first man's skull that moved, who did not swear to forgo rebellion. He turned this way, and that, crouched and intense, the belaying pin held high. At last I knew that he was right. His very own stance made a mockery of our scheme, for while he might smite one of us, had we all rushed him his belaying pin was as nothing. And our opponents had guns. Grumbling and dispirited, we went on about our duties, and our plan sank without trace there in the night.

"We now bore further south, until at the beginning of December we came round to a heading south-west through the Le Maire Strait, with the ugly blacknesses of Staten Island on our port beam, and began to tack against a most unexpectedly fierce current which flowed from the Pacific beyond, in great haste to join the Atlantic. This is to say, some of us knew of this current, but Downs and his henchmen appeared neither to know of it, nor to be much distressed upon discovering it, except in that it impeded our progress. However, when we had sailed a number of leagues on our south-westerly course, against a stiff west wind, there suddenly rushed upon us a most frightful squall, with heavy cold rain and gusts of wind that buffeted us sorely, and carried away the main course before it could be reefed. Now Downs saw the danger, and turned every man to take in canvas, for the squall, while it passed as nimbly as it had approached, left him in no doubt as to the humour of the weather. The sky ahead was a most eerie combination of dull hues and light, growing darker by the minute, until the light patches were almost non-existent, and the wind had shifted a few points to the south-west, so that it now blew directly on us with ever-mounting fury.

"I think Downs had no notion of what was really in store, having failed to appreciate just how sickly and weak even the fittest men were, and what a toll the scurvy had taken on the run south. In fact, when we entered the Le Maire passage on December the second or third, we had lost nine men, and there were a further four expected to die presently.

"I cannot adequately describe the tempest which all but over-whelmed us during the ensuing week. Reduced as we were from forty-one to a mere half of that number by the scurvy, six more men fell ill with constant retching, and a seventh, my shipmate Bute, slipped down the fore ladder and broke his arm so that the bones pierced the flesh. And Downs, terrified by the constant screaming of the wind, and the slashing, horizontal rain driven before it, went below to the cabin and refused to come again on deck, saying he had to plot our course and so forth. If it had not been for our stubborn determination to get all possible canvas furled, I think we must have foundered certainly. As it was, it took three men to hold the wheel, even though it were lashed, for we had to keep bringing her head up when the mad wind shifted this way and that, a few points here, a few points the other way, and so on, and thus the wheel had to be untied and held, and forced spoke by spoke, and tied again.

"Then, too, we had to be at the pumps for four days, since she began to take water under the constant pounding and smashing of the sea, and altogether we were exhausted so extremely that no man worked except in a kind of daze that was half delirium, and half aching, smarting wakefulness. I myself remember vividly going for'ard with two others to take in the jib (which while it was meant to keep her head into the wind, made her more sluggish), and without the aid of foul weather deck ropes we all but lost our foot-ing half a dozen times before reaching the bows. Then when we reached the bows, a monstrous wall of water reared up sheer before us, and broke over the ship. The bowsprit was entirely buried, then

Scurvy

the bows themselves, and I remember diving headlong and clinging to the port cathead with all my strength as a great mass of green, freezing water flooded over me, tearing at my trunk, lifting me high, so that my legs trailed out aft, several feet above the deck timbers, and only the instinctive severity of my grip saved me from being carried against the foremast and smashed to a pulp.

"During the time the storm raged it was impossible for Downs to plot anything at all, for as soon as the storm struck we were all but blinded, and did not see the sun again for above a week, let alone stars in the night. Our food had dwindled to the few scraps and sodden lumps of casked beef we could lay our hands to, foul water, and weevil-ravaged biscuit, plus the only thing I believe kept us going at all, a great cask of grog that stood broached and lashed next to the galley, and from which Downs allowed each man a double tot four times a day, so that we were able to dismiss the worst aches and distresses from our bodies and minds, replacing them with the fiery warmth of the rum.

"On the fifth day, which was the worst day, the wind veered constantly, then dropped a little, so that we went aloft at great cost to our strength, and set the topsails and the foresail, only to see them all torn from the yards by a sudden mad gust which leapt out of the west without warning, carrying away the canvas, and all the running rigging. We were now grievously short of sails, the lockers holding only torn and frayed remnants, and although our rope lockers still held a good supply of hemp, there had been no time to spin yarn, nor to see to even the most trivial of repairs to the rigging. Vainly we attempted to salvage the forecourse (which we had set with a deep reef) for it was only half gone, and flapped like a mad thing from the larboard yard arm and quarter, held by the larboard sheet, the starboard half of the sail having been blown out. At length the sheet gave, and the block whipped up and knocked a man senseless, the sail flew like a great demented flag briefly from the yard, then the whole – sail, yard and parral – tore free and carried over the side, and would have carried us with it like a giant tangled shroud had we not taken refuge upon seeing the parral ropes part.

"After the fifth day, when we had all but despaired, the weather began to abate, and on the eighth morning the sky had cleared and the wind dropped sufficiently for us to take stock of our position and assess the damage we had suffered. Downs now emerged from his cabin, white and considerably reduced in spirit. A fix was taken on the sun, and a new course set for the north-west, since we had drifted south. Five men had died during the hurricane, including my poor friend Bute, whose smashed arm had become rotten with the gangrene, and our surgeon having already died of the scurvy, there had been no person to aid my shipmate. He had lain in his swinging hammock without complaint, and on that first tranquil morning we found him dead and staring.

"Those of us who had been active in trying to handle the vessel throughout the storm were like walking dead by now, so complete was our physical exhaustion and our mental fatigue, and I remember little more of the following week than that I was in my bed, and that when I was not in a swoon, my thoughts followed a like course always; that was – in my mind's vision – my presence atop a hay wagon, drawn by a powerful horse, that rushed through valleys and over hills at a great rate, so that the wagon tossed and jumped, and I had to cling on for dear life, to the hay itself very often. I know that during this period of my illness, the carpenter's mate was able to fashion makeshift spars, and enough rope was found to enable certain essential repairs to be carried through so that we did not risk losing an hour of the favourable weather to tack north as best we were able.

"When I was again able to take heed of my circumstances, and to recognize the man lying next to me, and to tell him apart from those who came in and out, we had rounded the Horn and were sailing up the broken, barren coast of Tierra del Fuego, which seemed nothing more than endless islands, each as inhospitable as the last. I had not witnessed something I sorely regret missing, even now, which was the actual sighting of the Cape itself.

"Thus we made good progress up the western coast, until we were past Desolation Island, and only then would Downs relent and agree to a landing on one of the smaller islands that lay to the north. By now, of course, the condition of those men still left on their feet was very poor, and of those of us who had fallen ill, even worse. Yet Downs had so inspired the crew with his promise of relief, if they only sailed north a matter of days, and so impressed them with his navigation and success at avoiding lee shores in the still forceful west wind, that they did as he commanded readily enough. I think when we sighted the island on which we were to make landfall there was not a man aboard who was not suffering in some degree from the scurvy, and certainly no man who was not near to collapse from hunger, and from pains in the bowels.

"I know not the name of the island, which was one of a group to the north of the Magellan Strait, lying on the fifty-second parallel, but there was a tolerable anchorage there, free of treacherous reefs, and something of a beach, though nothing that might compare with the superb beaches of the Caribbean isles. The jolly-boat being our only means of getting to and from the shore, this was launched, and a small party of men managed to give way to the shore, which lay perhaps the quarter part of a mile distant. Upon their return, they reported that there was water on the island, but little evidence of food. The only trees were stunted and tangled in a mass of low vegetation, much of it rotting, and the whole appearance of the place was one of desolation and barren, unrelenting harshness. This did little to cheer us, but when the shore party produced from the boat several large bunches of a green stalk-like vegetable, a kind of celery, every man who could work his jaws fell upon these plants and chewed and sucked at them in a kind of dementia."

There followed a long account of their stay on the island. They had been reduced by scurvy and accident to twenty-three in number, and existed now on a diet of shellfish and the celery plant. Makeshift repairs were carried out, and after three weeks Downs began to discuss various schemes with them, and proposed that they should attempt the Pacific crossing. The majority eventually agreed, and the matter was resolved. They broke camp, taking what food and water they could.

"I remember that before the jolly-boat was taken in, a turtle was sighted and this was chased and captured, and made good eating. Also, that as we weighed anchor several canoes were seen rounding the point of our little cove. Downs – because of our small number – thought it best to avoid any sort of encounter with the natives. We stood out to sea in a steady, filling shore breeze, and none of the canoes, which were primitive vessels indeed, could keep pace. I had chance enough to observe that each canoe appeared to contain a family, and that in some of them fires were burning for'ard, o'er which men – rather than women – crouched, and that all the occupants, both men and women, were greatly wizened of countenance, and withered in their flesh, and appeared of a great age, yet their movements and agility in paddling belied that appearance.

"We sailed north, standing off the coast for fear that the wind, always unpredictable, might drive us back upon a lee shore, and smash us upon a place even more barren and unfriendly than that we had just departed."

Daley laid aside the sheet he had just read, and reached for the next. Involuntarily, he yawned, shivering. His eyes watered and he felt that his whole body was aching. He was suddenly so aware of his great tiredness that it was an effort for him to move from his chair to the bed. He fell on the bed gratefully, on his back, reflected briefly that he had done this countless times when he was so drunk he was numb, then slipped into total sleep.

He woke some hours later, and instead of the blind terror of so many of his recent wakings, he knew at once where he was, and what his life consisted of, and that it had constructive purpose. He was going to finish reading the account. Then he would have something to eat, because it would be time for breakfast. He got up from the bed, went to the wash basin and splashed more cold water over his face. The vellum page he had not yet read lay beside the bed; he bent and picked it up, noticing that his body was beginning to work properly again, because he did not stagger or lurch any more, or get sudden, thudding pains in his belly and chest, or his head; he felt – and by God, it was a good feeling – that he could probably make love and be a success at it.

The reading lamp was still burning, and he sat down again at the writing desk, stretched for the third time, and plunged eagerly back into the account.

Everything went wrong aboard the brig after they left the island. Sailing northward along the coast of Patagonia, they sought, but did not find, an island that would provide them with food, shelter, timber and refuge. All they saw were islands exactly like the one they had left, in ceaseless archipelagoes, with countless bays and channels between. And the weather again deteriorated; the tireless west wind grew in strength and they had to beat west-nor'-west into the Pacific to avoid the lee shores. Their rations were soon so depleted that they were little better off than before they had made landfall. Their health, no doubt due to the relief from the scurvy, held up surprisingly well, but within ten days they had begun to feel weak again. Downs, combining ferocious curses with moderately skilful sailing, managed to ride the weather out, but when the wind abated after almost a fortnight they had lost sight of land completely, and because the sky was still overcast, could not get a fix on the sun and so calculate their position. Downs believed that they had been blown a long way south, possibly as far as the fifty-sixth parallel, and accordingly sailed northward again into a much lighter wind. In fact, he must have been much farther north than he realized – his tacking to the north and west having successfully countered the efforts of the wind – and when they were at last able to get a fix and make a reading, Downs was astonished to find that they were far out in the Pacific, under the fortieth parallel.

He now had a daunting decision to make. Beneath the decks in the hold, acting very effectively as ballast, were four chests filled with enough gold and silver to make every man on board richer than he had ever dreamed. To the north-east, not much more than a week or ten days of steady sailing distant, lay Valparaiso and certain relief from their physical discomfort and distress. But it also meant the end of their dreams, for if they were not to suffer execution at the hands of the usually liberal Spanish authorities in colonial Chile, they would have to heave the chests overboard. Even then, they faced the prospect of long months of confinement, perhaps years. To the west, four and a half thousand miles across the Pacific, lay Canton. Downs put the choice to his crew, giving it as his opinion that while Valparaiso was certainly the safest course, it meant throwing away the gold, and giving up their liberty; while Canton, on the other hand, offered them the chance to dispose of the treasure and remain free, the price being an appallingly arduous voyage with all the odds against them.

In the end, it wasn't much of a choice, in Carter/Cogswell's opinion. He favoured Valparaiso, not because he wanted to give up his share of the treasure, but because he simply wanted to live. By a narrow margin those favouring Canton carried the day, for Downs put it to a vote. Carter/Cogswell sensed that Downs knew it was hopeless; the ship was short-handed, short-canvassed, leaky, and with much of her spars and rigging in a pathetic condition; they had almost no food, and their water was getting low – soon they would be relying on rain; they were weak; worst of all, as the narrow result of the vote had shown, they were divided. Before long, Carter/Cogswell knew, they would begin to fight amongst themselves. After that, only disaster could follow. He resigned himself, and set himself to wait.

"When the port watch turned to and I went below, I was so dis-spirited and cast down that I could eat nothing, and lay in my hammock in a stupor of self-pity, and answered nobody's questions, which seemed to me to be trivial in the extreme, as was all the conversation in the fo'c'c'le. This humour enveloped me for several days together, during which I thought we made a few leagues only, the winds being very light, and we tacked north. But since I was so sorely aggrieved by what I regarded as my ill fortune, I paid little attention to where we were going, in what direction we bore, and at what speed. I was sure of one thing only, and that was that we were all doomed to die at sea ere long. After that time, I remember very little, for I fell ill once more, greatly weakened not only by my parlous state of mind, but by a most unnatural fasting, which I adhered to as tho' trying to hasten my demise. Undoubtedly I knew not what I was about, with any clarity, for no man beckons Death unless he be either a fool, or mad. I was most fortunate, at that time of extreme despondency and sickness, in having a shipmate who was also the most loyal of friends – Tom Crigg – who nursed me. He brought me through the worst of my fevers as if I had been his own brother, asking no relief from his other duties. In short, he saved my life, and I think of him warmly to this very day.

"It was now two months since we had rounded Cape Horn, and we lay below the thirtieth parallel, about one hundred and ten degrees west of Greenwich, for during the time that I had lain ill, we had in truth caught the south-east wind and made good progress. But we were still an immense distance from China, and there was literally no food, the last of the biscuit having gone. The scurvy was again beginning to show itself. We fell back exhausted from the least labour, and the suffering I saw around me every day made me dread the sunlight almost as greatly as I dreaded the night. For long periods the ship was left to sail itself, for we were too weak to haul on the sheets and braces, much less furl canvas, or man the wheel, which was lashed and left. I think that my own illness, of despond and despair, had saved me from a more severe debility, for I was rested, and when I emerged from it, tho' weak, I was not so weak as many. Two men died on about the twentieth day of February. I cannot now recall their names, having fixed in my mind only those names which bear importantly upon my story. We drifted north-wards, with not much westing, until the close of February, and March found us in the tropical regions, hot and still for days together and no land in sight. We had not seen land for many weeks, and we were desperate. The divisions and fighting I had expected did not occur; no man was strong enough to fight, nor had the breath to quarrel; over the length of the ship settled an invisible miasma of defeat, and I had the cheerless satisfaction of believing one of my predictions was to be realized, and that we should perish on the vastness of the sea, not in a terrible storm, but in light and favourable winds.

"On the fourth of March, or thereabout, I was lying for'ard on the deck by the carrick bitts, when I raised myself to try and capture a sea bird which had alighted on the bow rail. It flew up as I made a clumsy lunge at it, and hovered just above me briefly, so that in a vain hope I stood on one of the cats. The bird flew off, but the strength this effort had cost me was not wasted, for rising on the larboard bow, at about three leagues, was a line of low hills. I think that my tongue clove to the roof of my mouth, for I could not raise the longed for cry of 'Land ho!' but jumped to the deck and whirled this way and that in agitation, a tumult of emotions coursing through me. At length I managed to give a kind of strangled shout, which brought Downs – ever the alertest of us – on deck. I ran towards him, pointing for'ard over my shoulder, and when his eyes followed the direction of my outflung arm I knew by their expression of wonderment and joy that I had not deceived myself, and that land was really there ahead.

"All hands were soon on deck, and drawing on our last reserve of strength, we brought the ship up to bear directly on the island and closed it in not more than two and a half hours. Of course, this seemed a deal longer to us, so dearly did we desire the shore beneath our feet, and fresh water in our throats, and the smell of growing things in our nostrils. Indeed, this smell drifted across the water to us, and made us almost delirious with expectation. However, as we came up to sounding distance, we saw that the island was very small, not more than a mile square. The hills I had seen first lay on its western side, and we drifted in upon its south shore, which thrust out in a kind of promontory, or more accurately a spit, ending in a reef. Tom and I eagerly made the soundings with the leadline, and when the line had given five fathoms some three or four hundred yards off a pleasant sandy beach, Downs ordered the anchor let go.

"To the north of the spit were a considerable number of palm trees, and a great density of smaller, thicker trees, clumped close together and surrounded by lush vegetation. The trees were not so many nearer the hills on the west side of the island, and although the hills were covered more or less wholly by vegetation, they supported no trees. All this we could make out from the deck, and even though the island was diminutive, we anxiously assured ourselves that it contained game, and plenty of other food, and a plentiful supply of sweet water. Being one of the strongest members of the

54

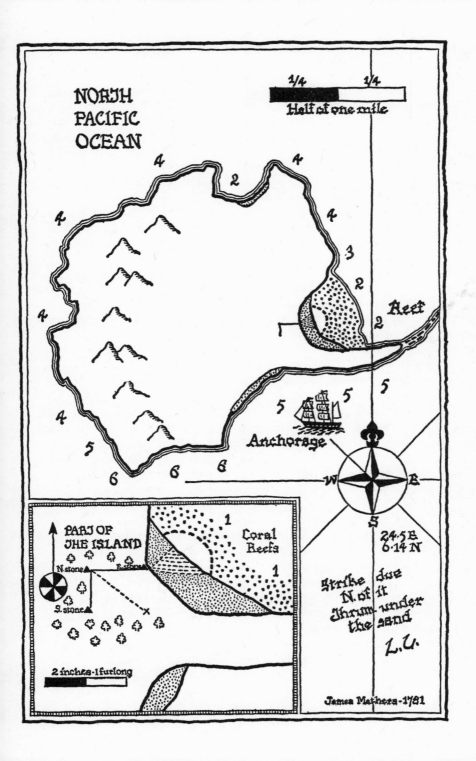

crew, I was detailed to an oar in the jolly-boat and was able to discover for myself without delay the truth of our fevered expectations.
When we had beached the jolly-boat, and ventured a little way into
the foliage, our muskets loaded and primed, we found much evidence of game in tracks and droppings, and some way to the west of
our landing place, a small stream running from the nearest of the
hills. Throwing our weapons aside, we fell down at the edge of this
brook – as splendid to us as the mightiest river – and drank deeply
of the cool, clean water. This so revived us that we might have
drunk brandy; it seemed to go to our heads, hearts and limbs all at
once, and when we had soaked our faces and quenched our thirsts
sufficiently we all at once fell to laughing, and continued until we
were breathless. Shortly afterwards, I remember standing up and
looking about me, and was amazed to see a wild pig staring back
at me, equally startled, not five yeards distant. Fortunately, I had
the presence of mind to grab my musket, and before the pig had
recovered its sense of self-preservation, I killed it outright with a
ball through the shoulder.

"By nightfall, Downs had all the ship's company ashore, leaving
no man aboard, since to do so would have been a cruel business, and
would have served no use – the anchors were away at her head and
stern, and biting well in a firm bottom that could be seen from the
deck, and multitudes of brightly coloured fishes. Two more wild
hogs were shot during the afternoon, and the lamest and weakest
men were set to gathering the abundance of fruits, coconuts and
roots that were everywhere about. Downs had the topgallant masts
and yards sent down, and these, with tools and other essential articles
were got ashore on a raft rigged up from the main hatch cover and
some casks. Tents were set up with the yards and sails, and a very
tolerable camp established, which, when we recalled the hardships
on the southern island, and the long weeks of our torment and
hunger since, seemed as grand as a country seat.

"Downs also had a cask of grog brought ashore, tho' not a large
one. We feasted that night, and drank a good deal of wine from the
late Captain Gough's stores, but not too much rum, as our guts
were still spasticked from being not much used of late. In truth,
many of us were sick with the richness of our repast, and benefited
not at all. However, the eating and drinking were taken up again

on the morrow, with more cordial results, and we began to feel stronger and easier in our minds and to take stock of our circumstances, now so thankfully transformed.

"First, two small parties scouted the island thoroughly, to make certain that it was not inhabited by savages; the search was as barren as had been hoped for it. Then a rough estimate was made of the number of wild pigs, and it was found that there were probably upwards of several hundred of these creatures; later we realized that they must have been introduced by natives who had briefly inhabited the island, when we found the remains of an old camp, with a huge pit of ashes. Thus, the question of our supply of food was answered, for apart from the pigs, the roots, fruit and coconuts grew in such quantities that there was no need to think of conserving or rationing them. Next, came the business of making the ship seaworthy for the remainder of the voyage to China, a process that would take several weeks at least. Here I must relate the events which led to my devising this account, and which pertain to the charts which accompany it."

Here it was at last. Daley stiffened in his chair, and hunched involuntarily forward in his excitement. His sense of well-being was replaced by one of utter concentration, as if he were straining to hear directions that would save his life over a long-distance telephone wire.

"Myself included, there was not a man who believed that we would not reach China now. Our luck had changed, and all that was required was that we should get back our strength, repair our vessel, lay in victuals, and resume our voyage. Downs held a council on these matters, and disagreements concerned only the time it would take us to reach Canton, some saying two months, others less, and so on. But in truth getting the ship right was easier said than done, for there was scarcely a foot of her – from stem to stern, and from trucks to keel – that was not greedy of attention and care. Those of us who had made long voyages, including Tom and myself, and Downs and several of the others, knew that the work of repair would take at least a month, if not six weeks, since we were short of men who could be called skilled. The wales would have to be caulked the length of her, and the decks. Half the yards at least were sprung, and the topgallant masts greatly weakened. Lifts, braces, halyards, shrouds, stays – all needed either replacement, or splices, or strengthening of one kind or another. Sails would have to be extensively patched, and many bolt-ropes replaced, and cringles. In short, false optimism was our worst enemy, and Downs made this plain, so that after he'd spoke we were more subdued.

"When we had had time to digest his words, and were generally in no doubt of the labours that lay ahead, Downs came to the details of how we should tackle the work. As on board, we were divided into watches, which would work through the hours of daylight. The first thing was to careen the ship, for apart from the need for caulking, the copper sheathing – for the protection of the hull against the frightful ravages of the tropical teredo worm – was loose in many places, and wanted hammering firm against the timber. Now, to careen even a small ship like a brig is a major undertaking, since it involves heaving her over to one side or t'other by a careful weighting on that side, and by ropes at the masts bringing a further purchase to the lean. Downs supervised the building of a second raft on which we might work, and we managed to bring ashore half of the cannon, thus causing her to list noticeably. Now it became clear that to leave the four great chests – quite forgotten briefly – in her hold would adversely affect the degree of list, and that they would have to be brought out of her, and carried ashore like the cannon.

"From the moment we began to get the chests up from the hold, setbacks occurred. That is the only way I have of describing the difficulties, accidents and injuries that now beset us. The first chest, as it was brought on deck through the main hatch, slipped from its cradle of rope and fell on a man's foot, crushing it to a mangled pulp. This man later died of gangrene. Barely had we rove up the blocks on the loading boom, to swing the chest outwards and lower it to the larger of our rafts, when a sudden swell made the ship lurch and the massive oak oblong, with its dead weight of precious metal, began to swing wildly on the boom, so that we were fearful of losing it. In the end we lost none of the chests, and they were placed together by the tents at our camp, a little way from the beach in a small clearing. But the troubles continued when the work of careening and nailing down the copper sheathing began. First, we lost one of the cannon, the trunnion rests on the carriage had rotted and when a greater strain was placed on them by the angle of the list, the trunnions broke free and the gun slipped into the water through the port. Then, more seriously, the ship began to take water at an alarming rate, so that for a short time we believed she would founder. However, the leak was discovered, and caulked, but at great inconvenience, for the whole careening exercise had to be reversed, then once more performed, before we were able to resume work on the copper.

"I cannot recall all of the other hindrances, but they culminated in what was the decisive incident of that whole ill-fated voyage. The work of repair, under Downs's able supervision, and under the secondary direction of the carpenter's mate, was about half done, and it was the beginning of April, when we woke one morning to find the oak chests missing. The ship's company was roused, and it was found that Farley, second mate under Gough and now simply one of us, had also disappeared, and eight men with him. Since all told we had been reduced to twenty, that left eleven of us, under Downs. We soon established that Farley and his men had dragged the chests away to the north, through the foliage, on a kind of cart they had rigged up out of raft timbers and wheels from the cannon carriages. Also gone were the muskets – all we had between us were half a dozen pistols, our knives, and some cutlasses. Downs checked the guns, and found that all the carriage wheels were either missing or broken to pieces, and the muzzles and vents choked with a mixture of sand and pitch."

Daley turned over the page he had just read, and placed it on the pile to his left. He reached for the next page from the bundle containing the rest of the account. The bindings lay in front of him, draped across the glass ashtray like discarded ribbons, faded and dry. He had read a couple of sentences of the new page before he realized that it was out of sequence. The pages were not numbered; he flicked hastily through the few that remained unread. He could not pick up the thread. A page, or pages, were missing.

"Dammit to hell," he muttered angrily, feeling cheated.

Carefully he checked all the pages again. Still he did not find the missing section. Either Carter/Cogswell had lost it, or deliberately removed it. Daley decided to finish reading, then worry about the setback. The narrative resumed:

"Since I knew that Farley was dead, and probably Downs, and my faithful friend Tom Crigg, I reverted to my original notion of stealing the jolly-boat. I could not hope to sail the brig single-handed, and in any wise the spars were all sent down, and the sails ashore. I made all speed to the camp, took from Downs's tent his sextant, a telescope, and what charts I could find, stripped the sail from its poles, and went to the landing place, where the jolly-boat lay. I returned once more for a yard to act as a mast, and some rope, plus all the stores I could carry. I managed to take a good number of fruits and roots, and a whole hog that we had cured and salted down. Also a small cask of grog, and several large flagons of water. I then put to sea, rigged my sail roughly, but effectively enough to fill away, and bore west away from the island.

"For sixteen days I maintained a westerly course, carefully noting my position each day on the chart, by means of the sextant and a compass that was in the boat; I had learned the way of these instruments well, on my first long cruise, in the sound opinion that they might one day be the means of my salvation. It is not every seaman who can boast this advantage, but in the end it was the very sun from which I calculated my position that brought me low, for during the heat of the day I had little protection from it, and my head swam dizzily. In short, 'tho I had enough food to keep me going for another two weeks, or perhaps three with careful husbanding, I was sunstruck and ill after only a fortnight, and on the morning of my seventeenth day at sea, I passed into oblivion. How long I lay in a burning torpor in the bilges I know not, for I woke in the fo'c's'le of a French frigate, feeling very weak, and was a week abed more ere I was able to stand. My good fortune in being saved from certain death was tempered by the fact of being saved by an enemy ship, but in truth I was treated very decently, and when I was well, given time to walk about on deck and anywhere else I pleased. This began to seem odd to me, until I discovered the second cook spoke a little English, and he declared that the war between our countries was at an end; the peace had been negotiated only a matter of a day or two before their ship had sailed. At first I was disinclined to believe him, but when he repeated the information several times, most emphatically, I saw that he spoke the truth, and was further gladdened.

"The story of my return has no place here; it is an eventful one, and a long one, too, but has no bearing upon my theme. Suffice it to say that I set foot in England again some two years after I had left it, and by my circumstances was forced to do so under a false name, which I retain to this day. Of the great riches spoken of in this account I brought to England a small handful only, amounting in value to no more than thirty guineas, which I have set aside to cover expenses. In gold and silver upon the island is a fortune – in my rough estimate – of at least four hundred thousand guineas. May God go with you, join you with this bounty, and bring you safely home, so that all the sufferings, madnesses and deaths I saw and was party to, might have some vindication.

(Signed) William Carter."

Daley went to sleep in the bath, and woke with light streaming through the window. He could hear the early chitterings and warblings of birds, and knew that he was better for the sleep. He stepped from the tepid water with his eagerness returning. An expectant well-being possessed him as he dressed, as if he were about to set out on a day in the hills. The memory of hunting trips as a small boy came back to him as he opened his bedroom window wide; the air which drifted in was redolent of wet grass and the rich saps of trees.

"Well, I'll be damned," he muttered to himself. "I'm hungry."

He found Miss Gorm in her office beyond the dining-room, after breakfast. She was checking accounts, her half-moon spectacles glinting like chips of ice. Wherever she was, Miss

Gorm contrived to conjure an atmosphere of cold disapproval. Ideal for reforming boozers, thought Daley as he closed the door. Miss Gorm laid down her pen.

"Is there a church in the village?" Daley asked.

"There was until the First War," said Miss Gorm. "Some anarchists burned it down, and it was never rebuilt. There is another church over at Storton Leigh, but the vicar calls only on alternate Sundays."

"Well, I don't want to *go* to church," said Daley. "I'm looking for a grave."

"I see," said Miss Gorm. She adjusted a paperweight.

"Not my own," added Daley. "Someone connected with this house."

Miss Gorm brightened. "I *see*," she said. "A member of the Storton family."

"Sort of," said Daley.

"The graveyard at Storton Devrill is intact, I believe," said Miss Gorm. She paused, then: "Can you be trusted, Mr Daley?"

"Yes," said Daley, and meant it.

"You know that there is a public house in the village?"

"Yes."

"The landlord has instructions."

"I'll bet he has."

"Very well," said Miss Gorm. "But be back in time for luncheon, please."

"I will," said Daley. He turned to leave.

"Oh, Mr Daley?" said Miss Gorm as he put his hand to the doorknob. He turned, sighing.

"Mr Daley, I understand you missed your cocoa last evening."

"Yes, I did. I was busy."

"Please try to understand," said Miss Gorm. "It's the only way we have of making sure you're all here at bedtime."

Daley nodded and smiled. "OK," he said. "I'll be there

tonight. But I don't promise to drink it."

He crouched beside the headstone, which leaned back at a
decrepit angle, its base hidden in weeds and tufts of grass.
Carefully he scraped the moss and lichen away from the
inscription, and read:

MOLLIE BOSCOMBE
aged 37 years,
Spinster of this Parish.
Died February 14th, 1793.
Laid to Eternal Rest.

He sighed and got to his feet. Brushing the moss off his
trousers, he resumed his slow, methodical pacing, checking
each pitted, cracked and drunken stone in its bed of green. He
came to the end of the last row, and slapped his notebook
against his leg in exasperation. Then he glanced back at the
ruined church, turned and walked to the gaping arch of the
door. A few minutes later, having examined the stone floor of
the church and found no additional graves, he was about to
leave when something caught his attention.

At the far end of the churchyard there was a long, low wall.
Almost hidden under blackberry bushes and weeds in a corner,
where the wall met the fence, was a gate. Quickly Daley
threaded his way through the headstones and approached it.
At once he saw it was hopelessly jammed under the tangle of
bushes, and he turned his attention to the wall, which was
chest high. Leaning on it, he peered over into the patch of
ground beyond.

Part of it had been cleared and made over into a vegetable
plot. The rest lay as it had for a very long time, overgrown,
neglected, littered with an assortment of tins and broken
bottles, but unmistakably the original burial ground of the
village.

There were far fewer headstones than in the yard next to the church, and some of them were in even worse condition. But there was more space between them, and the plots, originally, had been arranged with some care. With renewed hope, Daley clambered over the wall and began searching. Within five minutes he had found it. In a group of a dozen stones was a simple slab with the weathered inscription:

WILLIAM CARTER
Died November, 1781,
aged about 65 years.
A True and Faithful Servant
of Storton House.
Rest in Peace.

2

Preparation

"I can only say again that I think you are making a mistake."
Miss Gorm turned from the fireplace, joining her hands in
front of her. "We have an excellent record here at Storton,
deservedly so. In the doctor's opinion, you are not yet ready to
leave."

"That's too bad," said Daley, making an effort to keep his
voice polite. "I'm leaving tonight."

"Won't you reconsider? At least stay for the evening meal,
and think it over."

"I'm sorry to sound rude, Miss Gorm, but I don't need to
think it over. I've made up my mind."

"Very well," said Miss Gorm with an irritated little sigh.
"There's no more to be said."

"There is just one thing," said Daley. "I've been wondering
about it for some time. Who . . . Who's paying for me?"

"Why, didn't you know?" said Miss Gorm, in genuine
surprise. "Your wife."

"My . . . I haven't got a wife."

"I'm sorry, I don't understand, Mr Daley. Your wife has
telephoned several times to enquire of your progress. And, I
assure you – " Miss Gorm gave a disciplined cough – "the bills
have been promptly paid."

"My wife divorced me seven years ago," said Daley. "I
haven't seen or heard from her since."

"I'm sorry," said Miss Gorm with prim rectitude. "We never *delve*, you understand."

As the taxi took him to the station to catch the evening train, Daley remembered the card in his wallet. He took it out and looked at it. It was a standard cardboard slip he'd been given several years before in the casualty department of a large London hospital. On it was printed in blue:

NAME: Michael W. Daley
ADDRESS: 6 Bedloe Place, London S.W.6.
AGE: 33
IN THE EVENT OF AN EMERGENCY PLEASE CON-
TACT
Mrs Helen Daley
29a Radnor Gardens,
London, S.W.3.

Drunk, bloody-faced, his world spinning and disintegrating, he'd given her name to the clerk behind the glass window, taken the typed form, stuffed it into his wallet, and forgotten all about it. They must have contacted her, he realized, after they brought him in concussed – how many weeks ago? She had arranged the nursing home, and paid for it, and left him guessing. Why?

"Why the bloody hell did she do it?" he said aloud, as the taxi drew up outside the station.

"That'll be one pound exactly," said the taxi-driver firmly. He did not hold a high opinion of Miss Gorm's patients. Daley paid him with his last fiver, stuffed the change into his pocket, and went to buy his ticket.

The woman living at number 29a Radnor Gardens in Chelsea said she did not know Helen Daley's address. But she did know her telephone number, and gave it to Daley willingly enough. He was gratified to see that people were beginning to take him seriously again. He was no longer a bleary-eyed

monster mumbling incoherent pleas and curses, but a rather
thin, grey-haired man going about his business. In the telephone kiosk he dialled Helen's number, and when she
answered almost forgot to push the coin home. Her voice took
the wind right out of him. Tears rose in his eyes, and his legs
felt weak.

"Goddammit," he muttered, his hand over the mouthpiece.
He recovered, and pushed the coin into the slot.

"Hello . . . it's me. I mean, it's Michael."

"Oh, you're out. They said they were going to keep you for
another month. I've just posted the cheque."

"Oh, did you?" said Daley. For a moment all words de-
serted him, and his mouth opened and shut; he began to sweat.
At last he managed: "How are you?"

"I'm fine," she said. "I expect you're wondering why I paid
for the nursing home?"

"Well, yes . . ."

"I don't want to see you, or anything, we'd better get that
straight. I happened to have a bit of luck, that's all, and when
the hospital got in touch with me, I thought I'd do you a good
turn. That's all there was to it, really."

"Luck? . . . I don't?"

"I sold a couple of pictures. Things Mummy left me, that I
didn't want. They fetched quite a lot, so I – "

"For God's sake!" said Daley. "Don't talk at me like this.
Can't we meet? Let's have dinner. It isn't too late. Where are
you? I'll come and pick – "

"No. Absolutely no." Her voice had a quality he couldn't
remember. There was an authority about it that hadn't been
there when they were together.

Dismay welled up inside him.

"Why not?" he said, trying not to plead. For the first time
in weeks, he wanted a drink. The desire for a drink was so
strong he could taste down the back of his throat a metallic
dryness.

". . . point in going on about it. Shall we say goodbye now?" said Helen.

"No! No, please don't hang up. Look, why don't we just meet for a drink?" Even as the words came out he knew what her reaction would be.

"I can see the money was wasted," she said coldly, and the phone went dead in his hand.

"Damn!" he said and kicked the panel beneath the phone. He replaced the receiver and pushed out of the kiosk into the mild summer night. Holding in a breath and concentrating, he fought down the near-manic urge to cross the street and go into the brightly-lit pub on the corner. A taxi turned out of the King's Road and puttered down the street; he hailed it, and gave his address in Fulham. As he got into the cab, his legs began to shake with relief.

Mail lay scattered on the rug inside his front door. The flat smelled stale; he felt that he was an unwelcome visitor in a sickroom, and opened the one window at the rear. The dull London bricks of the house next door faced him, and he knew with certainty that he would have to quit the flat soon, or suffer depression so acute he would not be able to bear it without alcohol.

He did not open the mail, but instead lay on the broken-down settee in the cleaner of the two rooms, and drank a cup of tea. At length he rose and took the oilskin packet out of his suitcase, opened it and laid the bundle of vellum pages out on the stained coffee table.

"I cannot, repeat cannot, pass this bloody thing up," he said.

But he knew no way of not passing it up without unacceptable risk. He needed money. He needed help when he got to the Pacific. He needed one or perhaps two good men he could trust. Here in his frowsty rooms in Fulham, he had none of these things; they were so remote as to be the fancies of a dream; possession of the faded pieces of parchment seemed to him an irony of the bitterest kind.

He did not bother to undress, but brought a blanket from the cupboard in the other room, and fell asleep under it on the settee.

Sleep, as it does so often, refreshed his outlook. As he came awake next morning he knew that the trip to the Pacific was possible. He arranged it very simply. He rang Helen, and asked her if she would cancel the cheque to Miss Gorm and instead pay the money into his account. After all, he argued, the money had been earmarked for him anyway, hadn't it? On learning that he planned to leave the country, Helen was relieved enough to agree at once. Daley hung up, then dialled a travel agent, and fixed a cheap flight to the Pacific. At ten, he left his flat, and went to the British Museum. On the way he posted a letter to an address in Bristol. As he gazed down on them from the top of the bus, people in the streets seemed to him to be carefree and happy.

M. W. Daley, Esq.
6, Bedloe Place,
London, S.W.6.

Maritime House,
Anchor Road,
Bristol 6
June, 12, 1976

Dear Mr Daley,

In reply to your letter of yesterday, I am happy to tell you that a search of our records was productive.

A vessel registered in this port under the name of *Severn Gull* traded between here and the West Indies from 1754 until 1762. The last mention that is made of her is in that year, when she was posted missing with all hands after sailing from Kingston upon the homeward leg.

Her captain on that last voyage was Benjamin Clyde, and her owners Messrs. Pool & Sons of Bristol. No record has survived of the names of her crew, nor of the exact number. Her cargo is described as "principally glassware, and stuffs".

Trove

In the hope that this information will be of some help with your forthcoming book.

I remain,
Yours faithfully,

J. N. Coames
(Vaults)

MEMO   BRITISH MUSEUM   ROOM 916

No record of a galleon – or indeed any Spanish vessel – slipping out of Havana before British attack. Possible rumours in Kingston of impending attack, but doubtful. Only Brit. commanders, and Sea Lords, knew of attack – unless someone v. indiscreet.

As regards vellum page, it is of fine quality, dating from latter half of C 18th. Ink also fine, and has not faded, indicating that specimen has been preserved with some care.

Please find attached, ref. to Havana from Argyle's *British Naval Engagements – Drake to Nelson* (Ribbon & Falk, 1938)

PHOTOSTAT   BRITISH MUSEUM
– 96 –

On August the 14th, 1762, in a counter to the Spanish attacks on Rio de Plata, a British Fleet closed Havana and effected the capture of the port and city. Relying on surprise and speed, Admiral Keppel in the *Valiant*, and Admiral Pocock in the flagship *Namur*, sustained the British advantage throughout, proving once again the truth of the axiom (attributed to Admiral Lunkeek), "Surprise is the greatest."

One week later, Daley watched Papeete harbour float away at

70

an angle below, then right itself as it receded in the distance. The big Catalina climbed without haste into the cloudless Pacific sky, her two 1200 horse-power Pratt and Whitney engines pulsing above the cockpit. In the co-pilot's seat Daley felt elated. It was the first time he'd been on a flight deck in eight years, and even if this wasn't exactly the computerized layout of a jet, it had an atmosphere of professional certainty, that businesslike quality common to all large, long-range aircraft. Daley glanced again at the instrument panel, the throttles, the self-start buttons in the central console. He looked down at his feet, at the rudders, and gently grasped the twin prongs of the stick in front of him. None of the tremors or vibrations found in many prop-driven aircraft were evident here.

"She's a beautiful old ship," he said, turning to his left. The man in the pilot's seat, Crabtree, smiled and nodded. Wraparound aviator sunglasses prevented Daley from seeing if Crabtree's smile was genuine, but he had no reason to doubt that it was. He seemed an uncomplicated type: dependable, easy-going, carrying his forty-five years without strain or regret; the ideal pilot.

"What's our maximum range?" asked Daley.

"You asked me that last night," said Crabtree, glancing at Daley. "With the extra tanks, we're good for three-two-fifty. Don't worry about it, we'll make it there and back."

"Yeah," said Daley. "I forgot about the reserve tanks." He hadn't forgotten.

"Those photographs you want to take," said Crabtree. "We could overfly this island of yours long enough for Rembrandt to paint it. You'll get all the shots you want."

Daley nodded, and told himself to stop trying to find fault with all his careful planning. Everything was going along smoothly. So far, there had been no hitches at all. The one thing that sometimes made him sweat a bit was that he wouldn't be able to pay Crabtree. Still, he would fix all that up when he got to Frisco with the photographs, and the story.

He stretched, and settled in his seat. Crabtree would wake him when he wanted a break. The pilot set one part of his brain on automatic alert, and allowed the other to relax. Presently he began to hum the score of *South Pacific*. It was his favourite music; he'd seen the movie seven times.

The aircraft droned on, heading west-nor'-west over the Tuamotu Archipelago, its great wing carrying the burden of the hull at a standard cruising speed of 130 miles per hour. At that height and speed, he knew there was no possibility of danger from jets. In fact the Catalina will travel at almost 200 miles per hour, but Crabtree was in no hurry. Where they were going, there was no need to rush things.

It was six hours later that Crabtree noticed a slight change in the beat of the port engine. He craned his head round, staring up through the sectioned perspex at the massive radial engine. He could see nothing amiss, but the altered throb was more distinct now, and he was beginning to be worried. He woke Daley, and gave him the controls. He'd had the aircraft on George for some time – having got up to check details on the charts once or twice, and to stretch – but in these new circumstances he wanted to take no chances.

In the wartime Catalina – of which Crabtree's was a stripped and modified model – there was a crew of not less than seven men, one of whom was the engineer. His little nest was located in the massive central wing root, with ports on either side for close-up examination of the engines. Crabtree went up there now, and carefully scrutinized the port housing, listening to that ever-mounting metallic shudder. Still he could see nothing out of the ordinary, then, as he was about to slip down into the aircraft proper, a wisp of smoke came back from the housing, fanned instantly away by the wash of the great propeller. A chill crawled up his spine. He waited, and the smoke came again. This time it was thicker, and there was an ugly black tinge to it. Crabtree scrambled down, and for'ard into the cockpit.

"Hit the port extinguisher!" he shouted.

"Where is it?" asked Daley. His eyes swept the dials, levers, buttons, toggles.

Crabtree vaulted into his seat, and punched a red button by the port throttle, shutting the throttle off as he did so, feathering the engine. Both he and Daley swivelled in their seats to look up at the prop as it spun slower and slower, then was driven only by the wind. From behind it came a thick gush of smoke, oily and black. Again Crabtree stabbed hard at the red button. A white puff joined the black flow, then the entire stream of smoke issuing from the feathered engine turned white. In a few seconds, the smoke stopped. The fire was out.

"I'm going to bring her round on a one-eighty," said Crabtree, "and try to gain height."

Daley glanced at the altimeter and saw that they had lost a thousand feet.

"I'll try and get her up to about eleven thousand," contined Crabtree, as the horizon canted port down. "That way we'll glide quite a few miles if the other engine blows."

"That isn't likely, is it?" asked Daley. He was familiar with one-live-one-dead flying, but not in old prop-driven machines.

"I'd say it was pretty unlikely," conceded Crabtree. "She's got a wingspan of over a hundred feet, and we're not loaded up, so the one engine stuff shouldn't strain her. But our speed is way down. We'll be up here an awful long time before we see Papeete."

"Do you think it's a good idea to try for Papeete?" said Daley. He could not keep the anxiety out of his tone. "Wouldn't it be safer to put her down somewhere in the Tuamotus?"

"Bugger that," said Crabtree flatly. "This baby's my living. The people who can repair that engine are in Papeete. The spares are in Papeete. I don't want to waste time bringing her down in some chickenshit place where they haven't seen an aero engine since God was a boy."

"OK," said Daley. Crabtree wasn't the type you argued

with. It was his aircraft and this was his ocean. He knew best.

It was already dark when the Catalina cut a white, folding wound in the harbour at Papeete, and both men were exhausted from the strain of willing the aircraft to keep going. Crabtree had radioed ahead for lights on the water, knowing they wouldn't make it before sunset. As they stumbled back through the hull to the painted-over port gun-blister, Daley remembered how thankful they had been for the coffee Crabtree had heated on the little hotplate by the bunks. Without the strong refreshing brew, he would have succumbed to sleep. He hadn't wanted to sleep, because he couldn't stand the idea that he might die before he woke up, as the aircraft hit the water and broke up, or caught fire and exploded in mid-air.

As he lay in bed that night, Daley saw that it wasn't going to be as simple as he'd thought. He had never thought that it would be easy, but since Helen had given him the money and he'd come out to the Pacific, since he had arranged the hire of the aircraft and camera equipment with Crabtree, he had had something positive within his grasp. It would not be easy, but it would be uncomplicated. That was the way his mind had been going when they took off that morning. Now, all that was gone. It would be complicated, all right. It would be hard. It might even be dangerous. Above all, it was going to take time. And he still had to get to Frisco after finding the island, and sell the idea to McNally.

Crabtree – because he understood that Daley would not want to talk through the business of the cracked engine – had left him at the hotel and gone home to his rambling stilted house across the harbour. Crabtree had not wanted to think about the engine himself. The whole damn thing would have to be taken down. The starboard engine would also have to be checked, after its long solo run. Crabtree granted himself a second large gin, and sat down to write up the events of the day in his log. One day, he hoped to turn the log into a commercial property, by offering it to a film producer he had met in Hawaii. Or perhaps write a book based on the log, and offer *that* to the film producer. One day, thought Crabtree, he would make a million. Meanwhile, he reflected, tossing down his pen in abrupt irritation, he would have to be up early to supervise the stripping of the engine, watching all the time so that the boys did not steal tools, guarding his precious aeroplane while surgery was performed. And the mechanics would have to be paid; it meant going to the bank, and arguing with the manager, a dyspeptic, sour Frenchman who had been too long in the islands. Crabtree swore, and swallowed his gin.

As they took off into the Pacific dawn three days later, Daley was not unduly worried about money. Helen had been generous, doubling the amount of the cheque to the nursing home. He had had enough, on his arrival, to pay the deposit on the hire of the Catalina, and the aerial camera. Swallowing his scruples, he had told Crabtree a number of straight lies about the expedition; Crabtree had believed him. And he knew enough to fix a fly-now-pay-later trip to the States on their return from the island.

The one big doubt – now that he'd had three further days to think about it – was whether the island was actually there. Detailed area maps of the Pacific had shown nothing within many miles. A cartologist he had consulted, in London, had been reassuring – "Many, many hundreds of islands are recorded on no maps" – but Daley had not been reassured. Crabtree, who knew the islands well, had no knowledge of it. The trouble was, it was so small. If the bearings on Carter/Cogswell's last scrawled sheet were not accurate, Daley knew he was sunk.

They found it in the late afternoon. Crabtree had taken the aircraft down to one thousand feet, and Daley had crouched over the charts at the navigation table crammed in behind the seats. Crabtree called out that he could see something.

"Ten right," he said. "See those little humps?"

"No," said Daley, then: "Yes, I see them now." Three minute dots floated in the distance on the vast, flat sea.

"That's your island," said Crabtree. He sounded pleased.

"Christ," said Daley, in absolute wonder. The whole damn thing was true. It was going to be all right.

"Yeah, I told you it'd be small," said Crabtree, nodding. "And I told you I'd find the bastard." He nodded again, and grinned. Daley had fallen silent. "You OK?" said Crabtree, glancing at him.

Daley's head stopped rocking, and the dizziness faded. For a moment he had thought he might pass out. He passed a hand over his face, ran it back through his untidy grey hair. Would Crabtree wonder about this?

"Better get strapped in," said Crabtree. "I'll take her in south of that little spit. Reefs on the other side. Don't want to rip her gut open." His voice was calm and matter of fact.

Daley climbed into the co-pilot's seat, and strapped on the safety harness. Crabtree brought the Catalina into a wide, sweeping turn that took them over the island and the line of low hills on the western side, and into the shallow bay on the south-eastern shore, below the spit. All the features on the charts were there, Daley noted – the hills, the trees, the beaches, the rocks and reefs. Elation was replacing the sudden faintness of a few minutes ago.

The pilot brought his aircraft down smoothly, in a clean rush of spray, and taxied in until they were about fifty yards off the beach. They launched the rubber dinghy through the modified gun-blister. Its small outboard engine started first time, and they puttered in to the beach, leaving the aircraft riding easily on a single bow anchor, like a great gull.

The trees and vegetation appeared to Daley to be as thick and lush as Carter/Cogswell had described them, but the beach was slightly wider than indicated on the old map, no doubt due to the storms and shiftings of two centuries. Daley walked up the beach and stared into the trees, the sand clinging to his wet canvas shoes. He wondered if the wild pigs were still in residence; he could hear no sounds of wildlife; the whole island seemed unnaturally quiet. He looked through the palm fronds at the brilliant sun over the western hills, then down into the vegetation which covered the ground in dense thickets. Everything was still. Behind him he heard Crabtree dragging the dinghy well clear of the water. He approached up the beach, his feet making a soft, heavy sound as they sank into the fine sand.

"Bloody quiet," said Crabtree, staring about him with a hand on his hip. "Engines must have frightened the birds."

"Mmmm?" said Daley. He rubbed his forehead, and his hand came away dripping with sweat.

"Quiet," said Crabtree, coming level with him.

"And hot," agreed Daley. "Perhaps we should sleep on board."

"Those bunks are narrow as hell," said Crabtree. "We'll be a whole lot better in a tent here on the beach." He lit a cigarette, then added, "You'll feel better when you've had a stiff drink and something to eat."

"I don't drink," said Daley too quickly, and cleared his throat.

He felt compelled to qualify this statement. "I've been in hospital."

"So that's it," said Crabtree. "I thought you looked a bit shaky before we landed. Did they cut you?"

"No," said Daley. "No, I was in . . . an accident. Busted ribs, that kind of thing."

"Uh-huh," said Crabtree. "I've never been under the knife. That's one thing that scares me silly. Listen, you take it easy. I'll fix the tent, and the bedding. Maybe you could get a fire going. We'll need it after dark."

Later as they sat over mugs of Crabtree's coffee in the flickering firelight, Daley said: "I'm recovered, now. I used to

77

get dizzy spells a lot, but I'm fine."

"Sure," said Crabtree. He had no wish to embarrass Daley; he wished he would drop the subject. He had guessed about the alcoholism as soon as Daley said he had been in hospital. That worn, beaten look about the eyes was something they never lost. He had seen it too often in the islands. He had been careful not to offer Daley gin before the meal. He probably was over it, but you never knew for sure.

"I'd like to start as early as we can tomorrow," said Daley, after a silence. He stood and threw the dregs of his coffee away across the sand. "I want to get a comprehensive set of pictures. Once I've got them, we can head for Papeete whenever you like."

"We'll take off at dawn," promised Crabtree, and stretched. "I'm just going for a bit of walk down the beach. I sleep better after a walk."

When he returned twenty minutes later, Daley was already stretched out in the tent. Crabtree crawled into his sleeping bag, and blew out the lamp. Everything was still so quiet that for a while he found it difficult to sleep. But long after Crabtree's breathing had settled into the rhythmic pattern of slumber, Daley lay awake, listening.

Crouched over the camera housing in the little well below the for'ard gun turret, Daley saw the anchorage flash blue below, then the sand of the beach. He peered through the viewfinder and pressed the button. The high speed motorized shutter made a series of whirring clicks as the island sped beneath in a blur of green.

Crabtree made a dozen passes from east to west, then another dozen from north to south. Then Daley was satisfied he had as complete a set of photographs of the island as it was possible to have. He climbed back into the gun turret, and from there into the cockpit. He gave Crabtree the thumbs up, and the pilot took them in.

Daley had discussed with Crabtree, before they took off, his desire to tread the ground north-west of the spit. He had not yet taken the pilot into his confidence, so was unable to show him the charts and explain that he wished to look for the stone markers. Instead he had told Crabtree that "his company" required him to find a suitable place for a large camp.

They went ashore in the dinghy, and while Crabtree struck the tent, Daley stumbled the half mile to the north beach through the undergrowth. The sun was hot, and he began to sweat, cursing himself for not bringing a canteen of water. The beach north of the spit was very wide, a lot wider than shown on the old chart. It shone with a brilliant whiteness, and hurt his eyes. Chart in hand, he began pacing the inland edge of the beach, in search of the east stone. Before long he realized that he was not going to find it in a few minutes. Two centuries had altered the width of the beach; certainly they had altered the spread and density of the undergrowth also. The marker was hidden somewhere in these green thickets, but until he examined the photographs, he would not be able to judge where. Then there was the other point: the charts themselves were not more than guesswork, based on Carter/Cogswell's memory. Again Daley began to feel twinges of unease. He needed to find at least one of the markers before returning to Papeete. The photographs, even when combined with the charts, might not be enough. He had to present McNally with a concrete reality, otherwise the trip to Frisco would be wasted. Waste was something Daley could not afford, not only in terms of money, but in terms of time, and the strength of his resolve.

As he stumped through the sandy soil above the beach, tearing at the sappy leaves of the ground plants, pulling them aside, treading them flat, he decided that he would have to tell Crabtree the truth. He could hear him starting the outboard engine on the dinghy. Soon he would return to the beach, having stowed the camping gear. He would wonder where Daley had got to. He would begin to grow impatient.

He heard the dinghy puttering out to the aircraft in the distance. Panting with exertion and heat, he squatted for a moment, felt dizzy, and sat down heavily. His left hand, as he stretched it out to prevent himself from falling flat, connected with something solid beneath a scrubby bush. Getting on to his knees, he tore the bush aside, his dizziness dispelled. Before him, firmly rooted in the dry soil, was a roughly carved pyramid of stone.

On the long hop back to Papeete, Daley told Crabtree the story. At first the pilot was incredulous, then angry, and at last – as it sank in – excited. He put the aircraft on George, and examined the vellum charts with the eagerness of a child. Then he read the account right through.

"If I can raise the money in Frisco," said Daley, "are you in?"

Crabtree thought for a moment. To hell with the bills, to hell with the French bank manager. "I'm in," he said.

"With the ship?" Daley gestured round the cockpit.

"Hell, yes."

"OK. Ten per cent," said Daley. He adjusted his sunglasses and looked ahead through the windscreen, waiting for Crabtree's reaction.

"I guess that's about fair," said Crabtree. "Sure, ten per cent." He grinned, and they shook hands.

McNally stared at the bridge from the thirty-second floor of the Rolar Building. Three hundred feet below him, traffic undulated on the steep streets of San Francisco. He spread his feet a little further apart on the beige tiles of his office floor, and stretched. A late night had left him with a mild hangover, and a craving for coffee.

Turning to his desk, he buzzed his secretary and asked for another cup. When she brought it in, he asked, "What's my schedule? Can I duck anything?"

"No," said his secretary. Her large round spectacles emphasized the moulding of her face, her high cheekbones. They also drew attention – discreetly – to the round shape of her breasts.

He looked at her for a moment. "Why don't we lock the door and make love?" he said.

"Because you have a very heavy morning," said his secretary.

"And a heavy afternoon?"

"Very heavy."

"That's too bad, Janice," McNally sighed, and sipped coffee.

"It is," said Janice. "Oh, I nearly forgot. This cable just arrived." She handed him the yellow strip. He read the tele-printed words:

**** CRABAIR PAPEETE TAHITI ***** MCNALINC
SAN FRANCISCO USA ****

ARRIVING FRIDAY JAL 207 HAWAII STOP BUSINESS
PROPOSITION STOP CAN YOU ACCOMMODATE
STOP REGARDS

MIKE DALEY

"What's today?" asked McNally, looking up.

"Wednesday," said Janice. "You did have a late night."

"I want you to cable an answer right away. Reads: Crabair, Papeete, Tahiti. Can accommodate, stop. Will meet flight, stop. Bring a nut-brown maiden, stop. McNally."

"Do they have nut-brown maidens in Tahiti?" said Janice, as she finished jotting.

"Have a car meet that flight, yes?"

"Is he a friend, or is this strictly business?" asked Janice.

"Why the hell does my secretary have to know that?"

"Well, I need to know whether I should send someone with the chauffeur, or just the chauffeur."

"Yeah. Tell Roy I'd like him to meet the flight. Tell him to stop the car on the way here. Make some excuse. Cigarettes.

Tell him to call me. I want to know if Mike is drunk."

"Drunk?"

"Tell Roy to use a chauffeur on our payroll, not one from the pool. If Mike is drunk, I don't want it talked about."

"He is a friend, isn't he?"

"I haven't seen him in almost ten years. But, yes, he's a friend."

Roy Sewerd sat in the back of the big limousine, watching the traffic on the freeway slide past the darkened windows. Beside him, in light tropical clothes sat Michael Daley. Between the two men was Daley's only luggage: a grip, and a skinny leather briefcase.

Sewerd was nervous; he did not like assignments like this. Since joining McNalinc two years before as a lower echelon executive with prospects, he had done well. Of the many holdings of the organization (including computers, race car components, and two small domestic airlines), Sewerd had seen most from the inside. He knew he was being groomed as a top trouble-shooter; his degree in economics from the Harvard Business School had started him on a ladder he was eager to climb. But he loathed having to baby-sit difficult clients, sit through their drunken life stories, their dull obsessions. He knew that he was given these jobs as part of his training, and he sweated them out, knowing also that the experience would never be really valuable. When he was calling the shots, other young men would be there to do what he was doing now.

Still, at least this guy wasn't drunk. He'd been warned that Daley could prove awkward. So far, he was a model of good behaviour. He turned to him and gave him the frank grin he had practised for months.

"Mr McNally was very sorry not to be able to meet you personally," said Sewerd. "He was sure you'd understand."

"Of course," said Daley. The kid was nervous, he could see

that. Small bubbles of sweat lay along his upper lip, despite the air-conditioning in the car.

"We'll go right to his house, and he'll join us there from his office. He wanted me to see you had everything you need."

"Yes, you already told me," said Daley. He was courteous, but not deferential. The kid would be reporting back to McNally, of that he had no doubt; once a drunk, always suspected.

Sewerd pretended to fumble in the cigarette box in the cocktail cabinet. He snapped the cabinet shut with an exasperated click of his tongue. "Uh, we don't seem to have any cigarettes. Mind if we stop while I buy a pack?"

"I bought some on the plane," said Daley, making the kid's job tougher, just to see if he would handle it smoothly.

Sewerd allowed Daley to haul the carton of Kent out of his grip, then said, with an apologetic smile: "Thanks, but I smoke Trues." He pressed the intercom button. "Pull over, please, Manuel." He turned to Daley. "Won't be a minute," he said and grinned again.

"Go ahead, go ahead," said Daley, and then, as if on an afterthought, "Why don't you call your boss, tell him I made it OK?" He had the satisfaction of seeing the kid flush with embarrassment as he hurried across the sidewalk.

McNally's ocean cruiser slid easily through the long Pacific swell, travelling at less than half its maximum speed of 26 knots. A custom built seventy-footer, she could sleep ten, and three crew. In the big fuel tanks below there was 500 gallons of dieseline; the twin 250 hp engines gulped fuel at the rate of 18 gallons per hour at full speed; McNally liked to be able to make the trip down to Santa Barbara and back without having to refuel. This trip she carried two crew and six passengers. Daley was one of them.

McNally showed him over the cruiser as they headed into the open sea. She had been designed as a deep water boat, and rode without fuss or slap through a minor squall that hit them as the Golden Gate fell away astern. And aside from her sea-worthy character, she sported luxurious appointments throughout, including a saloon with colour TV, a bar and shelves of books. The wheelhouse (beneath the flying bridge) featured multi-band radio, 50-mile radar, short range radar, auto-pilot, and an array of small television screens with compass headings, speed readouts and weather conditions. The triple-panel weather screen was fitted with heavy duty wipers. Electro-hydraulic trimming tabs kept the boat stable in heavy conditions. Everywhere there was evidence of electronic efficiency, and practical design. Daley was impressed and said so.

"I like my toys to work," was all McNally said. He turned to leave.

"Mind if I take the wheel?" Daley asked.

"Sure," McNally said, then turning to his skipper, "Keep an eye on this guy, Pete. He's a hell of a flyer, but he doesn't know boats from a monkey's ass."

Neither the skipper, Pete, nor the other crewman aboard, a thin Mexican whose name Daley didn't catch, seemed anxious to talk, and Daley was glad of that. He had had no opportunity yet to put his proposition to McNally. Since arriving in Frisco, he had seen McNally in brief bursts, over meals at expensive restaurants, and between the endless meetings McNally attended from eight in the morning on. Now, days later, he had hoped that the weekend trip aboard the boat would leave McNally free to talk, listen, make up his mind. So far, life on board had been almost as hectic as life ashore.

The other passengers, or "weekenders" as McNally called them, were a middle-rank television actor and his girl; the development engineer from McNally's race car component company and his wife. Daley found the actor a self-centred bore, and his girl vacuous. The development engineer was humourless, a high-energy achiever; his wife, Daley noticed with a flicker of something or other, looked as if she liked a good time in bed and wasn't having it. Daley had found the only meal they'd eaten since clearing port – lunch – a strain. The development engineer, Harris, had dominated the conversation. Since only McNally appeared to understand the technical jargon Harris used instead of English, the actor had turned to the others and regaled them with name-dropping anecdotes.

Now, with Frisco falling below the horizon, Daley wanted time to think. Somehow, he would have to get McNally away from his goddamn development engineer – they were apparently planning a new suspension system for an Indianapolis car – and show him Carter/Cogswell's account, the charts, and the photographs. The photographs had turned out even better than he had hoped. Although the stones shown on the chart – one of which he had found – did not show up, a faint line was visible between the beach and the position of the north stone. The east stone – the one he had found – looked solid in the separate set of photographs he had taken of it. These he planned to show McNally last.

He decided to tackle him after dinner that night. If he waited until they reached Santa Barbara next day, there might be no other opportunity. It was a long time since he'd really known McNally; they'd both changed so much that all the old easiness between them had disappeared. As pilots they had been firm friends – even intimate friends – but since Daley had begun to crack, ten years ago, then fall, McNally had done nothing but climb. He was a different man, now; power had come with success, and his former courtesy and warmth had been replaced by the kind of social momentum politicians acquire – a sort of swift certainty about people and things that obviated emotion.

Idly, knowing that Pete was there to get him out of trouble if need be, he guided the powerful boat through the water. With his pilot's quickness, he picked up the trick of reading the screens, the trim, the speed and direction of the wind, and the rest. After a while, he asked Pete if he could increase the speed and take the boat through some easy turns. Pete buzzed McNally in the aft cabin and got his OK, explaining that McNally liked to be informed of all manœuvres. Daley knew that Pete was saving face. As captain he liked to think of himself as the guy in charge; there was little doubt that McNally ran things, even here.

He put the boat through her paces under Pete's eager tuition, learning how to turn tight by putting one engine full throttle ahead and reversing the other, how to bring her head up into the wind, and how to adjust the trim. Pete was frankly admiring.

"You learn pretty fast, Mr Daley," he said. "Most people come on this ship don't know from nothing when they come aboard, and they don't know from nothing when they go ashore. Makes a man happy to see someone who *likes* to learn. You ever do any sailing?"

"A little, a long time ago. I think I remember the difference between a cleat and a sheet. But don't hold me to it."

"No chance of that on this ship, anyways," Pete said. "I'm not complaining, see. This is a helluva job. But it isn't sailing. Compared to sailing, this is a bunch of shit. Excuse me. Sailing is skill. Sailing is knowing. This is just driving on water."

After dinner, McNally apologized to his guests and withdrew with a cigar and a roll of blueprints to the aft cabin. Daley followed him.

"I'd like to talk to you about that proposition of mine, Mac. Is now a good time?"

"Frankly, no," said McNally, then, as if sensing he had been churlish, he grinned. "But you're right, we should get to it soon."

"Later tonight?"

"I'm busy tonight, Mike. Let's make it tomorrow, then I can give you my full attention. Yes?"

Daley found himself growing impatient. He resented

McNally's bluff rudeness, his offhand, I'm-in-charge manner. Instead of sitting down at the table, thrusting the blueprints aside and selling McNally hard on the island, he nodded once and left the cabin, not trusting himself to speak.

The actor and his girl were watching a cassette movie on the TV set in the saloon. Daley passed Harris – on his way to the aft cabin – as he went for'ard for some fresh air. For a while he stood on the foredeck in the moonlight, enjoying the sound of the sea hissing back from the bow along the chines, and feeling the throb of the big diesels beneath his feet. Looking aft to the wheelhouse, he could see the glow of the instruments behind the weatherscreen.

Suddenly it rushed him. He was back on the carrier deck; he could see the glow from the bridge, and the running lights. The elevators hummed, bringing the Phantoms up to flight deck level from the hanger decks below. The raised canopies gleamed as the ship altered course into the night breeze.

Daley shook his head, and faced the bow of the cruiser, taking a deep breath. It was no good; the memory would not leave him. Like a film in his head, it ran on.

He strapped in, felt the tap on his shoulder. Twin arms of light beckoned him in to position. He felt the slight metallic jolt as his aircraft connected with the steam catapult. His belly clenched as they were flung forward along the grid and out over the dark sea. Under power he hauled the stick into his gut, then the sickening lurch as the twin GE turbos flamed out. The instrument panel went crazy. His aircraft – his coffin – tipped heavily, loaded with 8000 pounds of rockets and anti-personnel bombs, and plunged downward. His co-pilot's voice, choked with panic, on the intercom. Frantic fumbling, a frightening kick and a rush of air as he ejected, then he was falling, falling. Brine bit into the back of his throat, choking him. His life-jacket would not inflate, then at the last moment it ballooned around him. He'd seen the white eruption of water as he came down. His aircraft going in, dead, taking his co-pilot with it. In the shivering cold waiting that followed his nerves were strung out to breaking point. And the fear that would haunt him popped at the base of his spine and fled up into his brain.

Daley clung to the rail, and forced himself to breathe slowly, calming his insides. His face was damp with sweat. In the cool night air, it felt good. His legs stopped shaking, and he began to feel better. All those years ago – with airline service in between – and it could still hit him like that, almost as if he were being physically attacked. The old nightmare, his "moment of truth", or whatever the hell they called it; the thing that had reduced him, in the end, to gibbering in bars to people who did not listen, to vomiting in washrooms, to shaking like a malaria case in the mornings as he clutched at the bottle by the bed.

He was all right now, the vivid memory – it was always vivid – receded into the depths of his mind. He rubbed a hand across his face, then ran it through his hair. He gazed at the long, glittering reflection of the moon on the sea, peace returning. Then a voice less than a foot from his ear made him start.

"Do you have a cabin all to yourself?"

Daley turned. It was Harris's wife.

"What?" he said.

"Do you have your own cabin?" She put her head on one side, looking at him.

"Yes. Yes, I do."

"Let's go there."

In his cabin she turned off the overhead light, leaving the bulkhead light burning above the bunk. Daley locked the door, then kissed her. Her lips were soft and moist, and he felt her tongue push between his teeth, dart over his own tongue. He tasted her, feeling clumsy and exhilarated at the same time. She leaned into him, and he felt the shape of her breasts and belly against him. He ran his hands over her back, feeling the warmth of her, then brought his hands up to her slim neck, and touched her there, behind her ears, under her hair. He pulled her closer and ran his hands down her firm, curved buttocks. She pushed away from him.

"Wait," she said.

She slipped out of her light dress and let it fall to the floor. She wore nothing else. Her skin was fine and lightly tanned, with a small mole above her navel. Her long, pointed breasts shook slightly as she sat on the edge of the bunk, the coned nipples growing stiff and grainy. She caressed them with her fingertips, scratching them gently, until they were rigid. Daley felt his heart thudding as she leaned back on the pillows, and drew one leg up. She arched her neck, and her long hair hung back over her shoulders, then fell forward over her breasts as she bent forward to watch herself.

Daley gave an involuntary groan, and moved towards her, loosening his belt. She looked up.

"Not yet," she whispered.

As her excitement grew, Daley found the sight almost unbearably erotic. At last she sucked in her breath through clenched teeth, closed her legs over her hand and arched her back. A shudder swept through her, she gave a long, whimpering cry, and fell back as if in a faint. Presently she regained her breath and opened her eyes. Daley was beside her, naked. She seemed dazed with sex, and he went into her at once, thrusting with an energy he had not felt for years. His desire was so great that he could feel himself coming within seconds. She wrapped her legs around him, her feet in the small of his back. Unable to hold back, he came wildly, jerking and thrashing, breathing in great gasps, then rolled on to his back and lay stunned and panting.

Daley woke some time later. She lay on her side, facing him, watching him. They made love again; it was almost as explosive as the first time, but this time she came with him. Her scents and warmth, the way her hair fell spreading on the pillow, the moans that came from deep in her throat, all made him feel like a man with superhuman powers and gifts. Instead of exhaustion, he now felt an alertness, a clearness of mind, that seemed to demand action. He kissed her shoulder and swung his feet to the floor.

As he dressed, she said: "Where are you going?"

"I have to arrange my future," he said. She looked both puzzled and annoyed. "I have to talk to Mac," he explained. "I'm sorry, but it can't wait."

"What about me?"

"I'll come back," he promised.

"My husband will want to know where I am by then."

"Don't give me a hard time," said Daley with a new assurance. "Be a good girl, and I'll see you tomorrow."

"What a lousy way to talk to someone!" she flared. "What do you think I am?"

"I think you're fantastic." He bent and kissed her again.

"Do you mean that?" she whispered.

"I do," said Daley. "Now I have to go."

She pulled his head down and licked his ear. "He gets up early," she breathed. "To do his exercises. Call me around seven-thirty."

"You mean, come to your cabin?" Daley pulled away and looked at her in surprise.

"No, dummy." She smiled and pointed to the telephone fixed to the bulkhead opposite. "The number is two-six."

"What if he answers?"

"He won't. I told you, he does physical jerks. The trouble is, they're not my kind."

Daley found Harris and McNally poring over the blueprints. The aft cabin was hazy with cigar smoke. Clouds of it eddied in the beam of the desk lamp. Daley came straight to the point.

"Would you excuse us?" he asked Harris. McNally looked amazed at this intrusion, but said nothing. Harris looked at him, then back at Daley, gave a little shrug and left them alone.

"Mike, I don't like people to interrupt me when I'm busy," said McNally, cutting a new cigar. He stared Daley straight in the eye. "And I don't like people ordering my executives around, either."

Daley pushed the blueprints aside, and dropped his brief-case on the polished teak of the desk. He opened the zipper, then paused as McNally went on.

"Maybe you didn't hear what I said." McNally leaned on the desk. "You've had a rough time. The airline weren't very generous. I heard all about it. I'm trying to help, but I can't just let you bust up conferences with my executives this – "

"I don't give a shit about your executives," Daley told him equably. He shook out the vellum pages of Carter/Cogswell's story, and the charts, then spread the glossy photographs of the island beside them. "If you want in on this deal, Mac, read these papers through, and look at these photographs. Then let me have your answer. I'll be in my cabin."

Then he turned and walked out. One hour later, McNally ordered Pete in the wheelhouse to bring the boat about, and head for San Francisco at full speed.

3

The Island

The sound of engines grew out of the distance and became a throbbing roar on the quiet tropical air. McNally stood up and moved outside the hut. He watched the Catalina as it banked low, levelled out and came in fast, the hull cutting the water cleanly. The aircraft came to a gliding halt, its bow wave rolling smoothly in towards the shore. A figure appeared in the for'ard gun turret and the anchor splashed into the rippling water. After a minute the rear gun blister rolled open, and Crabtree stood there, wrestling with the dinghy. He threw it out on to the water, paused to strip off his shirt, then dropped heavily into the small craft and started the motor. As it droned in towards the beach, McNally threw away his cigar and put his head back into the hut.

"He should have the seismic equipment. I'll go down and give him a hand."

Daley looked up from a mass of papers on the trestle desk, rose and rubbed his eyes.

"No, I'll go," he said. "I want to stretch my legs."

McNally grunted and went to the portable fridge behind the table. He took out a can of Budweiser.

"How are the calculations coming?" he asked.

"The same," said Daley. He paused in the doorway. "They don't make sense."

Crabtree was wading ashore as Daley came down the beach towards the dinghy. The pilot looked hot and tired. His thick torso was blotched with red, and sweaty.

"Did you pick up the seismic gear?" Daley asked him.

"It's still aboard," said Crabtree. "Jesus, I'm beat. I need a cold beer."

"Go and get one," Daley said. "I'll bring the equipment ashore."

"Right," said Crabtree, scratching under his arms. "Be careful of the meter itself. It's cased in foam rubber, and it's delicate. You'll have to untie the ropes before you move it."

"Don't worry. That thing's important to me," said Daley with a smile.

"Yeah, and to me," said Crabtree. "Get any further with those bloody charts?"

"I'm still working on them." Daley was careful to keep his voice neutral. Crabtree gave a mirthless laugh, sniffed, and went off up the beach to get his beer. Daley pushed off in the dinghy, started the motor, and swung the tiller over, heading for the big flying-boat. The water beneath him was pellucid, and even though it dropped away quickly to thirty feet, the bottom was visible in every detail. Shoals of brightly coloured fish hung almost motionless in the water, then darted away as the shadow of the dinghy passed over them.

As he tied the dinghy's painter to the ring inside the gun blister, and went for'ard to where Crabtree had stowed the special seismometer, Daley thought about the progress they had made so far. It was true that McNally – once he had had time to examine the documents and photographs – had been as enthusiastic as Daley himself. But the enthusiasm was beginning to run out. Crabtree seemed all right. He was used to long flying hours, and as long as McNally paid the bills, and his high retainer, Crabtree would stick around. It was McNally Daley was worried about. Like many men who make good through their own efforts, McNally had an enormous capacity for enthusiasm. But men like that, Daley knew, often grew bored with things that a week or a month before had aroused their greatest interest. Daley had a feeling that was beginning to happen now. Somehow, he had to come up with a positive advance in their struggle.

The charts had proved to be the stumbling-block. Once he and McNally had returned to the island with Crabtree, it had been a matter of a few hours' systematic search to locate the remaining two stone markers which made up the triangle on the charts. Using a theodolite, tapes and a calculator, he and McNally had established that the east stone and the north stone were exactly one hundred and ten yards apart, and that the north stone and south stone were just half that distance apart – fifty-five yards. The dotted line on the detailed chart, running south-east from the north stone, was something of a mystery. The spot at the end of it, marked with an X on the chart, proved bare in reality – rather, it was a sandy, scrubby area, with no discernible features. Following the instruction to "strike due N of it," they had, by means of a compass and the theodolite, made a line that ran due north from this spot, and then had been at a loss what to do next. Already the enlarged version of the chart was beginning to be criss-crossed with lines and dotted with calculations. Daley, sensing the need to think their strategy through called a halt. Supposing that "strike due N of it" meant striking north of some point other than the spot marked with X?

McNally had argued against this. It did not seem logical to him for Carter/Cogswell to have gone to all the trouble he had gone to, simply to confuse whoever got hold of the charts and documents. Daley had pointed out, then, that part of the account was missing; a vital part.

McNally had been impatient, and sent Crabtree back to Papeete to buy a core drill. Crabtree had had to stay in Papeete for a week while the drill was flown in from Hawaii. When he got back with it, McNally began drilling every few feet along the line north of X, to a depth of ten or twelve feet. He got nowhere. Time after time the core attached to the drill produced nothing but sand, soil and occasional layers of grit and shells. He began to get angry, and for a few days sat in his hut (they all had pre-fabricated huts, which McNally had flown in in sections) and made calculations. Daley then hit on the idea of the seismometer, an instrument that worked like the war-time ASDIC, sounding through earth rather than water, and producing read-outs which indicated underground rivers, caves, rock faults and the like. McNally was enthusiastic about it at once.

Daley untied the ropes and eased the seismometer out of its protective foam rubber mouldings. It was quite heavy, but he could lift it. He carried it aft past the bunks to the gun blister and set it down with care, bending right down with it so as to prevent the slightest jarring. As he straightened up, he felt dizzy. He shook his head, and went back for the ropes. Hitching them round the khaki metal housing of the instrument, he lowered it carefully into the dinghy. He was about to drop down after it when another wave of dizziness made him stagger, his vision blurring for an instant. He gripped the rim of the blister, and steadied himself. The dizziness passed. He took a couple of deep breaths, felt better, and climbed down into the dinghy. As he headed for the shore, he wondered why the dizzy spells had come back. Perhaps he should get Crab-tree to fly him back to Papeete, where he could see a doctor. He dismissed this idea as soon as it came to him. He had more important things to do.

The small drill rig stood behind them in the distance, at the beginning of the narrow strip they had cleared through the tangled vines and undergrowth. The seismometer stood close by them on a wooden crate. McNally set the dials and sig-nalled to Daley, who began the check. Twelve sensor probes stuck out of the earth in a rectangular pattern stretching for thirty feet along the strip. Each probe was connected to a wire lead, and each lead was patched in to the main cable, which ran along the ground through the middle of the rectangle. Daley reached the last of the probes and gave McNally the thumbs up. McNally flicked switches, and UHF sonic waves passed along the leads through the sensors into the earth. The six-inch-square screen on the seismometer registered the waves in a complex grid of white lines. The grid pattern was consistent, and McNally knew within seconds that the excavation they were looking for, the mysterious shaft in the diagram chart, was not beneath their feet.

"No good," he called.

"Shit," said Daley, and frowned with disappointment.

They had now covered a hundred and twenty feet, going due north, lengthening the strip with machetes and shovels as they went. After three days Daley was already beginning to doubt the relevance of the expensive seismometer. Unless they could somehow interpret the charts with more effect, they would be on the island for months, searching the area bounded by the stones and the X on the chart for a hole that might not even be there. He knew that McNally would never last that long. And if McNally left, Daley knew he could never carry on alone, without funds.

The light was fading. He disconnected the leads and wound them into individual rolls, then went along pulling out all the metal probes, making a bundle of them under his arm. The methodical work calmed him. McNally hefted the seismometer, leaving the crate behind. They walked together back to the huts overlooking the south beach and the anchorage.

McNally stripped off his sweatshirt, towelled himself dry, and took a can of beer from the fridge. Daley flopped in one of the canvas chairs. McNally opened his beer and drank deep.

"I've been having me a little think," he said. Daley tensed; this was the moment he had been dreading, and it had come sooner than he had expected. "I think we should take another look at those charts. I think we should take the goddamn things and work through every possible combination of figures we can come up with. Based on the measurements."

Daley almost laughed with relief. "I think you're right," he said.

"Get Crabtree in on this, too," McNally went on. "He should go over those aerial shots with a fine comb. He might just come up with something. He knows islands like this one a lot better than we do."

Daley nodded. "Good idea," he said. He did not mind that McNally was talking like a military officer at a briefing, delegating, issuing orders. So long as McNally retained his interest, felt the challenge of the thing, that was all that mattered. Daley understood that for his partner it could never be a question of the gold and silver alone. He was rich. He enjoyed the power running his own corporation gave him. And he was not by instinct a gambler. He was a man who liked to succeed on his own terms. The difference between them was that McNally saw this as a challenge to his abilities, whereas for Daley it had become an obsession.

Crabtree was working on the Catalina, replacing the glass face of the altimeter, which had cracked. He had been carrying the new disc of glass in the cockpit for weeks, but had not until now had time to get to the job. He prided himself on keeping his aircraft in A1 trim. Little things like a cracked dial, or a loose panel, irked him. They offended his sense of order, which although he was not a fussy man, made him the careful and dependable pilot he was. Daley swam out to where the Catalina lay tranquil in the dusk. He pulled himself up into the gun blister and went for'ard, dripping. In the cockpit, Crabtree stared at him with what looked like horror.

"You swim out here?" said Crabtree hoarsely.

"Yes, I swam. What's the matter?"

"Jesus," said Crabtree, with feeling. "Haven't you ever heard of sharks?"

Daley felt the hair at the nape of his neck prickling. "Sharks?" he said.

97

"Long, pointed things," said Crabtree. "You know? With teeth like saws."

Daley began to feel cold. He shivered. "All right, don't rub it in," he said. "Have you got a towel on board?"

"There's one in the locker by the starboard bunks. Under the hotplate. You're lucky to be alive, my friend."

Daley came back, rubbing the towel over his shoulders. "Have you actually seen any sharks?" he said.

"Oh, I've seen them," said Crabtree. "Listen, I grew up with the bastards."

"No, I meant here, around the island?"

"So did I," said Crabtree, putting his screwdriver into the toolbox on the seat beside him. "They're here, all right. Right underneath."

"Well, I haven't seen any," said Daley.

"Come with me," said Crabtree, climbing over the seat. He went aft. Daley followed him to a stowage locker aft of the gun blister. Crabtree took out a powerful Exide handlamp, beckoned Daley to the blister, and shone the brilliant beam down into the water. Shoals of fish, attracted by the light, flitted like shadows beneath them. Crabtree played the beam slowly over the bottom of the anchorage, until it revealed a narrow shelf about forty feet beneath the surface, beyond which the water got rapidly deeper. Lurking under the lip of the shelf was a dark shape. Crabtree played the beam over the shelf, moving it back and forth. The shape moved sluggishly, and Daley saw, with a nasty thrill down his spine, that the shape was a fish. Its body was long and sleek, with a dorsal fin. But it was the head that drew his attention. The eyes were fixed on bulbous stalks that stuck out at right angles from the squat shape; the effect was grotesque and frightening.

"Hammerhead," said Crabtree beside him. "Ugly, vicious, and probably hungry."

"Christ," said Daley. "I see what you mean."

The big fish, uneasy in the light, moved suddenly away into

the deeper water, flicking its tail with a swift, powerful grace Daley found totally unnerving.

"What made you swim out?" asked Crabtree as he put the handlamp back in the locker.

"I wanted to see if I could," said Daley. "Don't worry, I won't be doing it again."

"No luck with the electronic echo-box, I suppose?"

"No, not so far."

"No, you'd have said something by now," Crabtree nodded. He hauled on the painter, bringing the dinghy back to the blister from under the hull where it had drifted.

"Mac and I have decided to take another look at the charts."

Crabtree gave one of his snorting, mirthless laughs. "I thought you'd given up on those."

"Could you go over the aerial photographs again, too?"

"If you say so."

"You don't sound very optimistic."

"What we're looking for is underground, right?" said Crabtree. He dropped down into the dinghy.

"Yes, I know. But some sign of the excavation might be visible on the surface. You know, the way graves are sometimes from the air."

"Graves?" Crabtree looked at him as Daley dropped after him into the dinghy.

"Murder victims' graves."

"You're a cheerful bastard, aren't you?" Crabtree pulled the cord and the motor sputtered to life in a cloud of blue smoke. "Anyway, things like that are usually recent. This is two hundred years old. Undergrowth, fallen trees, shifting sand . . ."

"It's just one more angle," Daley said patiently. "We have to check them all."

"All right, I'll take another look at them. You could be right."

While Crabtree went over the aerial shots in his hut, Daley

and McNally spread the photographic enlargements of the original charts on the trestle desk in the main hut, under the big gas lamp. Daley brought a red crayon and a long rule.

"OK," he said, leaning on the desk, "let's forget all the calculations we've made so far, and start from scratch."

He placed the rule at an angle on the chart and drew a thin red line.

"What's that?" said McNally.

"It's the base of an imaginary triangle," Daley told him. He wiped sweat from his forehead with the back of his hand. "If you take the line between the east stone, and the north stone, that's one hundred and ten yards, right? Now, the line between the north stone and point X is also one hundred and ten yards."

"If you insist on using non–metric units," said McNally. He drank some beer.

"I'm sticking to the measurements they used in 1762," said Daley. "Fuck metrics."

"OK, OK," said McNally. "So the line you've just drawn, between point X, and the east stone, is the base of a triangle. So what does that prove?"

"Wait a second, and I'll explain," said Daley, keeping his voice patient. He did some rapid calculations. "The base of the triangle is eighty-four yards."

"Eighty-four yards," repeated McNally. He drank some more beer, and lit a cigar.

Daley placed the rule at a different angle, and drew another red line. "That line runs due north of point X. I've made it long enough to intersect the line between the north and east stones."

"I can see," said McNally. "But we've already investigated the goddamn due north line with the seismometer."

Daley finished doing some more quick figuring. "Yes, but only for about one hundred and twenty feet. Or, forty yards. As near as I can make it, we should be looking for a point forty-five yards due north of X."

"How in hell do you figure that?" McNally was beginning to be caught up in Daley's enthusiasm. Now, he leaned over the desk beside him.

"Because I'm using the base of the original triangle, as the base of a second one," said Daley. "The apex of which is forty-five yards . . ."

"Due north of X," McNally finished for him. "I get it. You think that's where the excavation is."

"Yes," said Daley. He ran a hand through his hair, and straightened up, "We can try it in the morning. It means hacking away some more undergrowth, but it will be worth it."

McNally sat down, and puffed on his cigar in silence for a moment. Then he turned his head and said: "I think it's the best guess we've come up with, Mike. But somehow I don't feel convinced."

Daley's heart sank. "Well, neither do I. Until we uncover the opening of the shaft, it's all just guesswork. But I'm hopeful."

"For example, that other instruction or whatever – 'Thrum under the sand.' What the hell is that? He wouldn't have written that if it didn't mean something."

"Thrum is a kind of rough matting used on ships of that period," explained Daley. "I think it simply means that the top of the excavation was protected by a thrum covering, which was probably covered in turn by loose earth and sand."

"Yeah, but why put that on the chart?" asked McNally in a thoughtful tone. "I'm not trying to be difficult, Mike. But if we uncovered the shaft, we'd find this thrum stuff anyway."

Daley frowned in turn. "That hadn't occurred to me. Now that you bring it up, I have to agree. It's strange." He paced up and down behind the desk, then paused and sighed. "He was old. By the time he wrote that on the chart, he knew he was dying, and he just wanted to make sure that whoever the charts went to would know when they'd hit the shaft. That's all."

"I'm sorry, Mike, but for me it doesn't gel. My hunch is we'll strike nothing but sand tomorrow. I think 'thrum' is some kind of clue, or code-word."

"I hope you're wrong," said Daley. "Let's get some sleep. I'd like to start early."

McNally nodded. Although neither would admit it, both men were feeling something close to hopelessness. If the search in the morning proved fruitless (and Daley felt as doubtful as his partner, now), they would be facing stalemate.

In his hut, Crabtree worked on, minutely examining each separate photograph under a large magnifying glass. He worked with a concentration born of long experience examining survey maps of the islands he had made home. No detail escaped his attention.

Morley Jarquell was one of the senior vice-presidents of McNalinc. He was fifty-one years old, tough and unsentimental. He owned a ranch north of Yuba City in the Sacramento Valley. He liked to shoot; his only other relaxation was reloading his own shells for his large collection of shotguns, rifles and handguns. He was possessed of considerable cunning and foresight, a limited imagination, and a desire to be independently rich.

He nodded his satisfaction and the waiter withdrew. After two minutes, Jarquell grew impatient and glanced at his watch. He was about to call for a phone when Burnes appeared, threading his way through the other tables, shooting his cuffs. I wish to God he wouldn't do that, thought Jarquell. It makes him look like a cheap phoney.

Burnes arrived at Jarquell's table, smiled and sat down. "I'm a little late," he said. "Did you order yet?"

"Yes," said Jarquell, "I'm having the soup."

"The bouillabaisse? That's a little heavy for me at lunch. I'll have a salad." Burnes ran a manicured finger down the menu. "And the cold salmon."

"Here's the waiter," said Jarquell. "Tell him." He wished that he did not have to deal with Burnes at all. For a start, he was young, only thirty-six. He was good-looking, and slim. He drove a foreign car, and knew nothing about cattle, rifle-shooting or the flying characteristics of the mallard. He read books, and listened to music. He liked women who could talk, and talk back. In short, he was everything that Jarquell disliked in a man. But he was also in a very powerful position in McNalinc's second echelon, and Jarquell needed him.

Burnes chose the wine, and they ate for a while in silence. At length Burnes sat back and looked hard at Jarquell. He knew this would disconcert the older man, and he did not give a damn. He knew Jarquell wanted something from him, and he would make him spell it out.

"The food's good here," said Jarquell, wiping his lips and belching behind his napkin. "You can get a table where you can't be overheard."

"This is clearly one of them," said Burnes. He held Jarquell's gaze for a few seconds, then said in the same mild tone: 'Morley, you didn't buy me lunch so we could bat eyelashes at each other in a quiet corner. You don't even like me. Why don't we get to the point?"

"All right," said Jarquell, with some relief. Even after all this time, all the planning and figuring, he disliked conspiracy. If only there were another word. Yet younger men, men like Burnes, seemed to be able to handle it without a qualm. "I think the time has come for a group of us to . . . dismantle the corporation."

Despite himself, Burnes showed his surprise. He leaned forward, staring at Jarquell with none of his former composure. "Jesus Christ, you're serious, aren't you?" he said.

"Damn right," said Jarquell. He finished his wine, and pushed aside his plate. "Let me give you the basic details. There are three of us, four if you come in. We all feel the market's due to take another slide. The airline operations are our weakest component. They're not breaking even, and we don't think they ever will. The race car projects are crap. The plastics merger in the East was a mistake. Unless we unload all these weaker elements, the corporation will fall apart within a year." Burnes opened his mouth to interrupt, but Jarquell waved impatiently. "Hear me out, please. Now, the trouble with dumping those operations is that it will weaken us on Wall Street. Then the healthy part of the corporation will collapse before we can do a damn thing about it."

"That depends on how it's handled," said Burnes cautiously. He felt off balance.

"You think so?" said Jarquell, and gave a short laugh. "Horseshit. There's only one way to do this thing, and that is for our group to sell – through a legitimate front – and retire before the roof falls in."

"You sound like some kind of godfather," said Burnes, shaking his head. "Suppose I decide not to cooperate? Will you have me silenced?"

"What's your holding in the corporation?" said Jarquell.

"It's quite small."

"It needn't be," said Jarquell. "We've been buying quietly for eleven months. We have effective control of thirty per cent of McNalinc stock."

"I don't understand," said Burnes with a frown. "I thought you wanted to sell."

"That's where you come in," said Jarquell. His eyes narrowed. "You see, this stock isn't paid for yet. We've been buying through redundant sections of the corporation, which have no actual cash assets. A feedback system of cheques. Now we've run into a problem, because the cheques are going to come out of the end of this system earlier than we planned. The way you're placed in the profitable part of McNalinc, in computers – "

"I know where I'm placed," Burnes cut him off.

"– you have access to –"

"To cash? Come on. I'm sorry, but what you're talking about is a very big Federal offence." Burnes shook his head "I'm just not into that kind of a deal."

"Will you let me finish?" said Jarquell angrily. "We don' *need* any goddamn cash. What we need is someone to fake th payments."

"You what?"

"Through the bank. All legitimate."

"Jesus Christ, how can it be legitimate if it's faked? And it's still an offence."

Burnes stared hard at Jarquell. Then he said: "Program-link. Uh? Program-link?"

Jarquell nodded, and breathed out with relief. "If you authorize these transactions, back-dated, no one is going to question a damn thing. You're a computer expert. And you're in an executive position. You simply link everything into the accounting system. It'll go through our system, and the bank's system, like a breeze."

"Yeah, but –"

"The only person who might question this is McNally himself. He likes to keep his finger on the corporation pulse. But McNally isn't here. He's fucking the sand on some goddamn island in the Pacific."

"It's too simple," said Burnes after a short silence. He smoothed his napkin and toyed with the edge of his wine-glass. Jarquell watched him with a hunter's alertness. He did not say a word.

"But you might get away with it for . . . maybe two weeks." Burnes looked up. Jarquell grinned, nodding encouragement. "That'd give you just enough time to transfer your money to Europe, convert it, and disappear." Burnes stared across the restaurant, then back at Jarquell. "You couldn't hope to stay in the US."

"I've made my arrangements," said Jarquell. "So have the others. There are still places left outside of this country where a man can live pretty good, where there's space, and air to breathe."

Burnes almost laughed aloud. "You know, if you weren't offering me a hell of a lot of money, I think you'd make me puke. Just how much are you going to offer me?"

"Twenty-five per cent of whatever we make. We're going for a bottom line of around ten million. If you do your stuff now, we can sell a week from today."

Burnes nodded slowly, and allowed himself to smile. "That's a hell of an incentive to keep from puking." He looked at Jarquell for a moment, then said: "I just thought of the right word to describe you. You're not a godfather. You're a kind of modern mutineer."

Daley woke early, and listened to the soft wash of the waves, and the shrill whistles and cries of the tropical birds. When they had first come to the island, the birds had been silent, terrified by this invasion of mankind and his machines. Now the birds had accepted their presence, and their songs and calls echoed through the trees and undergrowth all day long. Daley got out of his camp bed, stretched and walked down to the water for a quick swim. As he plunged in, he remembered the shark, and floundered in haste to the safety of the dry sand. McNally came down the beach towards him, putting on his sun hat.

"Too cold, huh?" He smiled at his own joke.

"No," said Daley, and coughed. "I forgot. There's a shark out there."

"I never swim, except in a pool," said McNally. "Have you seen Crabtree?"

"No, I came straight down here."

"He's not in his hut. Those photographs are spread all over, and his lamp's still burning."

Daley looked down the beach to where the dinghy lay, its motor hooded in canvas, high up on the sand beyond the tide marks.

"He's not on the Cat," he said.

"Maybe he swam."

"No. He showed me the shark."

"Uhuh." McNally squinted, looking out at the Catalina. "You think maybe he's on to something?" He looked at Daley out of the corner of his eye.

"If he is, he didn't say anything to me. I haven't seen him since last night. Let's get some breakfast." Daley picked up his towel and started back up the beach. McNally remained for a moment, staring thoughtfully at the wavelets breaking in a shallow rinse over the smooth sand. Then he followed Daley up to the huts.

When Crabtree had not appeared by eight-thirty, McNally showed signs of irritation and suspicion. Daley was troubled in turn, but hid his concern because he did not want McNally to think that he shared the other's obvious doubts about Crabtree's integrity. Daley was worried for the pilot's safety. If anything had happened to him, they would be in an awkward position. People would want to investigate; Crabtree was widely known and respected in the islands. But there was more to it than that. Daley realized, for the first time, that he had grown to like Crabtree; he was straight; he knew who he was, and what he was capable of; there was about him the air of a man who would not let you down.

Putting aside these thoughts, he said: "Let's get started. We have to clear about fifteen feet more before we can make the test." He drained his coffee cup, and stood up.

"What about Crabtree?" persisted McNally. "Where the hell is he?"

"He probably worked all night, went for a walk and fell asleep under a tree," said Daley. "If he hasn't turned up by noon, we'll look for him."

McNally lit his first cigar of the day and puffed on it, frowning. At length he rose, hefted the seismometer out of its corner and followed Daley to the cleared strip two hundred yards away through the undergrowth. Daley carried the machetes and shovels, and the cables and sensors. Wearing shorts, sweatshirts and wide sun hats, and light canvas work-boots – a uniform all of them had adopted – they made a start on the tough, scrubby undergrowth of guava bushes, chopping with the machetes, then scraping and grubbing with the shovels. It was slow and arduous work. As the heat increased they began to sweat profusely, and they were soon panting and cursing. McNally more than once swore that he'd have a bulldozer flown in.

After an hour and a half, they had cleared a further ten feet, and paused for cold drinks and a rest. There was still no sign of Crabtree. McNally made no comment, but Daley knew he was itching to go looking for him. They cleared another few feet, and had another short break, then set up the seismometer and the sensors. Daley checked that all the leads were patched in, and McNally switched on. The grid appeared on the screen, and trembled once or twice. McNally stared at it, fiddled with one of the controls, then switched off. He checked all the controls, then switched on again. Daley stood waiting at the far end of the rectangle of sensors.

"Well?" he called.

McNally threw away his cigar with a disgusted flick of his wrist. "No dice," he said. He spat on the ground, and switched the machine off.

"I'm sorry," Daley said, as he went along the lines of sensors and pulled them out, winding up the leads. "I'm sorry," he said again, when he had finished. "You were quite right, it's no damn good trying to guess our way to the shaft."

McNally said nothing. He hoisted the seismometer on to his shoulder and made for the huts. Daley followed. When they arrived, Crabtree was waiting for them.

"Where in hell have you been?" McNally demanded at once. Crabtree stopped drinking from his can of beer. It was clear he did not like McNally's peremptory tone. He stared at him without replying, then belched and finished his beer.

"You've been gone all morning," continued McNally in the same hectoring way. "We didn't know whether to search for you, or what the hell to do."

"I can look after myself, thanks," said Crabtree. Daley saw that he was angry now, and moved forward to cool things down.

"Take it easy," he said. "Mac was worried, that's all. We thought you might have gotten hurt, broken a bone. We can't afford to lose you, you know. You're the pilot."

"I wasn't worried about his goddamn bones," growled McNally, getting himself a beer from the fridge. "I think we ought to agree that nobody goes off alone without telling the others where."

"So that's it," said Crabtree, with his mirthless snort. "You think I'd deliberately hold out on you."

"Come on," said Daley. "This isn't the time to start arguing about –"

"What would make you hold out on us?" said McNally, putting down his beer unopened.

"Mac, for Christ's sake," said Daley. McNally ignored him. "You found something, didn't you, Crabtree?"

"You're making it very difficult for a man to keep his temper, Mr McNally," said Crabtree. His eyes had gone hard, and he stood with a hunched stillness.

"Fuck your temper," said McNally. "What did you find, that's all I want to know."

Crabtree crushed his beer can between his fingers, and turned to Daley. "I'm going out to my ship," he said. "If you want to talk about where I've been this morning, you'd better come along. I'm buggered if I'll stay here and listen to him." He jerked his thumb in the direction of McNally, then left the hut.

Daley waited a moment, then said: "I'd better go with him."

"I don't like the way he talked to me," bristled McNally, biting the end off a cigar. "I think he just talked himself out of a job."

"Pull yourself together, Mac," Daley told him sharply. "I hired Crabtree, and this is just as much my operation as yours. He stays."

McNally seemed on the point of rounding on his partner, but thought better of it, and lit his cigar in angry silence.

"If he has found the shaft, think what that means," said Daley, "instead of worrying about your injured dignity, or whatever." He paused in the doorway. "If I was Crabtree, I think I would have busted your nose for you."

McNally nodded, then gave a shamefaced grin. "I guess you're right," he said.

Crabtree had started the motor and was sitting in the dinghy waiting. Daley waded into the shallows and grabbed the gunwale.

"Hold it a second," he said. "I don't want to go out to the aircraft. If you did find a clue in the aerial shots, I'd like to know about it now."

"Fair enough," said Crabtree. "I don't know whether it's a clue or not. You know where the beach is shaded over on the chart, near where you found the first stone?"

"Yes, in a kind of fan shape."

"Right. Well, I went over the shots of that area with a magnifier. There seemed to be something under the sand there. So, I went and had a look this morning."

"And?"

"There's not much left, but it looks like there was a big pile of mats spread out on the beach, then covered over with sand."

"What kind of mats?" Daley's knuckles whitened on the gunwale.

"Most of them have rotted away, but they're made of some kind of fibre – manila hemp, I'd say. Kind of roughly woven together with twine."

"Thrum," said Daley, and nodded. "Anything else?"

"That's it," said Crabtree. "Well, except for the rocks."

"What rocks?"

"Semi-circle of rocks off that beach. It's on the charts."

"Go on."

"Well, they didn't get there by themselves. Looks as if somebody tried to build a kind of breakwater."

"A breakwater there doesn't make sense," said Daley in a puzzled tone. "There are too many reefs for boats to come in."

"Don't ask me to explain it, Mike," shrugged Crabtree. "I'm just telling you what's there."

"OK, thanks," said Daley. "I'll go and take a look myself."

Crabtree opened the throttle, then shut it off again, and let the motor idle as before. "What's that you said just now about a drum?" he asked curiously.

"Not drum," said Daley, and explained about the thrum.

Crabtree silenced the motor altogether. "Listen, we could be on to something here. I'll come with you." He jumped out and hauled the dinghy back on to the beach.

Daley was already making for the huts. Crabtree dug the little anchor into the sand and followed. In the new excitement generated by Crabtree's discovery, he and McNally quickly forgot their differences. The three of them took shovels and headed for the beach north of the spit. McNally was eager to dig up as much of thrummed matting as possible, in the hope of discovering its purpose. Crabtree said he would help and Daley left them and walked down the long, gentle slope of the beach. He wanted to examine the large semi-circle of rocks for himself.

He had noticed the rocks on the charts, and in the photographs (in which they showed as vague but discernible blobs amidst the maze of coral reefs under the water). But until now he had not considered them important. He waded into the water, still wearing his boots to protect his feet from the coral.

The rocks lay in water only two or three feet deep. A few of them were visible above the surface. As he came close to them, Daley could see – in spite of the years of coral growth, and the shifting of bottom sand – that the rocks had been carefully placed, making an even curve perhaps fifty yards across. He saw something protruding from behind the rocks a little distance away, and waded towards it.

What he found were several broken wooden stakes, blackened and worn by the sea, embedded in the sand. He pulled at one of the stakes. It remained firm. Moving along the line of the curve, he saw that there were stakes embedded behind the rocks every few yards. In the clear water he could see fragments of others lying in the sand.

"They did build a breakwater," he murmured to himself. "Only the bones are left."

A shout from McNally made him turn, and he saw his partner beckoning with an urgent, excited energy. Crabtree stood nearby, holding his shovel and looking down at something they had uncovered.

"What did you say?" Daley asked, as they sat down in the hut.

"There was no matting where we found it." McNally hefted the pistol in his palm. "Crabtree stopped for a drink of water, and dug his shovel into the sand a couple of yards behind him. And the shovel hit it."

McNally cleaned some more corrosion off the trigger guard and the pan of the pistol. "Must have been a fine piece once," he said, admiring the elegant lines of the weapon. "Maybe tomorrow we'll find the remains of the guy it belonged to."

Daley nodded, and sat behind the desk. "It might help us if we had some clue."

"How he was killed, you mean?" McNally looked up from his chair opposite, his face oddly youthful and expectant in the light from the doorway.

"No, I don't think knowing that would help much. Maybe

he wasn't killed. Maybe he just dropped it. No, we need to know what the hell all that matting was for." Daley took the pistol from McNally and turned it over. On the stock was a silver plate with the maker's name, "L. Downey – London".

"This probably belonged to the captain," he went on. "It's too well made to be standard arms chest issue. Probably one of a pair."

"So what?"

"Well, let's suppose the man who lost it on the beach was a leader. The guy who supervised the burial of the chests, let's say."

McNally rose and walked to the door, looking out. Then he turned, and his face was animated. "That's a good thought, Mike. A damn good thought."

"That semi-circle of rocks just off the beach," Daley continued. "It was a breakwater of some kind. Most of it has been washed away, but when it was built it must have held back the tides, so that the water inside it couldn't rise beyond a given level."

"Yeah, but why?" McNally rubbed his forehead and sighed. He was silent for a moment, then went on in an excited tone. "Unless they needed to hold back the water so they could lay the mats. Jesus, that must be it."

"I think so," agreed Daley. "The tide mark on the beach comes up over most of those mats. That's why they've rotted away, even though they were well buried." He pulled a copy of the chart across the desk. "It follows that the mats were of vital importance."

"Maybe they tried to build a big raft there, or a boat," suggested McNally.

"No, Mac, it doesn't add up," said Daley at once. "They had the ship. Our man even draws attention to it at the end somewhere." He fumbled amongst the papers on the desk, and found a photostat copy of Carter/Cogswell's account. "Yes, here it is: 'I could not hope to sail the brig single-handed, and in any wise the spars were all sent down, and the sails ashore.' He doesn't say how many men were left alive, but there must have been enough to sail a ship."

"You're right," said McNally reluctantly. "Anyways, they wouldn't build a boat on that beach. They'd use the one south of the spit. The anchorage beach."

"Our man probably helped with the laying of the matting," said Daley. "We don't know for certain, but it's probable he wrote about that in the account."

"I wish we didn't know some of it was missing, goddammit," said McNally with an impatient shake of his head.

"But he drew attention to the thrum on both of the charts," Daley pointed out. "We should have started by looking on the beach, but we got hung up on those damn stones. We have to solve the mystery of the breakwater and the mats before we go any further with the stones."

They heard the dinghy approaching the beach from the direction of the moored Catalina, and a few moments later Crabtree joined them in the hut, removing his hat, and wiping sweat off his face and neck.

"It still doesn't give us any idea about the shaft itself," McNally was protesting. He had opened a can of beer, and froth spilled from it as he gestured. "I don't see how they can be connected at all."

"What can't be connected?" Crabtree wanted to know. McNally ignored him, caught up in pursuit of his argument. He pulled a copy of the excavation diagram from the pile of papers.

"Look at this," he said, stabbing his forefinger at the diagram. "Here's something else we overlooked. The tablet. See what he's written on the corner here? 'Look to the tablet.' And there's the tablet, right there in the shaft."

"OK, Mac, OK," said Daley, holding up both hands. "Let's just take it one step at a time."

Crabtree moved forward, and popped a can of beer. "You

know what I reckon?" he said. "I reckon we ought to forget all about it for today. Relax, have something to eat, play some poker, get a good night's sleep. Start fresh in the morning."

McNally stared at him for a long moment, but was not really looking at him. "I have an idea," he said at last, snapping his fingers. "I'm going to fly Harris out here."

"Who's Harris?" Crabtree asked, looking at the others in turn.

"Mac, what the hell are you talking about?" said Daley. He spread his hands. "Why bring Harris into this? It's crazy."

"He's an engineer," said McNally in a tone of new confidence.

"He's an engineer," repeated Daley blankly.

"He wasn't always a mechanical engineer," explained McNally. "He once worked in mining."

"Oh, I get it," said Daley, beginning to be angry. "So you think, because he worked in mining, he'll be able to somehow discover where the shaft is. Am I right?"

"Not completely," began McNally.

"Listen, who is Harris?" demanded Crabtree now. "I might remind you that I have a ten per cent interest in this. If you bring somebody else in, are you going to cut him in? And if so, for how much?"

"Your percentage won't be affected," Daley said quickly. "I guarantee that." McNally had moved to the door. Daley followed him. "Where are you going?" he said.

"I'm not going to argue about this, Mike," McNally told him calmly. "I've made up my mind. I'm picking up the tab, and I say Harris comes out here."

"You mean you want to cut him in for a share? Because that's what you're going to have to do. Once he finds out what we're looking for, he'll want a lot more than his monthly pay-cheque."

"Look, Mike," said McNally, turning to his partner, "so far all we've done is go round in circles. What have we found?

Some stones, some rocks in the water, and some rotten mats. Oh, yeah, and one rusted-out pistol. Terrific."

"And you think Harris can look the ground over, and point right to the spot?" said Daley with heavy sarcasm.

"No, I don't," said McNally, in the same reasonable voice. "I think he can bring a new approach to the problem. I think he can look at all the facts we have, knowing there's a shaft there, somewhere close by, and he can deduce where it might be. As an engineer."

"I have never heard such crap in all my life!" said Daley. "Don't you see? It's only a matter of time before we deduce it ourselves."

"Now who's talking crap?" said McNally roughly. "We're up shit creek, and you know it. We need some expert advice here, and whether you like it or not I'm going to get that advice." Before Daley could protest further, he went on: "And now I'm going for a walk. On my own." Then he strode from the hut, going in the direction of the spit. Daley did not follow him. Instead he went back inside and played poker with Crabtree. They played for the kind of stakes that seemed appropriate. Daley lost five million dollars in the first four hands, and began to relax.

Harris received McNally's cable from Tahiti two days later. He cabled from his office to McNally's hotel in Papeete, asking if he could bring his wife. He had phoned her from the office; she had been so insistent that he had had to agree to make the request, at least. McNally, preoccupied with ordering new equipment and supplies, and disinclined to argue at a distance, cabled a curt negative. Crabtree had his aircraft checked thoroughly.

At the end of a week, Harris arrived in a chartered plane from Hawaii, bringing the equipment McNally had ordered, and his wife.

"She'll have to go back," McNally told him in the hotel

bar. He clinked the ice in his glass.

"I don't think she'll do that, Mac," said Harris, with a worried frown. "She said I never take her anywhere. She said we don't go on holidays together any more. I tried to tell her, but she wouldn't listen."

"Conditions are primitive on the island," said McNally. "She'd get bored. Bored women get in the way."

In their hotel room, Harris told his wife of McNally's decision. He tried to be tactful.

"OK," she told him, "I'll file for divorce as soon as I get off the plane in Frisco."

"Jill, for godsakes, don't give me a hard time with this," pleaded Harris.

"Then tell him I'm coming along."

"She can cook for us," Harris told McNally next morning. "She's a great cook, Mac."

"We take off at ten," said McNally. "Listen, if she –'

"She won't."

Daley had stayed behind. He preferred it that way; not because he relished being alone on a tiny, remote island in the middle of the Pacific, but because he wanted to go over the evidence in peace, and if possible come up with a solution before McNally and Crabtree returned with Harris. It was almost inevitable that he would fail. But he did not mind that; he needed to try.

In the big locker in the aft compartment of the Catalina, Crabtree had stored a second, smaller dinghy; an inflatable one-man life-raft. He agreed to leave this behind, so that Daley might paddle out on the anchorage water and observe the myriad tropical fish which lazed and darted there. At least that was what Daley told him he wanted it for.

Also stored – in the main hut ashore – were three wetsuits, with cylinders, masks, flippers, and transceiver head sets. There were spearguns with each of the suits. McNally had insisted on bringing these to the island so that they could relax and keep fit by doing some scuba fishing. None of the equipment had even been unpacked.

Daley took one of the suits from its plastic case, powdered it, and laid it out ready. Then he checked one of the double-cylinder oxygen packs, and the breathing apparatus and mask. When he had satisfied himself that everything was in perfect working condition, he took the gear down to the little dinghy at the beach, put it aboard, and paddled out on the water. He had done a short course in wetsuit diving as a navy pilot. He was confident he remembered enough to keep himself out of trouble. Thoughts of the shark – or sharks – worried him, but did not frighten him. His fear after swimming out to the aircraft at night had been instinctive and justified, but he had no intention of taking a similar risk now. He would be far safer under the water, suited up, than he had been swimming on the surface, splashing and kicking. To be on the extra safe side, he had brought one of the spearguns with him.

By leaning over the side of the tiny craft as he paddled, he could see the bottom of the anchorage with ease. He passed the place where the Catalina was usually moored; a small anchor buoy rode on the surface, its line stretching down to the smooth sand thirty feet below. When he was over the shelf beyond which the bottom fell away, he estimated the distance to the beach at about a hundred yards. He paddled out another fifty yards, and peered down into the water. He could now make out the bottom only dimly, eighty feet down. He became aware he was drifting, and realized that he was caught in a rapid current which was carrying him eastward towards the spit. He had been so intent on examining the degree of slope on the bottom that he had not noticed the ripple of the current on the surface. He tried to paddle his way out of the current. After a few seconds, he saw that it was no good, and began to be a little scared. Beyond the spit lay reefs. If the current swept past those reefs at the same speed it was carrying him now, the rubber and canvas dinghy would be ripped to shreds.

Again he tried paddling, digging the oval blade deep into the rushing water, and thrusting with all his strength. Soon his arms and shoulders were aching, and he was gasping for breath. It was becoming difficult to prevent the dinghy from spinning. If he lost control now, he would be swept on to the rocks and drowned. He paddled like a man demented, trying to head the dinghy directly for the southern shore of the spit; if only he could thrust himself clear of the main body of the current, he would be able to dive overboard and swim for it.

He was now halfway along the spit, and the reefs lay little more than two hundred yards ahead. And he was still no nearer the shore; the strip of water between the dinghy and dry land was at least a hundred yards wide even now. Summoning up a desperate strength, he flailed at the water with his paddle, sucking air into his burning lungs.

As abruptly as he had drifted into the current, he was clear of it. He was astonished. Behind him the water hissed and gurgled, rushing towards the reefs in a long, treacherous curve. Before him lay the peaceful shore of the spit, across a stretch of water that was calm and smooth. Shaking with fatigue, he paddled towards the shore, anxious simply to reach the firmness of land and safety. He leaned over the side and rinsed out his mouth, wetting his hair and face at the same time. As he spat out the salty water, he found himself looking straight down at a curved shape on the seabed. He grabbed the diving mask, and held it on the surface; through the glass disc the shape was more precise.

"By Christ," he said aloud. "I've found it."

"Found what?" said McNally, dropping his grip on the sand. Daley nodded to Harris, then shook hands with him as he came forward. Crabtree called a greeting from the dinghy, then shoved off and headed out to the Catalina.

"Found what?" repeated McNally. His face in the dusk was eager, despite the weariness of the long flight.

"Why is Crab going back to the Cat?" asked Daley. "Hasn't he had enough of her for one day?"

"Her is right," said McNally. He picked up his grip, and looked at Harris briefly; the engineer looked uncomfortable, hot and tired. "Listen, for Chrissake, Mike," McNally went on, "what did you find?"

Daley looked at him, making him wait. "Don't get over-excited," he said. "It's not what we came for. At least, I don't think so." Disappointment showed now in McNally's face.

"OK, wiseguy, if it isn't that, what?"

"The ship," said Daley, a touch of pride in his voice.

"What ship?" McNally looked blank.

"The *Severn Gull*." Daley started towards the huts. "Come on, I'll show you where on the chart."

Harris followed them, wordless and perspiring. Halfway up the beach, he paused.

"Mac," he called. McNally turned. "Mac, I think I'd better wait here on the beach. She'll expect me to wait. We'll find our own way."

"OK," said McNally. "See you in a few minutes. Our pilot knows the way," he added. Harris nodded and sat down on his bag.

"Did I hear him say 'she'?" asked Daley as they walked on.

"You did," said McNally. "He brought his wife along to do the cooking."

"Christ," said Daley, remembering the night aboard the cruiser. "Was that a good idea?"

"It wasn't my idea," McNally told him.

While they waited for the others to come ashore, Daley spread the aerial photographs on the desk in the main hut. They were from the batch showing the spit and the anchorage. McNally got a beer from the fridge.

"I'll have to give Harris and his wife one of the huts," he said, popping the can. "Mind sharing with Crabtree until we can rig up a new one?"

"That's OK," said Daley, careful not to show the resentment he was feeling. Harris was bad enough, but his wife was altogether a tougher proposition. He leaned over the desk. "Now. Look at this shape just south of the spit. Like a rock contour under the water." He pointed with a pencil. McNally examined the vague shadow on the photograph, and rubbed his forehead.

"It could be anything," he said at last.

"It's the ship. We missed it before, because we weren't really looking."

McNally swallowed some of his beer. He looked again at the photograph examining it closely. The gas lamp hissed in the silence. He straightened up. "What makes you so sure?" he asked, and his voice was full of doubt.

"I told you," said Daley, growing impatient. "I came across it by accident. I mean, I was looking for it – I'd started to look – but I didn't expect to find it there."

"You're not making a lot of sense, Mike," said McNally, growing impatient in turn. He drank some more beer and let out a long breath. "Guess I need some sleep."

"You can sleep in a minute. What I'm trying to tell you is that I've seen the ship with my own eyes."

McNally put down the beer can. "Why in hell didn't you say so? Jesus, I thought you were just talking about the photographs."

Daley told him about the near-disaster in the dinghy. "I've been out there a couple of times since," he went on, "but I need someone to come with me, to look properly."

"Do you think the chests could be in the ship?" McNally's weariness had vanished. Daley shook his head, and dropped the pencil on the desk.

"I doubt it. But we need to know for sure. When our man left the island in his open boat, he couldn't have known whether the others would leave the island or not. If they did try, maybe they loaded the chests back on board. There was some kind of fight, remember – there may have been a change of plan. And it's just possible, given the location of the wreck, that they struck the rocks east of the spit and foundered trying to double back into the anchorage."

McNally looked at the photograph for the third time.

"No," he said decisively. "That current you were talking about would have put them right on the rocks, and she'd have broken up. I think she was scuttled."

"Maybe," said Daley, and thought for a moment. "Maybe." He paused again then looked at McNally. "But what if we spend the next six months looking for the stuff on the island, when all the time it's lying out there on the bottom of the sea?"

The door opened behind them. Both men turned.

"Harris and his wife want to know where they're going to live," said Crabtree.

Roy Sewerd sipped his coffee, and thumbed the "record" button on his portable dictacassette. "And I would be grateful if you would check with the plastics people in New Jersey, and call me with your recommendations next week."

He paused again, and sipped more coffee. He looked at the reproductions of paintings on the walls of his office; they did not inspire him. He quite liked the Picasso, but not the others. He had not chosen any of them. Like all the offices of McNalinc's middle-rankers, his had been decorated by a design company which specialized in "custom individualization of the executive environment". The phone on his desk flickered on. He stabbed the lighted button, and lifted the receiver.

"Sewerd."

"Mr Sewerd, this is Janice Hartwell, Mr McNally's sec – "

"Yes, Janice?" Sewerd swivelled quickly to and fro in his chair.

"There's a meeting in the boardroom, and they'd like you to come up."

Sewerd was surprised. Even when McNally was around he was never invited to such meetings. "What time is that, Janice?" he asked.

"Now," she said. "They want you up here right away."

"Do you have any idea what this is about?" he said. "Can you feed me some names?"

"All the vice-presidents, except Mr Jarquell, and Mr Burnes."

"Any idea why they want me there?"

"I'm sorry, Mr Sewerd, it was all arranged confidentially.'

"OK, Janice, thanks. Tell them I'll be right up."

Sewerd hung up, and rose, pulling on his jacket. He felt his stomach tighten. Something was wrong. As he stepped into the elevator he began to sweat. It was like being summoned to the principal's office in high school for some unknown offence.

Janice met him at the boardroom door, and took him in. There were eight men seated around the big, polished table. He smelled cigar smoke. There was an air of tension. Davis, vice-president in charge of computer sales, pushed back his chair and came forward.

"Roy, won't you sit down, right here. That's all, Janice, thank you."

Sewerd allowed himself to be ushered forward and seated beside Davis. He recognized most of the other faces at the table as men he had met at various times but had never really had dealings with. He felt out of place, uncomfortable, and apprehensive. All the men looked at him. Davis spoke.

"I think you all know Roy Sewerd, Mac's trouble-shooter . . . ?"

There were murmured acknowledgements and nods. Sewerd smiled and said: "Gentlemen." His effort to sound confident seemed to work.

"Roy, we're in something of a quandary here," said Davis now. "We need your help."

Sewerd waited, unable to think of anything to say.

"Before I outline the problem, I have to ask you not to mention this conversation outside of this room."

"That's understood," nodded Sewerd. He wished he had gone to the men's room before taking the elevator.

Davis leaned forward and clasped his hands on the polished surface of the table. "It's apparent that during Mr McNally's absence, certain . . . transactions have taken place, which could not have taken place if he'd been here."

"Go on," said Sewerd. He did not know what the hell Davis was talking about. The whole scene had begun to assume for him a farcical quality.

"We were wondering if Mr McNally left any instructions for you as to how you might contact him in an emergency."

"No, he did not," said Sewerd. "Miss Hartwell has a number, I believe, in Tahiti where he can be contacted by the people there. But, uh, he led me to understand that all transactive business would be delegated before his departure. I mean, I just have no authority at that level, gentlemen . . ."

"There was no other arrangement?" said a bald man across the table. His eyes were flat and hostile.

"No, sir," said Sewerd. He glanced around at their faces. "Maybe if you told me what this is all about . . . ?"

Davis, in turn, glanced at them all, then turned back to Sewerd.

"Did Mr McNally, to your knowledge, have a personal bank account anywhere outside this country?"

"I don't handle his private banking, Mr Davis," said Sewerd.

"An account in Switzerland, for example, that you heard him mention?"

Sewerd let the question sink in. Now he understood. All these men believed that McNally had disappeared with the corporation's money. It was fantastic.

"Gentlemen," he said, "I can't help you. I can't help you at all."

"Think very carefully, Roy," said Davis. "You were pretty close to him, he confided in you."

"No, sir, he did not," said Sewerd. "I don't know what's going down here, but I'm not involved."

"We're not suggesting that, Roy," said Davis, a rough edge in his voice.

"We're asking you if you can recall anything that might explain McNally's prolonged absence."

"Gentlemen, I'm sorry, but I don't have to listen to this crap. I'm not going to be cross-examined. I've told you I don't know anything, and now I'm going to leave. Excuse me." He was already on his feet as he concluded this little speech. Davis held up both hands.

"Roy, Roy, Roy," he said. "Sit down, please. Nobody's accusing you, or trying to cross-examine you. I'm sorry if I gave you that impression."

Sewerd sat down. His palms were clammy. "Then tell me what this is all about," he said.

Davis sighed. "Someone has succeeded in embezzling ten million dollars from this corporation," he said. "Stocks were bought and sold between different parts of the corporation by a very skilful series of manœuvres. The corporation is crippled. Within a matter of days, we're going to begin to die. Mr McNally is not here. Mr Jarquell is not here. There are other people who are not here. There is no explanation for their absence from their offices. Do I make myself clear?"

"I guess you do, sir," said Sewerd, "but I still can't help. I don't know anything about it."

"All right, Roy. I'm sorry we had to grill you. You're not alone. We're talking to everyone who had close contact with Mr McNally before he left."

Sewerd rose a second time. "Do I still have a job?" he asked.

"For the time being," said Davis, "we all have jobs. But I'd be dishonest if I told you that won't change."

The men around the table had lost interest in him, and Sewerd rose. He felt a peculiar mixture of relief and unease. He wanted to run, but he controlled the urge, and walked to the door. As he closed it behind him, he heard one of the men at the table give a long sigh of defeat.

Jarquell blinked in the morning sunlight, as he stepped out of the bank. In the middle distance he could see the huge complex of offices which was the headquarters of the European Economic Community. He disliked Brussels; it was a cold town; the brown contact lenses hurt his eyes as he blinked again in the sunlight. He tucked the briefcase under his left arm, and flagged down a cab.

"Get me to the airport," he told the driver. In the cab, he examined the olive staining on the backs of his hands, and ran his hands over his face. The luxuriant moustache on his upper lip had begun to feel almost natural. He looked out of the window, and began to relax. Today's initial transaction at the bank had gone well. When he flew to Europe again in a few months time, he would sell the rest of his commodity scrip (purchased through a discreet acquaintance in London) and his financial manipulations would be at an end. It had taken a lot of organization, and a lot of planning to get him this far. His money was laundered. His tracks were covered. A million dollars in cash lay at this moment in the briefcase beside him on the seat. But it was not in dollars. And the name in his passport was not Jarquell.

"They'll probably catch the others," he said to himself, with some satisfaction. "They'll sure as hell catch that smartass bastard Burnes. But they'll never find me. Not in a million years."

McNally cut the motor and allowed the dinghy to drift until Daley held up his hand, peering over the side into the water.

Then McNally dropped the anchor. The dinghy steadied and lay motionless in the calm water.

Both men were in wetsuits, and now each checked his equipment. They had brought torches, small-headed underwater axes, and knives, but not the spearguns. Neither had they bothered with the radio transceiver helmets, or ring-pull inflatable life-jackets. They did not plan a long dive, they would not be going deep, and each would be in sight of the other at all times.

McNally entered the water first, toppling backwards over the side in the orthodox manner, and swimming down to ten feet, where he righted himself and trod water, waiting for his partner. Daley followed moments later in a cloud of bubbles. The surface of the water had a pearly brilliance; the dinghy seemed much larger from below, the bright orange of its skin darkened by the undershadow.

Daley joined his partner, and they swam over the long, humped shape below. He gave McNally the thumb down sign, then veered the flat of his hand to the right, indicating that he wanted to look at the bows of the ship first. McNally nodded and they kicked down. The light at thirty feet was almost as bright as just below the surface, so clear was the water. Yet thirty feet of water will mask some detail always, and Daley saw, as they closed in on the wreck, that his partner had been right about one thing. There were no masts; he had been hoping to find them lying along the seabed, embedded in the sand. And since there were no masts, she had almost certainly been stripped and scuttled. She lay on her port beam, coated from stem to stern in marine growth. No wonder she had appeared in the photograph as no more than a curved shape. The mossy growth was perfect camouflage.

Daley swam towards the waist of the ship from the bows. There was no trace of spars, tackles, blocks, or rigging. Even the bowsprit had gone. He scanned the decks and noted with satisfaction that the hatch covers had gone also. McNally swam towards him, having surveyed the stern. He held out his hand, palm up, the standard underwater interrogative. Daley shook his head – nothing – then indicated the main hatch. McNally nodded. They switched on their torches and swam cautiously through the gaping hatchway into the dark bowels of the ship. Startled fish swept past their faces. A squid shot for cover. Daley's backpack clunked against a ladder. They swung the powerful beams back and forth, and saw that most of the timbers were intact. But she had been gutted; nothing remained but the shell of her. They ventured further and played their torches along the length of the hold, the one place the chests could have been stowed. They were not there.

In the darkness the two men stuck close together, despite the reassuring brilliance of their torches. Beyond the narrow beams lay the unknown. It was the instinctive wariness of all living creatures in an unfamiliar environment, the knowledge that they were vulnerable. Daley tapped McNally on the arm, and they headed for the hatch. As they reached the opening, thankful for the green light of the water outside, Daley felt something thump against his left leg. McNally was ahead of him, had already reached open water. Against his training he let fear take over, and thrashed out wildly with his legs, shooting forward out of the hatch. He turned then, his torch tumbling from his grasp, and saw the shark.

The evil hammer shape of the head came at him. He sucked in air, was stricken for a moment by pure terror, and hung there helpless. His sudden immobility saved his life, for the shark, as frightened as himself, heeled sharply to the right, passed him in a rushing beat, its graceful body swishing, and fled to the green vaults beyond. He saw a pale flicker as it fanned its tail once more, then it was gone. His heart thudded so hard in his chest that he felt dizzy, and he took several seconds to compose himself. Forcing himself to be calm, he told himself the danger was past, and made for the surface. McNally was already pulling himself aboard the dinghy.

When he broke surface, he said to McNally: "Thanks for waiting, partner."

McNally did not look repentant. He pulled off the hood of his wetsuit, and ran a hand through his hair. "Want a hand in?" he grinned.

When he was in the dinghy, and stripping off his backpack, Daley began to tremble. He had to stop and grip the side of the little boat for support.

"What's wrong?" McNally was anxious now.

"I . . ."

"Hey, what the hell happened down there?" McNally took in his partner's ashen face and trembling hands, noted that his torch was missing. "What happened?" he repeated.

"That shark I was telling you about . . . it jumped me," Daley said, and abruptly vomited, McNally helped him out of the wetsuit, and wrapped him in towels. After a few minutes he felt better, and drank some cold water from the flask he had brought.

"That's the last time I ever go swimming around here," he said with great feeling.

"I didn't believe you about that shark," said McNally. "Not when you first told me about it. Man, you're lucky to be alive."

"I know," said Daley. "If I wasn't meant to find this bloody treasure, the fates would have killed me long ago."

"Yeah, well at least we know where it isn't." McNally sucked on a Budweiser.

"Where's Crab this morning?" Daley asked after a moment.

McNally nodded towards the Catalina lying a quarter of a mile away across the anchorage. "He's on his ship."

"Trouble?"

"The port engine coughed a couple of times on the way from Papeete. He's a little worried. So am I, but I didn't say anything to him."

Daley remembered his first trip aboard the old aircraft, the puffs of smoke and the metallic shuddering from the massive radial engine. If Crabtree was still having trouble with it, maybe they should suggest that he replace the engine. But that would be expensive, both in money and time. He might not be able to locate another engine for weeks, or even months. Daley did not mention the earlier mishap to McNally now, but instead changed the subject.

"What's Harris doing?" he asked.

"I gave him the charts, and the account, and all the stuff," said McNally, looking towards the beach. "Everything we have – photographs, calculations, everything. When he's been over them, he'll walk over the ground. Look at the beach, the stones in the water, and the stones north of the camp. I don't want to crowd him, Mike. I'm leaving him alone for a couple of days, so he can feel his way into the problem."

"Uhuh," grunted Daley. He nodded and drank the rest of the cool water. It refreshed him, and he felt a wonderful sense of calm and well-being. He'd been lucky. He was not going to go into shock. "I think I'm OK, now," he said. "Why don't we go ashore and have something to eat."

"I bought a new camp stove in Papeete," said McNally. "It's a pretty good one, the little guy in the store told me. Let's see what Mrs Jill Harris can do with it."

Daley looked at him in surprise. "Hell, you're not serious about her cooking for all of us, are you?"

"Why not?" McNally started the motor. "Haul in the anchor, will you?"

"I don't think she's going to like that, Mac," Daley told him as he coiled the anchor rope in a neat fake between their feet. "She struck me as a woman who doesn't take orders from people."

"I'll ask her nicely," said McNally, and tossed his beer can over the side. He headed them towards the anchorage beach. "Women like to cook. She's no different."

Daley saw that he was still wearing his flippers, and pulled them off. A thought occurred to him that was so fundamental he wondered why he hadn't considered it before. "Why did they scuttle their only means of escape?" he said. "I don't understand that at all."

"Come back to my theory," said McNally, as they grounded in the shallows.

"What theory?"

"They built another boat, or a big raft." The two men heaved the gear out of the dinghy, and waded ashore. "Not necessarily on the other beach. Maybe right here, on this one."

"If there were just a few of them left," said Daley, dragging the dinghy up on to the sand, "it makes some sense, I suppose. Unless they decided to settle here like the *Bounty* mutineers on Pitcairn."

"No, there'd be evidence of that." McNally glanced towards the Catalina. Crabtree was paddling ashore in the one-man dinghy. "They'd have built log cabins, cleared land for crops. Anyways, why would they stay? There was nothing for them here."

"I don't know," said Daley, shaking his head. "The whole thing's crazy. The hidden excavation, the ship deliberately sunk, that plan to sail to Canton. None of it makes sense."

"Listen, Mike, what the hell does it matter? So they were crazy. Who cares? We've eliminated the ship, and now we know the stuff is buried somewhere nearby on the island. We have a mining expert to help us. We can't lose."

Daley could see that McNally was ticking off these points aloud to reassure himself that a logical approach would provide a satisfactory answer. McNally was psychologically incapable of examining the problem from an intuitive position. And all along, Daley reflected, as they waited for Crabtree to beach the little dinghy, he had had an underlying feeling about the search, a feeling that logic was not the answer, but rather a grasp of the motivations of the men who had brought the chests of gold and silver so far across the ocean, against all the odds.

Trove

If they had been mad, then he would have to try to put himself in their place, feel as they had felt, think and act as they had done. That was why it was so important to understand why they had scuttled their ship. He decided to keep all this to himself, and to continue the search on his own, while outwardly going along with whatever McNally and Harris decided.

Crabtree waded ashore, and the three of them started up the beach towards the huts. Daley thought about Jill Harris. After that night aboard McNally's cruiser, he had not seen her again. By seven-thirty the next morning, the time appointed for their assignation, the cruiser was within an hour or two of San Francisco, and Daley was sure Harris would be in his own cabin, packing and working out the details of McNally's directives for the operation ahead. Daley himself had not slept. The planning session with McNally had taken most of the night, and as he watched the sun rise over the sea, Daley let the erotic memory slip away and dissolve in the clear pink light.

Several times she had called him at McNally's house to suggest that they meet, but McNally had set a tight schedule for getting to the island and he used this as an excuse. The real reason for avoiding her was that his commitment was now to the island, and he wanted no distractions. It had not been easy. The phone calls were very explicit, and he had been tempted. Now that she had actually arrived on the island, he felt irritated. Yet maybe she was not here because of him at all. Perhaps he was arrogant to assume that she was.

"Still thinking about that shark?" asked McNally. He had been telling Crabtree about Daley's narrow escape.

"I warned you, you mad bastard." Crabtree shook his head with fatalistic resignation.

"I'm still here, Crab," smiled Daley. "I'm indestructible." They reached the huts.

During the meal, which Jill Harris had prepared, Daley avoided meeting her gaze. She had spiced the canned meat and added other little touches of her own, including some of the wild

132

fruits of the island. They were all hungry; and ate quickly; the conversation was light and relaxed. Afterwards, Harris wanted to check a detail on one of the charts with McNally. They went to the Harrises' hut, which the engineer was using as a workroom. Crabtree announced that he was going back to the Catalina, and Daley was left alone with Jill. He felt uncomfortable, and rose from the trestle table, making a lame excuse.

"You needn't worry," she said.

Daley decided that a candid question was his best move. "Why did you come out here?"

"Oh, you think I came because of you, right? Well, I didn't." She collected plates from the table and stacked them on a beer carton. "Where am I supposed to wash these?"

"There's a stream behind the camp," said Daley. "I'm surprised you didn't see it when you were picking the fruit."

"I didn't come out here to wash dishes, and cook and sew, either," she told him.

"I didn't think you were that type. I was sure you weren't."

"What type?" She wiped her hands on a paper towel, and brushed her hair back from her forehead.

"Busy little housewife."

"Shit. No, I'm not, thank God. Want to help me rinse these off?"

"Not really."

She looked at him, putting her head on one side. "You're scared you'll give in, aren't you?"

"Give in to what?" Daley lit one of his rare cigarettes.

"Come on, do we have to talk like a couple of idiots? You know what I mean."

"You still haven't told me why you came out here."

"You're looking for something. I want to look, too. It's exciting."

"Didn't your husband tell you what we're looking for? Didn't McNally?"

"All they wanted to do was persuade me not to come. Which

only made me more determined." She picked up the pile of plates, and went to the door. Daley laughed. He found her refreshing, he realized. She knew what she wanted, and tried to get it.

"Don't you want to know what we're looking for?"

"You can tell me if you like," she said. "If you don't I'll find out anyway. What I'm interested in is the looking."

"Good," said Daley. "We're looking for four large wooden chests, containing something like twenty million dollars in silver and gold. It isn't less than that. It could be a lot more."

She looked at him for a long moment, then said: "Screw washing the dishes."

He laughed again, and the slight but nagging feeling that he would like a drink, which had been there ever since the shark nearly got him, evaporated in his lungs.

She put the plates back on the table. "Tell me all about it," she said.

"OK," he said. "But don't say I told you. The others mustn't know."

"Why not?" she laughed. "I was sure to find out. I told you I would."

"And you have. But I don't want the others to know I told you. All right?"

"Fine," she said with a shrug. "If that's what you want."

"I was opposed to your husband being brought into this," Daley told her. "McNally knows that, and so, probably, does your husband. I've decided to conduct a search of my own for the chests. Want to help me?"

"Yes," she said. "But please, could you call my husband Logan? That's his name."

"Is that his name? OK, Logan it is."

"You don't like him, do you?"

"I have nothing against him in any personal way."

"Don't cop out."

"No, I don't like him. I think he's a bore. But then, I don't really know him."

"I think you're underestimating him. But I want to help you. You're more honest than he is."

"You think he'll succeed in finding the stuff, do you?"

"I don't know how difficult that's going to be. But if bringing Logan out here is any indication, then I'd say you've got a problem. He's very good at solving problems."

"I'm better," said Daley. "I mean, I hate arrogance, but I know I'm better at this problem than he is. I can feel it."

Jill looked at him closely, and saw a look of commitment on his face she had not noticed before. It was almost like devotion, she thought. It was as though he was possessed by some kind of religious fervour.

"I want to help you," she said again.

Daley walked to the door, then came back to her in a restless, nervous stutter of motion. He did not appear to have heard her. "You have to understand that I change my mind a lot," he said, as if to convert her to his cause by first pointing out his shortcomings. "For example, I went looking for something the other day, which a few days before I thought could not be there. I found it."

"What was it?"

"A ship, I don't know why I went looking. It was an intuitive impulse, an instinct. That kind of thing keeps happening."

Her feeling that she was looking at a man in the grip of some powerful religious force was strengthened by this odd statement.

"I don't understand it," Daley went on, "so there's no use asking me why or how or anything like that. I'm beginning to think there's a sort of mental key to this thing that I don't have yet. Well, not really just mental. A psychic key. That probably sounds weird to you, but I've been living with this now for quite a while, and that's the only way I can express it."

"I don't think you're crazy, if that's what you mean. Tell me the whole story. Maybe I'll feel the same way you do."

"Good," he said, and smiled at her. "I've been wanting to tell somebody about that feeling for a long time."

He pulled one of the photostat copies of the Carter/Cogswell account out of the pile of papers on the desk behind them. He gave it to her, and said: "You'd better read this first. Otherwise you won't know what the hell I'm talking about."

Daley left her, and went for a walk. When he returned an hour later, McNally was unpacking the crates of equipment he'd brought back from Papeete. One crate contained a small but sturdy powered winch. Another, an air pump, with lengths of hose. The last crate, to Daley's surprise, contained a radio transmitter-receiver, and a large bundle of aluminium tubes.

"I meant to get this set up before now," McNally said. "I'll need some help with the mast."

"What do we need this for, Mac?" Daley was annoyed that McNally had not told him about the new radio.

"I need it to keep in contact with my people in Frisco," McNally told him. "If I'm going to be out here for an extended stay, I need to get information about my corporation. I have a man in Papeete who listens out. My office is in contact with him."

"I see," said Daley. "Wouldn't the radio on the aircraft have been enough?"

"Sometimes the aircraft isn't here," McNally pointed out.

Daley helped him rig the mast in silence. They placed it behind the main hut, in the clearing they had made. When it was all pieced together, and the wire guys anchored, it made quite an impressive sight.

"Going to test it?" Daley wanted to know.

"Later," said McNally, wiping sweat from his forehead, and replacing his sun hat. "The guy in Papeete only listens out at certain times."

"Suppose somebody picks up one of these conversations,"

Daley said. "Suppose they take a fix on the signal, and come snooping around."

"This island isn't even charted," McNally said with a dismissive gesture. "Anyone who happened to overhear would just assume it was a ship."

"Maybe," said Daley.

"What are you so worried about?" said McNally, with a rough edge to his voice. "Listen, this damn operation doesn't pay for itself, buddy-boy. I have to make sure the money keeps coming."

"I'm sorry," said Daley. "I'm getting over-cautious."

"It's the waiting," said McNally. "As soon as Harris is through with his preliminary study, we can get back to work." He lit a cigar, and blew smoke in a forceful cloud. Daley could see that his partner was anxious that Harris should prove his worth without delay. McNally still saw the whole venture in terms of a challenge to his ego. This knowledge made Daley suddenly weary of McNally's company, as if he was being drained of enthusiasm by the other's narrow view of life as a series of personal tests.

"I'm going to take a nap," he said. McNally grunted, and nodded, his cigar gripped in the corner of his mouth, between his teeth. Daley left him with a sense of relief, and went to his hut.

Jill was sitting on his camp bed, reading the last page of the account. As he came in, she got up and stretched.

"Have you read it?" he asked her.

"It's incredible," she said. "Where did you get it?"

"I found it. In an old country house, in England."

"Here, you'd better have it back. I'm not supposed to have it, am I?" She held it out to him.

"Did you look at the charts?"

"Yes. Everything."

"OK, I'll fill you in on the rest tomorrow."

"You want me to go?"

"Well," he said, feeling awkward, "Crabtree could come back any time."

She looked at him for a moment, then shrugged. "OK," she said. She moved past him, then looked round. "See you later," she said.

"Wait," he heard himself say. She came back to him, and as soon as he felt her against him, he wanted her so much he could hardly breathe. He kissed her mouth, her eyes, her throat, and they sank on to the bed. "Let's get undressed," she whispered. He sat up and fumbled with his clothes. She was naked in seconds. He kicked off his shorts, and she pushed him gently down on his back. "I want to sit on you," she whispered. She straddled him, and sank down with a gasp of pleasure, offering her nipples to his mouth. He abandoned himself to her tender carnality.

Davis stared at the TV console in despair. The mid-morning readouts from the Wall Street-linked computer downtown showed McNalinc had again fallen steeply. Other computer corporations were feeling the wind. In boardrooms in the East, and in Texas and Chicago and Los Angeles, anxious men would now be endeavouring to shore up their defences. In New York, brokers would be on telephones, trying to isolate the malignant disease of panic. Davis turned.

"Send this message to the people in Tahiti," he said, but was interrupted before he could continue, Johnson, from McNally Northwestern Airlines, was on his feet.

"What in hell do we want to send more messages for?" he demanded. "He's not there!"

"What do you suggest we do?" enquired Davis coldly. "Send another 'diplomat' out there to locate him?"

"He'd only get lost, like Tyson."

"Tyson didn't get lost, Bob," Davis said firmly, staring Johnson down. "He's on his way home right now. I circularized his cable; didn't you see a copy?"

"No, I didn't," said Johnson. "I'm trying to run an airline. I should be in Seattle right now. There's a strike threat. My wife also happens to be pregnant."

"All right, Bob," said Davis with a sigh. "We don't really need you here. Why don't you take the next flight? I'll call you when we hear."

"I want to hear what was in that cable first," said Johnson, annoyed at the way Davis seemed to be dismissing him.

"All right," said Davis, controlling an impulse to knock Johnson cold. He picked up the orange copy of the cable from the table and read: " 'NUMBER ONE NIX STOP NOGO INFO PAPEETE OFFICE STOP INQUIRIES NIX STOP PAPEETE SAY ONWAIT INSTRUX EX NUMBER ONE PACIFIC LOCATION BY RADIO STOP CABLE MY INSTRUX STAY RETURN STOP TYSON.' That's it." He dropped the flimsy copy so that it floated jerkily to the table and skidded to a stop on the polished surface.

"Outasight," said Johnson in disgust, and left.

"Any more news from Brussels?" said Davis, turning to Janice Hartwell as she hurried in with a sheaf of cables. She shook her head.

Later, at lunch in a restaurant overlooking the bay, Davis told his lawyer to stand by.

"The Federal boys will be all over us," he said. His lawyer nodded gravely, and ate a mouthful of scampi. "We're up crap creek," said Davis, tasting acid in the back of his mouth. "I want out of this. I don't want to be implicated, Arthur."

"You are implicated," said his lawyer, wiping his lips. "The whole executive structure is implicated. It's my job to prove that you, personally, are not guilty."

"Guilty?" said Davis, gripping the edge of the table. "What do you mean, guilty? I had nothing to do with this, Arthur. What in hell do you mean, guilty?"

"Don't panic," said his lawyer, sipping his wine. "I'm here."

At dusk Daley found McNally standing in front of the radio transmitter in the main hut. He was subdued and did not answer when Daley spoke to him. Instead he went to the door, and stared out at the palm trees. Daley was puzzled; his partner was not given to moodiness, and in company was never silent for more than a moment or two.

"What's wrong?" Daley asked, when he could bear the gloomy quiet no longer.

McNally turned slowly and took a long breath, then let it out in an uncharacteristic sigh. "Took a bath," he said. "Went down the pipe with the water."

"How bad is it?" said Daley after a moment.

"Kaput. Finito. Everything. A few days of trading."

"Stock market," said Daley. He did not make it a question.

"Slaughterhouse, buddy-boy." McNally lit a cigar. His hands shook. "The thing of it is," he went on, in a voice that was subdued, with an edge of bitterness, "for the first time since I went into business, I had nothing to do with what happened. I was robbed of ten million dollars, cold. And they think I did it. Isn't that something?"

"Robbed?" said Daley. "I thought . . ."

"Embezzled is the right word, I believe. Four of my key people. The bastards."

"I don't know what to say, Mac. I hope to Christ it wasn't my fault, bringing you out here."

"I came of my own free will," said McNally.

Daley could not fully understand McNally's position; he could not understand what had happened; but he realized that they on the island were now faced with the greatest threat of all, that they would have to stop.

"What are you going to do, Mac?" said Daley quietly. He could feel his chest tighten with apprehension as he spoke.

McNally looked at him, then out of the door. He puffed on his cigar, then grunted: "If I go back to Frisco now, I'm liable to be arrested. There's no hope of saving anything, anyways. So I'm going to do the only damn thing I can. Find that goddamn hole, and dig up that goddamn loot."

"It's one hell of an incentive, you have to admit," said Daley with a relieved laugh.

"It isn't funny," snapped McNally.

"I wasn't trying to make a joke of it, Mac. We're on an equal footing now, that's all."

"Because I'm broke, you mean? I guess we are."

"I think I can probably persuade Crab to stay," said Daley, already thinking ahead. "What about Harris?"

"I haven't told the others about this yet," said McNally. "I'd like to sleep on it, and decide tomorrow how to go on. They don't need to know anything till then."

"I agree," said Daley, nodding.

That night Daley did his best to be cheerful as they ate the meal Jill prepared. Even so, she noticed McNally's silences, and the scowl he seemed to have to make a conscious effort to dislodge from his face. If Crabtree noticed, he gave no hint. Harris as usual, was preoccupied with figures. They separated early and went to their huts. Jill touched Daley's hand briefly as she and her husband left the main hut; Harris did not notice.

Bright parakeets and king birds, their green, white and crimson plumage vivid in the early sunlight, chattered and whirred in the foliage. A small pigeon, or island dove, hopped between the huts, pecking at the earth. Already the insects were beginning to hum and tick in that special combination of sounds which rises to a crescendo in the heat of the tropical day, until the very air seems to vibrate. The tall palms were still; there was no breeze. The water in the anchorage was flat calm; only at the very edge, where small, gentle waves broke, was the endless movement of the sea betrayed.

Half a mile from the beach, and fifty yards off the end of the long spit, a tiny object bobbed and dipped in the water. A figure rose in it, and waved. There was an urgency about the wave. There was something about the way the figure balanced that was desperate. A faint shout came over the smooth anchorage, then the figure disappeared. The little object twisted about and was caught against something beneath the water. A moment later it rushed on, was caught again, and tipped up at an angle, revealing itself as the one-man dinghy from the Catalina. Then it fell back, floated sluggishly a little way, and was gone. Some gulls landed on the starboard wing of the Catalina, and strutted inboard towards the engines. Yesterday Crabtree had taken a snack out there while he checked the oil lines. On the beach, scuttling crabs pulled at the remains of a fish.

Half an hour later, Crabtree came down the beach from the huts, settling his sunhat on his head. He wore tennis sweatbands on his wrists, and in his shorts and light shirt, might have passed for a burly doubles player at some country tournament in his native Queensland. He paused to listen to the calls and chatterings of the birds.

"Noisy little bastards," he said to himself cheerfully, shook his head once, and stumped on down the soft slope. Then he saw that the small dinghy was missing. He shaded his eyes and looked out at his ship. Maybe Daley or McNally had gone aboard for something. The little dinghy was not there either. He stared beyond the aircraft, out to sea. There was no sign of it. A minute flicker of alarm passed through his gut into his chest. He walked along the beach, just clear of the water, and made sure the dinghy was not moored on the far side of the Cat. His lightweight boots sucked at the wet sand. He went back to where the larger dinghy was secured above the tide line. There were marks in the sand where the small dinghy had been dragged down to the water's edge. He felt the flicker again in his chest, and frowned.

"That bloody mad bastard," he muttered, again staring out to sea. He was thinking of Daley. He continued to stare for perhaps another half minute, then turned and stumped up the beach towards the huts, breaking into a clumsy trot as he neared the trees.

"She said she was going for a walk," said Harris, pulling on his clothes. "An early morning walk, before it got too hot. Are you sure that dinghy's gone?"

"It's gone all right," said Crabtree. "And she's the only one who isn't here."

Daley had not been in his bunk when Crabtree left the hut they shared. On returning from the beach, he had gone to McNally's hut, then he and McNally went to the main hut. Daley was there, brewing coffee. There was only one hut left.

Harris finished putting on his canvas shoes. He was very pale, and sweat shone on his forehead. "It might have drifted away by itself on the night tide," he said. He was clutching straws, now.

"No chance," said Crabtree, because there wasn't. "But she might have lost the paddle and drifted out to sea. So I'm going to have a look. You'd better come, too."

"Hey, that's a good idea." Harris brightened. "That's something I didn't think of. The aircraft. OK, let's go."

McNally came into the Harris hut. "Mike and I will take the other dinghy out," he said. "She might have got caught in the current."

"What current?" Harris paused in the doorway. Crabtree was already heading for the beach.

"Off the beach," said McNally. "It flows around the spit."

"Did anyone warn her about it?" Harris was prepared to be truculent, searching for someone to blame.

"I don't think so. Only Mike really knows where it is."

"Jesus Christ," fumed Harris. "Just how dangerous is this current?"

"How the hell could any of us know she'd do a fool thing

like this?" snapped McNally. "Get going, you're wasting time."

"If she's dead," said Harris, his eyes burning into McNally's, "I'm going to hold you responsible." He turned and left the hut, running for the beach.

Crabtree had the dinghy in the water, and was pulling the starter cord. Harris clambered in beside him in a flurry of haste. Crabtree brought the motor to life, and held the throttle down, waiting.

"Let's go, for godsakes!" yelled Harris. "What are you waiting for?"

McNally appeared, sprinting down the beach. He splashed through the shallows and jumped aboard. "Mike's checking the cylinders on the scuba gear," he panted. "It'll be ready by the time I get back to the beach. Let's go."

"Isn't using the scuba gear pushing your luck a bit?" said Crabtree above the chattering whine of the motor.

"What?" McNally cupped his ear.

"Forget it," said Crabtree. "I hope we find her in time."

They didn't find her. Crabtree spotted the ripped one-man dinghy hanging on the rocks beyond the spit, but when McNally and Daley got there, there was no trace of its occupant. They dived repeatedly, until the tanks ran out, but she was gone.

Harris sat alone in the hut he had shared with his wife; he could not bear to let the others see his grief; and he blamed McNally for her death, for bringing them out here on a crazy wild goose chase, and letting her drown. He knew that he was not in a rational frame of mind; behind his tears, he nurtured the belief that McNally should be made to pay for this, perhaps with his life.

Daley sat with McNally and Crabtree in the main hut, because he knew that alone he would not be able to go for long without a drink. The strenuous diving had made him tired, and that helped, too.

"We ought to report this, you know," Crabtree said for the fourth or fifth time. "If we don't and they find out in Papeete we had that radio, there'll be trouble."

McNally glanced at the large transmitter-receiver in the corner of the hut. Its blue metalled façade gleamed in the afternoon light.

"If it was just the Cat radio, there'd be no problem," Crabtree went on. "I could say it blew a valve, no worries. But they'd never buy the two sets going on the blink at the same time."

"OK, OK, report it, do what you like," said McNally in an exhausted voice. "Nothing can get any worse for us now."

"Come on," said Crabtree, glancing from McNally to Daley, "It doesn't mean we have to give up. We'll report a drowning by accident, and that'll be that. They won't send anyone out here, you needn't worry about that."

"That isn't the point," said McNally. "We're broke."

"What?" Crabtree's face was ludicrous in disbelief.

McNally told him about the collapse of McNalinc. He spelled it out with care, so that Crabtree knew just what the position was, could be in no doubt that they had reached a very low ebb.

"Strewth," he said at last. He got a beer out of the fridge, popped it, and drank it off in a single draught. He wiped his mouth, belched, and sat down. "Fuck it," he said, "Let's give it a go."

"You want to stay?"

"I want to stay, and I want to go on looking until we find the bastard."

"Listen, I can't even pay for your last tankful of fuel," said McNally. He wanted to be sure of Crabtree; there could be no turning back later. "My assets are being frozen. If I arrived in Frisco tomorrow, I couldn't drive my car out of the garage. I couldn't take my boat out of the harbour. The corporation owned everything."

"Stuff your boat," said Crabtree, and gave his snorting laugh. "My credit's good, even if yours isn't."

McNally turned to Daley, who had been sitting in silence for some time. "Mike, you still feel the same way you did yesterday?"

"I've got nothing whatever to lose," said Daley in a subdued tone.

"OK," said McNally, with a sigh. "Now all we have to do is talk to Harris."

"I'll leave you to do that, Mac," said Daley, without looking up.

"I'd appreciate it if you came along," said McNally. "I think he blames us for her death. It's crazy, but if he feels that way I'm going to need help to talk him around."

"Talk him down, you mean," said Crabtree. "A couple more days and he'll be ready for the funny farm."

"Crap," said McNally. "Harris is OK. He's a lot tougher than you think. Anyway – " he swung round on Crabtree – "he just lost his wife, for Chrissake. You can't expect him to behave as if nothing had happened."

Crabtree shrugged, and rubbed his face over with his hand. "You know him better than I do," he said. "But you'd better get him to give up the idea of blaming his old lady's death on any of us. That's a non-runner."

"He'll get over it," McNally said. He lit a cigar, and broke the match in two.

2 FINDING

Harris spread photographs and charts on the desk. Outside, in the noon daze, insects hummed. Harris glanced at the other three men grouped around him, then began to talk, pointing at features with a crayon pencil. They listened with respectful attention; his voice had a considered authority.

"The depth of the ocean in this area of the Pacific is approximately thirteen thousand feet. This island is therefore the peak of an undersea mountain. If you look at the western side particularly, you can see the abrupt deepening of the water only a short distance offshore. The soundings on the original chart are inaccurate, as you can see by looking at the photographs. The soundings are far more accurate for the eastern side, where the drop is more gradual. There's a shelf, reefs, and so on. My guess is that the shelf is a ridge falling away from the peak. There may even be a small plateau. OK, having got that basic information out of the way, let's look at the immediate area we're covering in this operation: the beach with the mats under the sand; the stones in the water; and the stones on land. I think we can forget about the wrecked ship for the moment."

He drew a rough circle with the crayon on the chart in front of him. "Now, having studied the aerial photographs, and having walked over the ground, I think I'm safe in making an assumption about the subsoil in this immediate zone." He adjusted his metal-rimmed reading glasses, looked up at the others briefly, then went on. "I think what we've got here is a natural depression in the rock, a kind of basin. Over thousands of years, as the weather and time have worn away the rock of the original jagged peak, this basin has filled with soil, layer on layer. All that's left of the peak is this line of hills down the western side of the island."

McNally shifted restlessly and cleared his throat. "Logan," he said, "can't you be more specific? I mean, how does this geological history help us? We need more definite hunches if we're going to start looking on – "

"Let me finish, Mac, please," said Harris with a touch of asperity. "I wouldn't give you this high school lecture if there was another way of explaining. OK, so here is the basin, and here are the hills. What it means is that aside from the basin, there is no other place on the island where the soil is more than a few feet deep. In other words, the basin is the only place where a shaft of a hundred feet could be dug. And the logical place to sink the shaft is right in the middle of the basin, where the soil is deepest."

"Yes, but how in hell would sailors know all this?" Daley interrupted. "You've been to college, studied geology, you've got aerial photographs . . . They were ignorant men, they didn't have that kind of knowledge."

"Exactly," said Harris, turning to Daley. "Almost without question they dug several shafts, before they found a place deep enough. That's what I think those rock markers are – we'll have to take some compass bearings."

Daley thought for a moment. "Hold it," he said, as Harris turned back to the desk to continue. "I just can't see it. There weren't very many of these men. They were split into two groups. Their ship still wasn't repaired. They simply didn't have the energy or resources to go digging up half the island until they found a perfect site. Anyway, what about the break-water, and the mats? What were they for?"

"One thing at a time, I'm not a genius," said Harris, and wiped his forehead with his handkerchief. "All I'm trying to do is proceed by logical deduction. I want to try another assumption on you." Again he glanced at all of them, getting their attention. Crabtree moved closer to the desk, folding his arms. "Suppose one or two of those men were miners?"

"Miners of what?" said McNally. "They were seamen."

"A lot of British sailors came from Cornwall," said Harris. "And in Cornwall they mined tin, and lead. The industry was well-established there in the eighteenth century. I know, because I submittted a paper on it once. Large numbers of tin miners ended up on ships. They didn't like the underground life; conditions were appalling in those workings. The only alternative was to go to sea. If my assumption is correct, and a couple of the crew were former miners, they'd have been able to show the others how and where to sink the shaft."

Daley shook his head in exasperation. "Jesus, I'm sorry, but I still don't see it. I'm not trying to make this more difficult, but really we're no further along than we were when we started. It's still all theory, and logical guesswork. We have to explain that damn breakwater, and those mats. And why they sank their ship. At least, that's the way I see it."

"May I please finish?" said Harris with an impatient glance at Daley.

"Yeah, let him tell us what he thinks, Mike. You keep jumping the gun all the time," said Crabtree.

"OK," said Daley with a shrug.

"Just go along with my assumption a little further," continued Harris. "They've found the spot they've been looking for, after several failures. They sink the shaft, and they set up the markers, so that when they return, they'll know where to look. There'd be no risk of a mistake. Now, what I suggest is that we find the central area of the basin with the seismometer. Then we can look at those stone markers again, take some readings, and locate the shaft with the minimum delay."

"Oh, boy," said Daley.

"Shut up, Mike," snapped McNally. He leaned over the table and stared at the charts and photographs. After a few moments he straightened up, and looked at Crabtree. "What d'you think, Crab?" he said.

"Seems fair enough to me," said Crabtree. "But I'm no expert."

"I think you're all wrong," said Daley, before McNally could ask him. "But we're all in this together, so I'll go along with whatever you say."

McNally sighed. "If you could only come up with something better, Mike, I'd listen to you. We all would. Forget the ship and the mats and all that stuff. We'll get back to it. Let's find the shaft first, yes?"

"What happened to that pistol we found?" Daley asked.

"It's on the desk, somewhere," said McNally, fumbling

amongst the mass of papers. "Here it is." He held it up.

Daley moved forward and took the corroded weapon from him. "If only we knew what the man who lost this knew," he muttered. "I'm going to clean it."

"What for?" said McNally. "Think if you clean it up it might talk to you?" He laughed.

Daley looked at him without amusement and without comment. He weighed the pistol in his palm, turned and left the hut, seeking the solitude of his own quarters.

It had taken a week to edge Harris out of his misery. Daley felt numb, as if his marrow had been reduced, his nerves deadened. But McNally and Crabtree noticed nothing out of the ordinary in his behaviour, since they were preoccupied with the rehabilitation of Harris. Daley did not participate in this, but spent the time walking endlessly over the ground bounded by the stone markers. Once he walked to the low hills on the west of the island, and passed an afternoon exploring the terrain, amidst the plantains and guavas, and the squat, dense trees of the slopes. From the highest of the hills, in the centre of the spine, he could see the whole of the island, including the wide beach and the coral shallows, the anchorage to the south of the spit, and the Catalina, small and still as a toy on a sheet of glass. He doused his face and neck with water from his canteen, and sat in the shade of some guava bushes, sipping.

He knew he was not really trying to find the shaft, or discover the solution to the puzzles which confronted them. He was keeping himself from losing control. He was keeping himself occupied away from the main hut, where Crabtree kept his gin. Both McNally and Crabtree were drinking more than usual in an effort to draw Harris out of himself, and Daley stayed clear of them all, except at meal times. Eventually, one evening, they got Harris drunk and he poured everything out in a long, ranting monologue: his rage, his self-pity, his sense of loss, his resentment. Behind it all was his knowledge that his wife had never really loved him; that had made her death worse. He spent the next day recovering in his hut, and by nightfall was whole and sane again. By then Daley was also able to come to terms with what had happened, because in a way Harris's recovery and his decision to help continue with the search was an incentive to Daley. It was, after all, his search; no one else was going to take it over, and Harris would try given half a chance.

The day before Harris's geological briefing, Daley and Crabtree checked all the equipment. They made a pit in the earth behind the huts for the fuel drums and cooking gas containers, to keep them cooler. They set up the new winch, and assembled the air pump, and tested the motor which served both. These would be needed when the shaft was located, and they began to excavate. Crabtree, as he had been meaning to for some weeks, also laid an ingenious makeshift night landing aid, for emergencies. On cork floats – which he strung out across the length of the anchorage on light cables – he fixed waterproof bulbs, in two lines. Thus, in any breeze, he could come in without fear of cracking up on the rocks, or the beach, in darkness. A small radio device made it possible to switch on the lights by remote control from the main hut.

Now that Harris had given his lecture (that was the way Daley thought of the briefing), the others would want to begin further seismological soundings right away. Daley was not impressed or heartened by this methodical, plodding approach. There might easily be several deep points in the basin, even fissures in the bedrock, or caverns. They could be hung up on conflicting evidence for weeks, like an archaeological expedition. For while the instrument was technically admirable, and accurate, it could not interpret its own findings. It was thus, in Daley's opinion, even though he had originally suggested its use, the clumsiest of scientific crutches. But McNally would be impatient to begin; that was his nature once a decision had been made. And Harris – his mind buzzing with calibrations, like the seismometer – would be blind to any more of Daley's doubts.

He sipped some cool water, and set to work on the pistol, taking care not to scratch the delicate scrollwork which the corrosion had not blemished. He used scraps of cotton waste from the Catalina's tool kit, which Crabtree had brought ashore, and cooking oil. After an hour, he had removed most of the top layer of corrosion, but it was clear the weapon was badly pitted and would need expert restoration if it was ever to assume its original gleaming elegance. However, he was determined to make the best of it, and found some metal polish in the tool kit, which he used with restraint and care. Within a further hour, the silver inlay of the butt shone brightly, and even the lock and pan had shed most of their gritty coating. He soaked the inlaid barrel and its wooden jacketing in more oil, and withdrew the rod from its groove. Wrapping it round with lint, he set about cleaning the bore. Crabtree came to find him as he laid the pistol down thirty minutes later.

"Well, well," said Crabtree in admiration, picking it up from the packing case Daley had been working on. "It's a real beauty, isn't it?"

"It is," said Daley. "Want to know why the ship sank?"

"You're not still thinking about that, for Christ's sake!" Crabtree was in no way prepared to take sides. He showed his impatience to protect himself.

"I'm not asking you to desert the cause, Crab," said Daley. "Harris might find the shaft in ten minutes, for all I know. It's just interesting to understand about the ship, that's all."

"All right, what about the bloody ship?" Crabtree found some fresh sweatbands and pulled them on to his wrists. He mopped his forehead with each wrist in turn, and waited for Daley to speak.

"Something I didn't even think about at the time," Daley made a ball of the cotton waste and threw it into the tool box.

"But now that I do, it's obvious. Our man even mentions it in his account."

"Stop carrying on like a two-bob watch," said Crabtree, "and get to the bloody point."

"Underneath the copper sheathing, which is still in place, the wood was eaten away. If we'd bothered to check the timbers of the ship, we'd have found they were eaten through. That hulk is literally as delicate as cardboard. One bad storm, and it would disintegrate. The only reason it hasn't is that that particular part of the anchorage is very calm and still, and storms apparently don't affect it. I'm thinking aloud," he went on, rising and pacing up and down, "but I'm sure I'm right."

"Eaten away by what?" said Crabtree. "Those old ships were made to last in the bloody water. Why would being under it rot this one?" He shook his head.

"Not rot," said Daley impatiently. "The damn thing didn't just go rotten. It *was* eaten away. By the teredo worm. While they were digging the shaft, don't you see? The damn ship was springing leaks all the time because the copper was loose. The teredo worms were having a ball. Of *course* it went to the bottom!"

"Yeah, but so what? What the hell does it prove?"

"It proves that the mats had something to do with the excavation," said Daley.

"Jesus H. Christ," snorted Crabtree. "The bloody mats again!"

"Shut up, Crab, and listen to me." Daley fixed Crabtree with a gaze so piercing that the other's protestations died. Daley was like a visionary, almost quivering with the intensity of what his mind was seeing. "OK, let's imagine what our man saw on his last day on the island. There was some kind of fight, some kind of fatal confrontation between the two groups. The work on the shaft was finished. Our man has been waiting his chance to escape, and this is it. Several men are wounded, or killed, there's confusion. He slips away, loads up

the boat, and gets away. The ship was still afloat when he left.
OK so far?"

"OK," was all Crabtree could say, a simple echo.

"Now, our man has gone, and the boat has gone. But the
men on the island are not concerned about the boat, or the
ship. They're in conflict. Maybe the fight continued through
the night. Maybe one group pursued the other into the hills.
Whatever happened, they don't notice that the boat has gone
for some time. By this time, the ship has begun to settle in the
water, and there's nothing they can do to save her. OK, how
many men are left? Half a dozen, ten? Only a few, anyway.
What do they do?"

"Try to get off the island."

"Right. So now they build their raft, or whatever. Mac was
right about that, I think. But they don't build it out of choice –
that was his suggestion – but out of desperate necessity. Now,
where is the logical place to build?"

"Has to be the anchorage beach," said Crabtree. He wiped
sweat from his face, and sat on his bunk. "I'm beginning to
get your drift." He looked up at Daley. "Those bloody mats
don't fit into any boat-building scheme, do they?"

"That's where Mac hasn't thought it through," said Daley.
"He's so anxious to find the shaft, he isn't looking at the other
evidence at all." Daley broke off and lit a cigarette. "I'm going
up to the other beach again," he said after a moment. "I'm
going to take a shovel and dig all around where we found the
pistol."

"You reckon the shaft could be on the beach?" asked Crabtree in amazement.

"No, I doubt it. But there has to be some clue hidden under
the sand there. That point – where the pistol was found – is the
narrow end of the fan of mats. They spread out over the beach
from that spot."

Crabtree got up, grunting, and put a hand on Daley's
shoulder.

"You've convinced me," he said. "But listen, don't go digging up the beach today. Mac and Harris will expect you to help them, and I reckon you should. They want to start in a few minutes."

Daley sighed with irritation, and shook his head. "I'm not going – " he began. Crabtree cut him off.

"If you want me to help, take it easy and don't antagonize them. In a couple of days, while they're still mucking around with that echo box, I'll come with you to the beach, and help you. Fair enough?"

Daley looked at him for a moment, and saw that he was right. "OK," he said, and nodded. He picked up the pistol and aimed it out the door. "We'll wait."

Roy Sewerd closed the top drawer of his desk and placed a set of poker dice, and a dog-eared copy of *Catch 22* in the small grip he had brought with him to the office that morning. He closed the grip, picked up his jacket and took the elevator up to McNally's office.

He opened the outer door, and went on into the main office through the big double doors that opened off the reception area. His feet made no sound on the carpet of the outer office, but clicked coldly on the tiles McNally had insisted on for his inner sanctum. Sewerd stared about him; nothing looked any different. It was the same large, beige-tiled room with the desk, the telephones and the television console, and the same tremendous view across the water. But this was the last time Sewerd would ever stand here, and his boss – cut off or simply hiding somewhere in the Pacific – was no longer a power here. Accountants, attorneys, and stony-faced men from Federal departments had begun to invade. Soon, filing cabinets and racks of tapes would be wheeled out of elevators in the basement. The board in the lobby at street level would have a blank space. McNalinc was effectively defunct.

Sewerd put down his grip, and tossed his jacket over the back of a chair. He wandered to the window and stood looking out over the spectacular and extraordinary city, teetering on its impossible hills. He could never quite get over the vivid blue of the water beyond, either. An Easterner, he was still caught in the spell of the Pacific coast, its paradoxes and disappointments, its constant ability to surprise. He was glad he had been based in Frisco instead of Los Angeles. LA was a smog-clogged luxury slum, hot, glittering and junked-out. This city had character, charm, and a kind of cranky vitality that was unlike anything else he had experienced. He would be sad to leave it. Behind him, the door opened. He turned and saw Janice Hartwell, dressed in denims and a headscarf.

"I just dropped by to pick up the last of my things," she said. "You too, huh?"

"Yuh, right," said Sewerd. "Not that I have any stuff in this office. Couldn't resist a last look. That view is something I'm going to remember."

"Are you leaving San Francisco?"

"Well, I come from the East, you know. I'm going back for a while."

"Uhuh. Do you think he really knows what happened here?"

"McNally?"

"Do you think he was involved?"

"It doesn't matter to me, one way or the other. It's all a bunch of shit."

"Oh. Well, yes. I guess you didn't even like him."

"Sure, I liked him, but – I have the rest of my life to live, that's all. Why pretend he matters any more?"

"What will you do?" she asked curiously. She put her head on one side.

"Me? Well, shoot, ma'am, there must be at least a hunert jobs waitin' fer me in copperations all over these United States. Why, in the kinda circles I move in, the re-cession jist don't exist. I can go right out and double my pay tomorrow."

Janice smiled. "I'm going to Santa Barbara. My sister and her husband run a seafood restaurant there. I'm going to learn the difference between crabbed crab and regular crab."

"Well, good luck," said Sewerd, returning her smile. He sighed. "If I was still in college, I'd drop out and grow vegetables and smoke dope. But it's too late."

"Come and eat in the restaurant next time you're in Santa Barbara."

"I'll bear it in mind, if ever I get enough bread together to come back from the East. What's it called?"

"It's called 'Sea Legs'," she said. "Silly, huh?"

Sewerd nodded and waved goodbye as she left the office. He turned and resumed staring out of the big window. A mist was rising out to sea, beyond the Bridge. The light was beginning to fade. He began to feel sorry for himself.

"Cut that out," he said aloud, and shook his head. He wandered over to the desk and looked down at the pen stand, the telephones, the neat wooden cigar box, the intercom, and the vast beige blotting pad that matched the tiles on the floor. He smiled, and sat in the swivel chair. The soft leather sighed under him. His smile grew broader.

"What the fuck is it all about?" he said aloud. "Hey, McNally, listen, man, what the fuck *is* it all about? Do you know, can you tell me? Even if you were right here, could you tell me why you gouged your way thirty-two stories up out of the garbage heap, so some motherfucker could kick your ass all the way back down again?" He laughed, and hit the blotter with the flat of his hand. The thick folds of paper muffled the sound. He took off his tie, and undid the button at the collar of his pale blue executive shirt.

"Those corporation bastards nearly got me," he said, and laughed again, shaking his head. "Jesus, man, they nearly got me!"

"You OK, buddy?" The voice startled Sewerd. In the doorway he saw a janitor, carrying a stack of towels. "You OK, buddy?" he repeated, peering at Sewerd doubtfully.

"Yeah, I'm OK," said Sewerd. "I was just kind of celebrating my freedom."

"Uhuh. Well, you better go and find a bar someplace, mister, 'cause we closin' up now."

"I know it," said Sewerd.

It was early afternoon, and the third day of the renewed seismic soundings. Harris and McNally had set up the seismometer and a square of sensors in a small clearing in the trees, from which Crabtree and Daley had removed the undergrowth. They were working in two teams, each taking turns to clear the ground while the other set up the instruments. McNally leaned over Harris's shoulder to look at an enlarged map of the stone markers and the imaginary triangle they formed.

"We're just about . . . here," said Harris, stabbing the chart at a point north-east of the south marker. "Judging by our last three readings, we should be over the area of optimum depth."

A few yards away, Crabtree and Daley, both dripping sweat, were clearing away more undergrowth in an area Harris had pegged out with wooden stakes. This would be used for the next test, should the present one fail. Daley was sure it would. He was tired and bored and irritated. Harris was beginning to get on his nerves; his enthusiasm for the tests was more appropriate to a laboratory experiment than to the hard slog of the search.

"Also," Haris continued in his earnest, pedantic voice, "we're now situated due north of the intersection between the south and east markers, and the line from the north marker to point X."

"Uhuh, right," nodded McNally, chewing on his unlit cigar. He was caught up in the other's eagerness.

"And if we don't hit the shaft here," said Harris, "we'll still be due north when we move to the next test area. 'Strike due north.' It's just a question of time, is all."

"Why should it be north of that particular intersecting line?" said Daley to Crabtree, keeping his voice down to an irritated growl. "It could be north of any fucking place."

"Yeah," said Crabtree, wiping sweat out of his eyes, "so why not here?" The sheer reasonableness of this remark forced Daley to grin and shake his head.

"You've got me there," he confessed. "It's the way he's so positive all the damn time that annoys me."

"Switch on," Harris called. At the machine across the clearing, McNally thumbed the metal stalk, and the grid appeared on the screen, pale in the bright sunlight which splashed over it through gaps in the palm fronds above.

"How does it look?" Harris called, peering at the sensors. "Have we got a full pattern?"

"Yes . . . but it looks kind of funny," said McNally. Something in his voice, an edge of tension, made Harris look up quickly, then hurry over to check the screen for himself.

"Yuh, yuh, yuh," he said, nodding rapidly as he stared at the small rectangle. "There's something there."

Daley and Crabtree dropped their machetes, and ran across the open ground, leaping over the wired sensors.

"Don't run on the grid!" yelled Harris. He turned towards them, his spectacles flashing in a shaft of sunlight.

"Is it the shaft?" said Daley.

"You have to take care of this equipment, you know," said Harris in an admonitory tone. "We can't replace it."

Daley was suddenly angry. He'd taken about enough of Harris and his fussy, precise self-righteousness. He knew that he couldn't go on working with him.

"Is it the shaft?" he repeated, keeping his anger in check with an effort.

"Possibly," said Harris. "I'm not sure. I'll have to evaluate the reading."

To Daley it seemed that Harris was being evasive, that he

did not know, really, whether the shaft might be there or not. The pattern on the screen told him little, and he looked again at Harris, trying to detect in his face some sign of what the reading meant. It was only then that Daley saw how hopelessly amateur their earlier efforts with the seismic equipment had been. If even Harris could not tell right away, then this method was probably no more effective in the long run than the core drilling they had first used. Again he wished that he had never suggested the purchase of the machine. He sighed, and turned to McNally.

"I'm sorry, Mac," he said, "but I've had a bellyful of this. If you want to go on, it'll have to be without me."

"But we might have found the goddamn shaft!" McNally was incredulous.

"Do you really think so?" said Daley. "You don't think so, do you, Harris?" he called over his shoulder.

Harris was adjusting some of the sensors to make a tighter grid. "What?" he said.

"It isn't the shaft, is it?"

Harris stood up and came over to them, brushing his hands free of earth. "It could be. There's some kind of irregularity in the subsoil, to around fifty or sixty feet. That's all I can say. We can test with the core drill as soon as I've taken some readings."

"There you go," said McNally. He turned back to Daley. "Don't be such a pessimist, man."

"You can test all you want," said Daley. Crabtree was watching them; he had squatted down on his haunches and was doodling in the earth with a twig. Now he rose and approached them. "I've had enough," Daley said with finality.

"Mike, what the hell's the matter with you?" McNally said angrily, staring into Daley's set face. "This is the first break we've had."

"Settle down, settle down," said Crabtree, stepping between them. "Mike, you need to cool off. So do I. Let's go and have a swim." Crabtree had his back to McNally, and winked. Daley saw what he was getting at, and nodded. "OK," he said.

"Swim?" said McNally. "You're both crazy. We find the goddamn shaft, and you want to go and get eaten by a goddamn shark! You're crazy." He gave a short, angry laugh, and walked away. He found his box of cigars beside the seismometer, bit the end off one and spat it out.

"Come on," said Crabtree, jerking his head in the direction of the wide beach. "If they *have* found the bloody shaft, they'll let us know quick enough."

Daley followed him through the trees. The thought of clear water lapping over his tired, sweaty body was already beginning to revive him.

After they had cooled off in the water, Daley went to the main hut, and brought back shovels and canteens of water. They began to dig systematically, keeping to a steady pace to conserve their strength. They dug in a rough circle around the point where the pistol had been found. They had been working for twenty minutes when Crabtree gave a shout. His shovel had hit something hard. He was two or three yards from Daley, nearest the edge of the scrub and undergrowth. Daley went to his side and they dug together, stamping the long blades down into the sand, careless of their strength now. Almost at once, both shovels struck the hard object. They quickly cleared a trench and, getting down on their hands and knees, they scraped away the loose sand. About two feet below the surface, they uncovered a rock about a foot across, and round. They looked at each other, then without a word grabbed their shovels and began digging furiously to widen the trench. In five minutes they had uncovered five more rocks, laid in a circle around the first. They worked on, clearing more sand, and found that the circle extended outwards. There were sixteen rocks in all; the diameter of the circle was five feet.

Crabtree broke the silence. "Jesus," he said reverently, "this has to be it."

"I think it must be," said Daley. He stood up, and took a deep breath. He felt elated.

"I'll go and tell the others," said Crabtree, and jumped up out of the trench.

"No, don't do that," said Daley sharply, caution dampening his elation. "We have to be absolutely sure." He squatted down beside the rocks again, and as he did so, noticed something gleam in the sand. He moved, so that his shadow did not obscure the spot, and again saw the gleam. He dug his fingers into the sand, bringing up a fistful. Turning his hand up, he probed the packed grains in his palm, and felt something hard and round.

"What is it?" asked Crabtree, bending down to look.

"I think it's gold," said Daley.

"Show me," demanded Crabtree, holding out his hand.

"Wait," said Daley and rubbed grit off the disc of dull yellow metal. He peered at it. Crabtree's shadow darkened his hand. "Get out of the light, Crab," he said impatiently. Crabtree moved, and Daley saw that it was a coin. On one side was a head and an elaborate coat of arms, with the words "PHILIPPVS IIII DG". On the reverse were some pillars and the words "PLVS VLTRA".

"What is it, for Chrissake?" said Crabtree again.

Daley looked up at him, and tried to speak. Suddenly his eyes were full of tears. Wordlessly, he held out the coin. Crabtree took it and examined it.

"It's gold, all right," he said excitedly. He kissed the coin. "You little beauty!" Then he noticed the tears on Daley's cheeks. "What's up with you?" he said in amazement.

Daley wiped his face over with his shirt, and cleared his throat. He took the coin back from Crabtree and stared down at it for a moment. "It's Spanish," he said. "Eighteenth-century Spanish." He shook his head, as if in disbelief. "We're going to be rich, Crab. It's here. The bloody stuff is here, and we're going to be rich."

"Course we are, you stupid bastard. That's why we came."
Crabtree dug his shovel into the sand beside the trench, and
rubbed his hands together. "I can't wait to see the look on
Mac's face," he said, and chuckled.

"Hold it," said Daley. He put the coin into the pocket of his
shorts. "Let's move a few of these stones. Just so we know for
sure this is the top of the shaft, OK?"

"For Chrissake, Mike, we know this is the bloody shaft,"
said Crabtree in exasperation.

"How do we know?"

"What the hell else could it be? The coin, the pistol. This is
where they buried the treasure."

"All right, let's move the stones and prove it."

"Move 'em yourself," Crabtree told him. "I'm going to tell
the others." He stumped off through the undergrowth, leaving
Daley standing in the trench. He sighed, then bent down and
grasped one of the outer rocks. It was firmly embedded, and
he had to get his shovel before he could move it. He worked
it loose with the blade, then tossed the shovel aside and pulled
the rock clear of the others with his hands. There was another
rock beneath. Working with all his strength, he pulled at two
more rocks and got them clear. There was another rock
beneath each, set at slightly different angles, so that each rock
was not directly beneath the one above it.

Then Daley noticed something else; something that in his
excitement he had missed before, although it was staring him in
the face. The rocks were damp; more, they were wet. On the
second layer of rocks little pools of water lay. And the surrounding sand – the sand in which they had been digging –
was damp, even soggy. He frowned, thinking of the corrosion
on the pistol, and the peculiar colour of the wooden stock.
Almost as if it had been lying underwater.

Again he grabbed his shovel, and levered two of the stones
in the second layer loose. He pulled them clear, and saw that
there was a further layer beneath them. This third layer

appeared to be set at a different angle again.

"It looks as if this can't be the shaft," he muttered to himself. He stood up, and hopped out of the trench, then stood staring down into the hole he had made in the rocks. It was an utter mystery to him what these rocks were for. He no longer believed they could be protecting the entrance to the shaft. Everything was damp, there was nothing on the excavation drawing about multiple rock layers at the top of the shaft. And in any case, the beach was a ridiculous place to have dug the shaft. It just didn't fit, any of it. He sighed with disappointment and frustration. At the back of his mind something nagged – something about the tides – but he shook his head, as if to rid himself of further complications, and headed in the direction of the main hut. He did not want to wait and talk to the others. He was too confused, and their questions and demands would only make that worse.

As he walked, he tried to go over in his mind what they had managed to discover so far. They had found the "thrum under the sand", that much was beyond doubt. They had found the ship, and eliminated it from their search. Drilling and sounding had so far produced nothing at all. And now there was this hole full of rocks. Yet they were no nearer to finding the shaft.

"Due north of what, for Godsake?" he said aloud. "What the hell do we strike north from?" Above his head a parrot shrieked in reply, mocking him. He reached the hut feeling depressed, his brain clogged with half-remembered calculations, angles, depths, suppositions. He sat down at the desk, lit a cigarette, and tried to think slowly, and clearly.

The stones under the sand would have to be dug out. They had to clear up the whole business of the beach sooner or later. And what about the stones in the water, the breakwater stones? They were part of it. His mind began to jam again, and he rubbed his forehead. He pulled the enlarged copy of the chart towards him, and saw the red lines he had drawn when he and McNally had first been sounding. Idly he picked up a plastic rule, and placed it along the line he had drawn due north of point X. The rule, extending beyond the end of the thin red trace, ran squarely through the line between the east and north markers. He felt a tingle in his spine, as an idea began to form in his head. Feverishly he scrabbled amongst the mass of coffee-stained papers, and found the red crayon. He steadied the rule on the chart, and extended the original line until it cut the east/north marker line at an angle of precisely ninety degrees. Staring up at him now was an exact replica of the stone markers triangle – in miniature. And the southern point of that triangle was directly north of point X.

"That's it!" he yelled, his voice cracking with excitement. He flung the crayon across the hut. It shattered against the wall near the door. A figure appeared in the doorway.

"What are you doing?" It was Crabtree. "Why'd you leave the beach?"

"I've found the shaft," Daley told him. "Don't ask me any damn fool questions," he went on quickly. "Get Harris and McNally back here, then you can help me get the drill ready."

"What – ?"

"Shut up. Just do what I tell you, will you?"

"Look, I don't like it when people talk to me as if I was a bloody sheepdog," said Crabtree. "I've had just about enough of your bloody crackpot – "

"I'm sorry, Crab," Daley cut in. "I'm a little excited. Forget the others. They can find us when they're ready. Just help me with the drill, will you?"

"What do you want the drill for?"

"Please, Crab. I've waited too long. We've all waited too long. I promise you, I've found it."

Crabtree shrugged, and went outside to the back of the hut, where the drilling equipment had been stored under a tarpaulin. He waited for Daley; when the other did not appear, he cursed in irritation and pulled the tarpaulin clear. Inside, Daley was making some quick calculations. He scribbled figures on a slip of paper, took a copy of the excavation chart from the desk, and grabbed up a tape-measure in its circular leather case. Then he hurried out to Crabtree.

It took them over an hour to carry the motor, the dismantled rig supports, and the drill sections to the beginning of the strip Daley had cleared with McNally north of point X. Still there was no sign of Harris and McNally; Daley reflected that that was just as well, for the moment. The stake which marked point X was still firm in the ground. Daley anchored the ring of the tape to it and set out along the strip. Crabtree sat in the shade of a tree on the bundle of equipment, and drank from his canteen.

Daley reached the end of the cleared stretch, paused to wipe sweat from his eyes, then fought his way through the thick scrubby undergrowth for another ten or twelve yards. The circular case in his hand squeaked, the brass winding handle turning as the tape unrolled like a ribbon behind him. He came to a small clearing amongst the palms and papaya trees. Here the undergrowth was much less dense and he was able to walk quite easily into the middle of the clearing. He looked down at the tape in his hand and saw that he had walked 180 feet, or sixty yards. He moved forward another three feet, and dropped the leather case at his feet. He found a fallen palm frond, and stuck it in the ground beside the case. Then he hurried back through the belt of undergrowth. Crabtree looked up as he approached. He was disgruntled.

"Now I suppose you want to lug this stuff through all that crap," he said, nodding towards the end of the strip.

"It's only a few yards," Daley told him. "It'll be worth it, I promise you."

"That's the second time you've promised me," said Crabtree sourly as he got to his feet. "You'd better keep it, or I'll knock your bloody block off."

Half an hour later they were ready to start drilling. Daley started the motor, and the greased gears began to turn. The drill hung poised above the earth.

"Looks just like all the other places to me," said Crabtree. "Waste of time."

"Cross your fingers." Daley's throat was constricted with tension, and his words were scarcely above a whisper. "Here goes." He pulled the governing lever, and the spinning drill bit into the ground, the rig supports quivering as they took the strain. Daley let the tip of the core travel downwards until it was twenty feet below the surface, then brought it up. Loose sand trickled from the core. When they had shut off the motor and detached the core, Daley saw that there were splinters of wood at the tip. He gripped Crabtree's arm.

"Look," he said. "It struck wood." His voice cracked.

Crabtree was unimpressed, and shook his arm free impatiently. "Ever heard of roots?" he said. "Things trees have?" His sarcasm was intended; he disliked Daley's obsessive, almost conspiratorial conviction.

"That's not root wood," Daley asserted. "Roots would be fibrous and pulpy." He ran his hand over the tip of the drill. "Crab, I know I'm right. Listen, if there are shells in the core, a layer of shells, will you accept that this is the shaft?"

Crabtree looked at him, then nodded slowly. It began to dawn on him – he bent to examine the splinters close to – that if they were not roots, they must have come from the first timber platform shown on the excavation chart. If there were shells – also shown on the chart – there could be no doubt that Daley was right.

"Let's see that drawing for a second," he said. Daley handed him the excavation chart. He studied it for a moment, then looked up at Daley and took a deep breath.

'OK," he said, and tapped the core with the edge of the chart, "OK, let's get this bastard back to the hut. All of a sudden I want to believe you."

When they got back to the hut they found the others there, drinking beer. They were red-faced and exhausted.

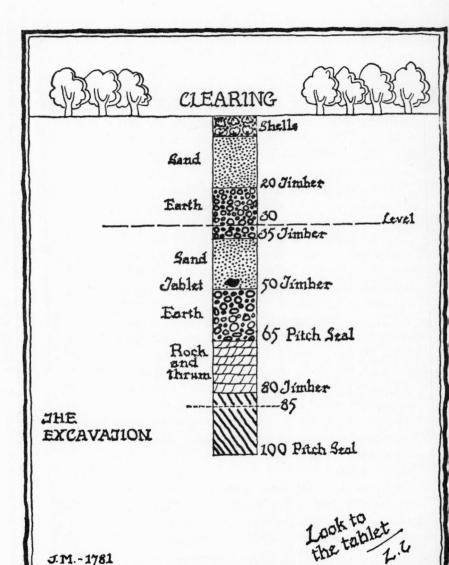

CLEARING

Shells

Sand

20 Timber

Earth

30 ——— Level

35 Timber

Sand

Tablet

50 Timber

Earth

65 Pitch Seal

Rock
and
thrum

80 Timber

85

THE
EXCAVATION

100 Pitch Seal

J.M.-1781

Look to
the tablet

L.L

"Where the hell have you been?" demanded McNally in a tone bordering on truculence. "We waited for you, then we started in without you." He took his cigar from his mouth and mashed it on an empty beercan. "We've moved the first two layers, and some of the third. There's a fourth layer under that." A note of disgust had crept into his voice. He drank from his can of Budweiser, then repeated, "Where were you, for Chrissake?"

"I shouldn't drink beer," said Harris to no one in particular. "I have ulcers."

Daley said nothing. He laid the core on the trestle table and went to the corner, where Crabtree had stowed his tool box. The box yielded a hammer, which he brought back to the table. Crabtree held the core while he tapped it. Nothing happened. He tapped again, and a tubular plug of sand fell out and crumbled as it hit the tabletop. Daley wiped his palm free of sweat, gripped the hammer and tapped again. The hammer made a light ringing sound on the hard metal. More sand fell out and collapsed silently. Daley tapped harder, several times. There was a rattle as something loosened high in the core, then from the hole tumbled a brittle white stream. In seconds the table was littered with shells.

Crabtree lifted the core, whirled it round his head, and flung it far out of the door.

"WOOOOOOOOO!" he yelled.

Harris and McNally stared at him in amazement, their mouths falling open. Daley stood looking down at the table, then reached forward and scooped up a handful of shells.

"She sells seashells on the seashore," he said.

"I'll drink to that," said Crabtree. "I'll drink to any bloody thing you like."

McNally let the brake off and the empty bucket, swaying on its hook, disappeared down the shaft. There was a shout from below, and he re-applied the brake, letting the motor idle. He sat down on the heap of sand and shells that lay behind the shaft, and lit a cigar. He was getting low on cigars, and the beer was beginning to run out. A week ago these would have been major inconveniences; now they didn't bother him at all. Like the others, he had ceased to care about what he ate and drank. All that mattered was getting to the bottom of the shaft. This was the third day of excavation and they were expecting to reach the first timber platform – at twenty feet – before noon. By the time they reached the second platform in a couple of days time, they would need the air pump. Exhaustion, heat stroke, dehydration – these were their worst enemies now. He glanced at his watch. In ten minutes it would be time to call a halt for lunch. He glanced across at Harris, who was filling the fuel tank on the winch motor.

"I talked to Papeete again late last night," he said. "I don't think they're going to send that plane, after all."

Harris screwed the top on the gasoline can, and took off his spectacles. He rubbed his eyes briefly, and replaced the spectacles, settling them on his nose. "I'm glad," he said. "We don't need officials nosing around right now. And I certainly don't want to answer a bunch of fool questions. She's gone. There's nothing anyone can do about it." He spread his hands, then turned away quickly and busied himself, screwing the cap back on the fuel tank of the motor, and wiping it down with a rag.

McNally was thankful that Harris seemed to be bearing up so well. He had been afraid Harris might sink back into his initial state of grief, with the added weight of bitterness to drag on his spirits. The constant back-breaking work helped. None of them really had time to worry about anything. They were so tired in the evenings that they fell asleep in the canvas chairs round the table in the main hut. And although Crabtree had insisted that they maintain a regular timetable for meals, there were times when they could hardly be bothered to eat. That was the trouble with the tropics. The evenings were seductive, and if you had been working hard, you felt only drowsiness and relief that the worst heat of the day had passed. Hunger didn't seem to come into it. But Crabtree had been adamant; he knew the dangers, and had seen too many men fall into their cots with nothing in their bellies but booze. That way lay fever. They could not afford fever, not now.

There was another shout from below, indicating that Daley and Crabtree had filled another bucket, completing their shift. McNally released the brake and put the winch on forward drive. The bucket came swaying up, heaped with sand and earth. He and Harris grabbed it and heaved it off the hook. McNally emptied it, and sent it back down the shaft – the bucket doubled as a one-man hoist. When both Daley and Crabtree had been hauled up, grimy-faced and drenched in sweat, McNally asked: "How close are we to the first platform?"

"We've just been standing on it," said Crabtree. "That last bucket left the timber bare. It's sound. They set joists into the sides of the shaft."

"One thing bothers me a little," said Harris, as they made their way back to the hut. "The danger of cave-in. The shaft wasn't lined, and we have no way of knowing how solid the sides are."

"Solid enough, I reckon," said Crabtree. "You can still see the marks of shovels."

"Yes, I saw those, too. But we'll need to check the sides every day as we go deeper," said Harris. "I'm not trying to be an alarmist. It's a sensible precaution, is all."

"Good point, Logan," said McNally. "We'd better work out some kind of signal for that, so whoever's on the surface will know if the others are in trouble."

In the event, Harris's fears proved groundless. The walls of the shaft were firm, and showed no sign of crumbling. They were rounded, and at no point was the shaft more than ten feet across. As Harris remarked more than once, it was obvious that the shaft was the work of a man with experience of mining. If it had needed lining, it would have been lined.

On the fifth day they reached the second platform, and McNally set up the air pump. It was hot in the shaft, and the steady blast of fresh air was welcome relief. The sheer drudgery of filling the bucket with earth was taking its toll in blisters, and aching backs, but hauling out the platform timbers required still further effort. It was a difficult task. The timbers were heavy oak planks from the ship, and had to be hoisted one at a time. They had been caulked with oakum, and much of this had rotted, but the platforms were still well sealed. The weight of earth and sand pressing down on them had caused the last two feet above each platform to set into heavy blocks which required a great deal of extra energy to loosen and break up. Below the timbers were corresponding gaps where the earth had settled.

A week after beginning, they reached the third platform. Resting on it, wrapped in rotted matting, was the tablet. It was a stone about eighteen inches across, worn smooth by the sea. Eager to decipher the inscription cut into this smooth surface, McNally and Harris – it was their shift – brought it to the surface. It was taken at once to the main hut and carefully scraped clean of the caked, clinging fibres.

Within moments Daley knew it was hopeless. The symbols scratched into the rock – probably with a chisel – were an intricate coded message. Without the key to the code, it was pointless to try and decipher the inscription. They would have to go on without its help.

McNally refused to accept that the code could not be cracked. "When I was in the service I knew a guy who was an expert. He could decode any damn thing. He showed me some of the tricks. It's simple once you know the tricks."

"What tricks, Mac?" Daley's voice was flat. McNally ignored the question.

"These are just symbols, that's all. It's like computers.

Everything is symbols. Listen, I'll work on this, try and spot the patterns. There are always patterns, and the guys who used this code were just sailors. They wouldn't have used anything too difficult, know what I mean?"

"Mac," said Daley, "the poor dumb sailors you're talking about mutinied, sailed a busted ship halfway across the world, dug this amazing goddamn shaft with the most basic equipment . . . I wouldn't underestimate them if I were you."

McNally smiled. "I'm not doing that, Mike. But I'm not going to let a kidstuff symbol code spook me. Give me a couple of hours."

"OK," said Daley, and shrugged. He walked with Crabtree and Harris back to the excavation. Harris was confident McNally would crack the code. Crabtree, whose inherent shrewdness had always kept him from being optimistic about things that looked easy at first glance, agreed with Daley. Their shift was due, so rather than wait for McNally, they decided to go down the shaft and continue. The planks of the third platform would have to be prised up and brought to the surface; it was better to make a start and get the job under way before dark.

In fact they had almost finished getting the timbers up when McNally appeared at the top of the shaft, and yelled down that it was time to finish for the day. When they had been hauled up, Crabtree and Daley saw that McNally had not cracked the code. His face said it all. Crabtree couldn't resist asking him how far he'd got.

"I'm still working on it," countered McNally, with an effort at cheerfulness.

"Oh, yeah?" said Crabtree. "Any idea when you'll have something for us?"

"Give it time, give it time," said McNally. He shut off the winch motor, and disconnected the air pump to check it for dust. Crabtree came and stood behind him.

"How much do you want to bet?" he said.

McNally looked up, pretending not to understand. "How d'you mean, bet?"

"I've got a hundred dollars that says you can't crack it," Crabtree said, scratching his chest.

"If you're trying to get me going, Crab, it's a waste of time." McNally got to his feet, threw the oily rag he had been using behind the motor, and headed for the huts. Crabtree laughed, and followed him.

When they had all eaten, McNally took the stone tablet to his own hut, leaving the others to play a game or two of cards. Soon they were yawning and nodding over their hands. When Harris had twice gone to sleep holding a royal flush, they agreed it was time for bed. As Daley passed McNally's hut he could see him bent over the tablet under his lamp, jotting on a pad, and making calculations on his pocket calculator.

When they rose next morning, McNally did not appear at the main hut for coffee. Daley went to his hut and found him slumped on his bunk, fully dressed, with his lamp still burning. The hut was stuffy and hot, and McNally looked exhausted. The tablet lay next to his bunk with a mass of calculations. Daley shook his head, and left him to sleep. He appeared at the excavation in mid-morning looking wan and tired. When Crabtree and Daley came up for a break, McNally looked at them silently for a minute, then gave a weary smile.

"You were right," he said. "I couldn't crack it." He drank some water from his canteen. "Uh, did I take that bet, Crab?" he asked.

"No, you wily bastard," said Crabtree with a grin. "You bloody know you didn't."

"I'd like to try," said Harris now, shutting off the motor and joining the others.

Crabtree untied his neckerchief, doused it in water from his canteen, and squeezed it over his head. "Well, you'd better try later," he said through the trickles of water that ran down his face. "Mike and I have dug two shifts in a row. It's time you and Mac went down."

"I think we should stop digging," said Harris quickly. "Until we've cracked the code, we're working in the dark."

"It's dark down there, all right," said Crabtree with his snorting chuckle. "What about that, Mac? Can we rig up a light?"

"Sure, I'll get some lamps from the huts," said McNally. "But I think Logan is right. Why don't we call a halt, at least for today? The information on the tablet must be important, otherwise it wouldn't be there."

"You've already wasted enough time on it," said Crabtree. He turned to Harris and in a blunt, brusque tone demanded: "What makes you think you can do it, when he couldn't?"

"I don't think you appreciate the point I'm making," said Harris, adjusting his spectacles. "Suppose we dig down for another ten feet and fall into some kind of pit, or trap? For all we know, the information on the tablet could save lives, here."

"You're a bloody alarmist, Harris," said Crabtree roughly, and spat on the ground. "I'm game to take the risk." He glanced around. "Anyone else want to chicken out?"

"He has a point, Crab," said Daley, who had been listening with a frown. "But I don't think we need to stop digging. We can drill down through the last fifty feet. If it's all clear, we can go on right away."

"And if it isn't?"

"Then we go back to the tablet."

"OK," said Crabtree, after a moment of deliberation. "That's fair enough by me."

"And me," said McNally. They looked at Harris. He nodded in agreement.

By noon they had dismantled the winch, and re-rigged the drill. Several sections were fitted together, with a standard rock bit. Everything was ready for the all-important probing of the final fifty feet of the shaft. It wasn't until McNally failed to start the drill motor for the third time that Daley felt a faint pulse of alarm. McNally tried again; the motor refused even to cough.

"Goddammit," he yelled in a sudden burst of anger. He stood back with his hands on his hips, then turned. "Crab, can you take a look at this?"

Crabtree checked the motor, and tried to start it. He failed. He tried again, and still there was no response.

"I'll have to strip the bastard down," he announced in a disgusted voice.

"To hell with that," said McNally with strident impatience. "We'll use the winch engine."

"Can't be done," said Crabtree at once. "We'd need a drive-belt and new gearing. If we want to use the drill at all, I'll have to fix this one." He tapped the dead motor with his foot.

He brought his tool box from the hut and worked for an hour on the motor, while the others waited in the shade at the edge of the little clearing. Birds filled the hot steamy air with their echoing cries and shrieks. The only other sound was the clicking and tapping of Crabtree's tools. McNally was lighting one of his few remaining cigars when Crabtree stood up and came over to them wiping his hands.

"She's seized up solid," he said, his voice flat.

"How long will it take to fix?" asked McNally, throwing away the match.

"Without the parts, I can't fix it," Crabtree told him. "It's the heat that's done it." He paused and sighed. "I dunno if I could, even with the bloody parts."

Alarm ticked again in Daley's chest. Surely nothing could go seriously wrong for them now? They were so close. He got to his feet.

"We'll just have to go on without the drill," he said with decision. "If we go carefully, we'll be OK."

"Come on, Mike, you can't know that," said Harris. "We agreed to go back to the tablet if the drilling didn't work out. I vote we stick to that."

"Stick your vote up your arse," said Crabtree. "This isn't a bloody election."

There was an uncomfortable silence. Open animosity – whether it arose from frustration, the heat, or straight dislike – was another enemy they could not allow to gain a foothold. Crabtree knew this as well as the others, and looked unhappy with himself over his outburst.

"Listen, I didn't mean that," he said to Harris. "I'm sorry."

"It's OK, forget it," said Harris. "We're all on edge, here."

McNally stood up and cleared his throat. "According to the chart," he said, "there's a pitch seal on the fourth platform. Why don't we dig down to that, and see how we go?"

"You aren't going to abandon the tablet altogether, are you?" persisted Harris, also getting to his feet.

"We can work on that at night," said Daley, sounding much more confident than he felt. There was something about this latest setback that had given him a feeling of deep unease, which he was at a loss to understand. He kept thinking about the hole full of rocks over at the wide beach. If only there were more than four of them, they could excavate that hole as well.

"It's still pretty hard," said McNally, looking up from where he was sitting behind the shaft. He took several deep breaths, and wiped off his grimy face. "But in the heat from the lamps down there, it'll soon start to melt." He leaned back against the stack of timbers they had brought up out of the shaft.

"OK, we'll go down right away," said Daley. He and Crabtree moved to the head of the shaft. Harris stood by the winch. They had improvised a new and much larger bucket from one of the equipment crates, so that two men could descend at the same time, and a greater volume of earth would be hoisted up in one load. It was now early afternoon on the ninth day, and the pitch-sealed fourth platform had been reached that morning. McNally and Harris had begun the work of prising up the timbers. Crabtree and Daley would now finish the job. It would not be easy. Even with the air pump pouring fresh air into the shaft, the lamps made the atmosphere close and oppressive. The seal of pitch was thick, and the timbers were heavy. The heat and smell would be barely tolerable soon, and if the pitch began to melt, their task would become a nightmare.

As the winch lowered them the sixty-five feet to the platform, Daley swore that when this was over, and he was back in civilization he would never ever travel by subway again.

By nightfall the last of the pitch-coated timbers had been hauled to the surface. All four men were smeared with sticky black patches. It took them an hour to wash themselves clean with buckets of gasoline, followed by detergent from their dwindling stores. None of them felt like eating, and it was agreed they would take the next day off, and relax.

In the morning Daley woke late, went to the main hut for coffee and found McNally and Crabtree checking the stores.

"We'll need more food in about a week," McNally was saying. "And we're almost out of gas for the stove and the lamps."

"As soon as we hit the bottom of the shaft, I'll make the trip," Crabtree said, sipping a can of beer. "But I'm buggered if I'll go before. I'm not missing that."

"I'm going to wander over to the top beach and take another look at that hole full of rocks," said Daley, pouring his coffee. "Anyone interested?"

"To hell with the beach, and to hell with the shaft," said McNally, stretching. "Me, I'm going to sit around and waste time."

Crabtree chuckled, and finished his beer. "That's good advice, Mike. Unwind, for Chrissake. In a week we'll be rolling in money."

Daley did not go to the beach. He went back to his hut when he had finished his coffee, and fell asleep. The long days of unrelenting effort had taken their toll, and he did not wake again until dusk.

They worked on for another three days, refreshed by their twenty-four hours of total idleness. Even so, the shifts grew shorter, because their work had become more arduous. The filling between the fourth and fifth platforms was a mixture of small rocks, matting and earth, bound together at two-foot intervals by layers of pitch. The fifth platform was also sealed with pitch, and consisted of two levels of timbers one foot apart, leaving a sealed space between. Both these sets of timbers were more deeply set into the sides of the shaft than those above. They discovered this on the fourteenth day of excavation. They had begun early in the morning, and when they had ascertained the nature of this last platform they knew they must be close to their goal.

McNally and Daley consulted the excavation chart during the first change of shift.

"That broken line at the eighty-five-foot level," said McNally. "That must be it."

They worked on with new energy, and prised up the rest of the timbers by mid-morning. By noon they had reached the eighty-five-foot level. They found nothing. Their disappointment was keen, but short-lived, and after a quick snack lunch, eaten round the head of the shaft, the work continued. It was almost night when Daley and Crabtree rode up in the crate and announced that they had hit the pitch seal at one hundred feet.

"And . . . ?" McNally stared tensely at the two grimy figures as they swung out of the crate to the safety of the ground beside the shaft.

"And nothing," said Daley with an exhausted sigh.

"Goddammit, there *has* to be something there!" shouted McNally.

"Well, I'll tell you what there is here, Mac," said Crabtree. "There's one man who needs a cold beer." He untied his neckerchief and threw it away. The lamps he and Daley had brought up with their picks and shovels sputtered in the cooler air of the surface.

Harris shut off the winch engine and joined them. "What do we do now?" he asked in a subdued tone.

"Let's sleep on it," said Daley. "It must be down there somewhere. Maybe hidden in the sides of the shaft, or under the last layer of pitch."

Nobody agreed or disagreed. They made their way to the huts in a silence broken only by the hissing of the lamps and the churning of insects in the foliage.

That night all of them slept soundly; the extra effort of completing the excavation had deadened their limbs and their minds. None of them had any suspicion of what lay ahead.

McNally and Harris had already climbed aboard the crate on the following morning, and the winch had been started when Daley, peering down into the shaft, gave a shout.

"Stop the winch!"

Crabtree, standing by the machine, cupped his hand to his ear.

"Stop the bloody winch!" yelled Daley, waving his hands in a rapid crisscross.

Crabtree shut off the engine and it coughed into silence. Daley was pointing into the shaft.

"There's water down there."

McNally and Harris tossed their picks and shovels clear, and scrambled out of the crate. Crabtree went to help them, then joined Daley on the far side of the shaft.

"The whole shaft is flooded," said Daley. Crabtree stared into the shaft. At first he could see nothing beyond the first fifteen or twenty feet; below that was shadow. Then he caught a faint flickering, perhaps thirty feet down. Reaching to his feet, he picked up a clod of earth and threw it into the shaft. There was a splash, and the flickering broke into myriad ripples.

"How the hell could it flood?" said McNally as if in a daze.

Abruptly Daley hurried away from the shaft and returned

with a copy of the excavation chart.

"Here it is," he said, pointing at the paper. "Thirty feet down – there's a mark. Don't tell me that's a coincidence." McNally seized the chart.

"We should have stuck with the tablet," said Harris, peering over his shoulder. "The explanation for this has to be in the code."

"It doesn't make sense," said McNally in an anguished voice. "How could anyone get the stuff out? It just doesn't make sense."

"I think it does," said Daley. "Let me see that a minute." He took the chart back from McNally and studied it for a moment. Then he went round to the other side of the shaft, and called out "Crab, start the winch, will you?"

"What for? We can't dig down there now."

Daley was already climbing into the crate. "Lower me down to the water," he called. Crabtree shrugged and started the winch. When the motor had picked up, he released the brake and let the drum unwind slowly. Daley sank into the shaft.

"OK," he shouted. "Hold it there."

They watched him bend over the side of the crate and scoop up water in his hand.

"What the hell's he doing?" said McNally.

"It looks like he's tasting it," said Harris.

"OK," Daley called, "bring me up." Crabtree reversed the winch, and the thick rope wound back on to the drum. Daley jumped clear.

"It's salt," he announced, and spat.

"Seawater?" said McNally.

"Right. To be more accurate, high-tide seawater."

"What are you talking about?" said McNally, totally at a loss.

"I think I know," said Harris. "Jesus, we've been really stupid."

"We have," agreed Daley.

Trove

"Crab, for Godsake, what are they talking about?" pleaded McNally. "I'm going out of my mind, here."

In the main hut, Daley cleared plates and coffee mugs off the table, and spread out the excavation chart and the island charts. McNally and Crabtree drank beer, Harris water. Daley drank nothing; he was too intent on his explanation.

"Here's how I see it," he said, looking up and glancing round at their faces. "The thrum matting on the top beach is the key to the mess we're in. It's probably all in the message on the tablet, but we don't have the code, so we blew it. OK, so they laid the matting; then they'd finished, so they destroyed the breakwater."

"They destroyed it?" exclaimed McNally in surprise. "I thought it was just washed away."

"No, because the hole full of rocks goes together with the matting."

"Right," nodded Harris.

"The matting acts as a giant sponge at high tide," Daley continued, circling the area with his pencil. "It collects water under the sand, to pour into the rock-hole. The rocks are carefully placed, so that they don't clog with sand. That's why they're in irregular layers. Now, below the rock-hole, which is simply an entrance, there's a tunnel. That's my guess, anyway. It may simply be a natural fissure that they took advantage of while they were planning to bury the stuff, but I doubt it." He pointed with his pencil, and traced a line.

"The tunnel runs from the beach to the shaft, directly along the line between the east and south markers. Again I'm guessing, but I'd say it runs into the shaft at eighty-five feet. See where that broken line runs across the shaft on the other chart. The reason we missed the opening while we were digging is very simple."

"It was plugged," said Harris.

"I don't get it," said McNally, throwing up his hands, splashing beer.

"It was plugged," Daley went on, "but only to withstand a certain amount of pressure." Again he looked up. "When we stopped digging yesterday, we'd opened up the whole of the shaft, but *before* high tide. The reason it didn't flood until last night was because the last platform – the double layer of sealed timbers – acted as an airlock. Once we'd broken that, the shaft was bound to flood. When the tide rose during the night, that's just what happened. The plug at the shaft end of the flood tunnel was forced out by the sheer pressure of water."

"OK," said McNally, "we know why the damn thing flooded. What I don't understand is how in hell we're supposed to get the chests out of there. That is, if they are there."

"I think they'll be there, Mac," said Harris. "They didn't go to all this trouble and then dump them somewhere else."

"Why not?" demanded McNally, putting down his empty beer can. "Listen, the guys who organized this whole thing were either very clever, or completely crazy. Let's say they were clever. Why risk putting four chests full of bullion at the bottom of a hundred foot shaft, if they knew it would flood as soon as they tried to dig them out again?"

"But it wouldn't flood," said Daley, shaking his head. "It wouldn't flood."

"Oh, it wouldn't? What the hell is that in the shaft, Mike? Seventy feet of water, for Chrissake!"

"Yes, because we didn't block off the entrance to the flood tunnel," said Daley. "You see, that was all they had to do. Once they had sealed the rock-hole, the only water was the water actually trapped in the tunnel from the tidal flow. Not enough pressure to blow the plug in the shaft. They could have excavated the shaft, taken the chests out, without even getting damp. But for anyone who didn't know the secret, disaster. It's only luck the tide didn't rise while we were still digging."

"At least we know the secret now," said Harris. "It's simply a matter of sealing the rock-hole against the tide, and pumping the water out of the shaft."

McNally was still far from satisfied. "Something else that's bugging me," he said, getting another Budweiser from the fridge. "Why such an elaborate plan in the first place? Why *not* just bury the stuff in a shallow pit, or cover it with palm fronds? I mean, apart from the guys who buried the stuff, who was there to find it? Who else would come looking, way out in the Pacific, for booty that was taken in the Caribbean?"

"Jesus, I don't know, Mac," said Daley. "You've read the account. We just don't know. How can we, when the vital pages are missing? Anyway, does it matter now?"

"I guess it doesn't. Except that this thing is getting so complicated and weird, you can't help searching for reasons."

Harris drew a breath. "Towards the end of the account, one of the crew took some men and absconded with the chests while the others were asleep." He flipped his fingers. "What was his name . . .?"

"You mean Farley?" said Daley.

Harris raised a finger. "Farley, right. If Farley was from Cornwall, that could be the answer. Or part of it."

"There's nothing in the account about him being a Cornishman," said McNally. "What's Cornwall got to do with it?"

"Mining," said Harris. "Remember, I was talking about that the other day? This kind of excavation, the engineering knowledge involved – only a miner could do it. Only a miner would think of it."

"Yeah, but the thing of it is, *why?*" said McNally, banging the table for emphasis. "What in Christ's name was the point?"

"You said these guys were either clever, or crazy," said Crabtree, breaking his long silence. "This bloke Farley was probably both."

Daley dropped the bundle of wood he had collected, and circled the fire. Sparks floated up in the column of quivering air above the flames. Over the centre of the fire, the old winch bucket hung on a makeshift cradle. McNally threw some more sticky chunks of pitch into the bucket, then stirred up the fire. More sparks rushed upward, snapping as they burned out. The chunks of pitch melted quickly, sliding into the viscous black ooze that now nearly filled the bucket.

"One more bucket after this one should do it," said McNally.

"Better make it two," said Daley. "There's plenty of pitch."

"OK." McNally coughed and backed away from the fierce heat of the fire and wiped his forehead with his forearm.

From behind them, south of the spit, came the sound of the Catalina's port engine firing into life. Crabtree brought the engine up to maximum revs and let it pulse for sixty seconds, shattering the calm of the anchorage, then slackened off and let it idle. The engine sounded crisp and steady.

"Where's Harris?" asked Daley.

"He's calculating the psi pressure on this new seal at high tide."

"I don't see that can really help us," shrugged Daley. "We'll just have to hope for the best."

"He's an engineer," said McNally. "He has a tidy mind."

"Let's just hope this is the only tunnel, that's all," said Daley.

"Don't even think about it," said McNally, pulling on a pair of stout gloves. He leaned close to the fire and gripped one end of the cradle cross-piece (a length of drilling rod). Daley pulled on his gloves and took hold of the other end. They carried the bubbling pitch to the hole, skirting the big pile of rocks they had dug out. They poured the pitch into the hole; it steamed as it spread over the filling. The plugging of the hole was now almost complete. It was filled with earth, layers of thick plastic sheeting from the huts, and a dozen buckets of pitch brought from the shaft. The tightly packed mass would act as a seal which in Harris's estimation would be as strong as a steel sluice gate – at least for a short time.

At dusk, as they ate their evening meal, there was a new

optimism in all of them. They had almost been defeated, but they were going to win through. The earlier animosities and tensions which had threatened to destroy their efforts were now forgotten. McNally smoked his last cigar, and he and Crabtree finished the last cans of beer. Even Harris was caught up in the euphoria.

"Boy, I'm going to enjoy being rich," he said. "I'm going to really enjoy it."

Crabtree drained his beer, belched, and rose. "I'm taking off at dawn," he said, "so I won't see you blokes till I get back. Behave yourselves."

"'Bye, Crab," said Daley. "Don't get drunk and forget the pump."

"If I can't afford to buy the bastard, I'll hire it," Crabtree assured them, and stumped off into the night.

Daley woke as the first rays of the sun played over the door of his hut, and listened to the pulsing roar that echoed off the anchorage. Presently, as Crabtree lifted clear of the water, and brought the big gull round in a climbing turn, the roar altered to a steady boom, then faded away. The birds resumed their exotic chorus, and Daley drifted back into sleep.

In the main hut, Harris rose from the desk, throwing down his pen, and pushing aside his pocket calculator. He took off his spectacles, rubbed his eyes, and stretched. Then he went to the corner where the wetsuits lay in their crates. He took out the one that had not been used, and looked at it, holding it up. He had never used one before. Laying the suit aside, he found the set of instructions, and read them with care.

Twenty minutes later, Harris adjusted his mask, and took the mouthpiece between his lips. He felt over his shoulder, made sure the backpack was correctly in place, and flexed his shoulders. He breathed oxygen, in–out . . . in–out. Then he gripped the rope he had tied to the winch bar over the shaft, swung out, and began to descend, gripping the rope with his feet and sliding a little at a time, as he had been taught all those years ago at summer camp. Soon his weight began to tell, and his hands began to slip, burning on the hard rope. He could not grip properly with his feet – the flippers were clumsy and awkward. He was still twenty feet above the water, yet his grip was going. Desperately he clung to the rope, swaying and slipping. At last his grip went altogether and he fell. He sucked in air, and felt his whole body jar as he hit the water. The backpack jerked, thudding at the base of his skull. There was a hiss, and his mouth was filled with water. He struggled, kicking out, choking, sinking. His head felt as if it was filled with a dense, hot mass of wool. He slipped into unconsciousness. One minute later, as his body drifted slowly downward, Harris drowned.

4
Nature

Daley woke late, feeling refreshed after his long sleep. He went to the main hut and found McNally searching through the remains of the stores.

"I'm sure I had one more box of cigars," he said, throwing aside empty boxes.

"You found that a week ago," Daley reminded him, opening a can of orange juice.

"I wish you hadn't said that," McNally grunted. "I could have gone on hoping."

Daley drank the orange juice, feeling the tart liquid cut away the fur of sleep in his mouth and throat.

"Did Crab say anything about doing some scuba diving while he was in Papeete?" McNally asked after a moment.

"I don't think so." Daley put coffee on the stove, and lit the gas.

"I'll have some of that when it's ready," said McNally, still searching. "If I can't find any damn cigars, I'll have to build myself up with caffeine."

Daley fixed himself a light breakfast, and ate in silence. McNally stopped rummaging and joined him at the table for the coffee. It smelled good.

"What time is it?" said Daley, a few minutes later. "I left my watch at the hut."

"A little after eleven," McNally drained his mug. "You make a good cup of coffee, Mike. Remind me to buy you a plantation." Daley laughed and lit a cigarette. He was smoking more recently. He coughed on a lungful of smoke, and ground the cigarette beneath his boot.

"What time did you say it was?" he asked again.

"Ten after eleven," said McNally. "You meeting somebody for lunch?"

"I can't get used to just sitting around," said Daley.

"Two days, three at the most, and we'll have the pump. Relax."

"I'm no good at relaxing," Daley confessed. "That's how I got started on the drinking."

"Yeah," said McNally. Other people's troubles made him uncomfortable, even those of old friends.

"That, and the crash. I used to think about it at night. Then I'd have to take a drink to get to sleep. I get the shakes when I think about what I was doing. Flying a hundred passengers with a blinding hangover – I must have been crazy."

"Yeah," said McNally, shifting in his chair. He coughed and cleared his throat.

"Don't worry, I'm not going to bore your ass off," Daley reassured him. He lit another cigarette. "Why didn't you ever get married?" he asked after a moment.

"I did," said McNally. "It lasted three weeks. It was about a year after I left the service. I was kind of preoccupied at the time, getting started in the air charter business. I came home one weekend, and she'd gone."

"Ever hear from her?"

"No, never. I kind of expected to, you know. When I made it, had my picture in *Fortune* and *Newsweek*. Thought I was king of the world." He paused, and smiled. "Shit, now I'm boring you."

"No, you're not," said Daley. "My marriage fell to pieces, too. It took longer, but the result was the same. She left."

"Hey, come on, this is a bunch of crap," said McNally, pushing back his chair. "We sound like a couple of eighty-year-old widowers, for Chrissake." He put his feet up on the table.

"What are you going to do with your share of the money?" Daley asked.

"I don't know. I think I might buy a ranch. I'd like to breed cattle, and whittle sticks, and lead a nice easy life. The hell with all that corporation bullshit."

"I'm going to buy a yacht," said Daley. He put his feet up on the table opposite McNally's. "A schooner, seventy feet, or longer, ocean-going. Then I'm just going to sail."

"Why not come in with me on the ranch?" said McNally, swinging his feet to the floor and leaning forward. "You were raised on the land, weren't you?"

Daley smiled. "I know I used to talk about that in the service. It wasn't really true. My old man owned an orange grove in southern California. But I grew up in the East. At least, that's where I was educated." He paused, then went on in a different tone. "One thing I know. I'll never live in England again. I went through too much crap there."

"Yeah, I heard," said McNally. "I guess I should have tried to help, but . . ."

"The airline wasn't to blame," said Daley. "I was. I was a drunk. They had every right to fire me. If they hadn't, I might have killed a planeload of passengers." His hand trembled slightly as he brought his cigarette to his mouth.

"Relax," said McNally. "It's history."

Daley glanced at him, then stubbed out his cigarette. "Right," he said. "Subject closed."

"Think about that ranch idea, will you?" said McNally.

"Why not?" said Daley. "I guess I can afford to own a yacht *and* a ranch."

Daley rose and wandered outside. He looked through the trees at the beach and the anchorage beyond. The anchorage looked strange and bare without the sentinel presence of the Catalina.

McNally came to the door of the hut. "You sure Crab didn't say anything about scuba diving?" he said.

"That's the second time you asked me that," said Daley. "He didn't say anything to me. Why?"

"One of the suits is missing."

Daley felt a tingle of alarm pass through him. He turned to look at McNally. He looked worried.

"Maybe he did take it with him," Daley said. "Maybe he –"

"Have you seen Harris this morning?" McNally interrupted him.

Again Daley felt the tingle of alarm. "No," he said. "You don't think he'd go diving in the anchorage, do you?"

"No," said McNally, shaking his head. "He knew about the shark. Anyways, Crab took the dinghy with him this morning."

They looked at each other. "The shaft?" said Daley.

"Oh, Christ."

When they found the rope dangling from the winch bar into the shaft, they knew that Harris was down there. Something told Daley he was dead, but McNally would not give up hope.

"He might have gone straight from his hut," he said. "Because we haven't seen him doesn't mean he's been down too long. For all we know, he might have enough air for another thirty minutes."

"Where are his bubbles, Mac?" Daley said, peering down to the smooth surface of the water thirty feet below in the shaft. "If he's still down there, he's not breathing."

"Jesus Christ," said McNally bitterly. Then another thought struck him. "Maybe he only made a fast dive. Maybe he climbed out and went to check the seal at the beach."

"He'd have left his mask and tanks here," Daley pointed out.

Then moving to the other side of the shaft, he found Harris's clothes, folded in a neat bundle by the stack of timbers. "His clothes are here," he said quietly.

"Goddammit," said McNally, kicking the winch drum. "Why did he do this alone? Why?"

"He probably wanted to make sure the tunnel opening was there. Maybe he wanted to prove something to himself – that he could do it alone."

"By Christ, I'll be glad to get off this island," said McNally. "It's jinxed."

He was silent for a moment, then said: "One of us going to have to go down and bring him up."

"Before we get the pump, you mean?"

"We can't just leave him lying down there."

"Mac, you're not making sense. It's too big a risk. We don't have any idea why he drowned. Maybe the shaft caved in on him."

"Yeah, I guess you're right," said McNally. "Poor bastard, I hope it was quick."

Late that night, as they sat in the main hut, disconsolate and subdued, Crabtree came through on the radio from Papeete. They recognized his broad twang at once.

"Hello, Delta-Zero-Niner. Hello, Delta-Zero-Niner. This is Papeete Papa-One. Do you read? Over."

McNally went to the transmitter and picked up the mike.

"This is Delta-Zero-Niner. Come in, Crab. Over."

There was a brief burst of white sound, then Crabtree's voice came through.

". . . Papa-One, Bad news, fellas. I'm going to have to wait ten days for the pump. There's nothing available that we could use. It'll have to come in from Honolulu. Over."

"Just a minute, Crab," said McNally. He turned to Daley. "What d'you think? We can't last ten days without supplies."

"It means an extra trip, but what choice do we have?" said Daley.

McNally spoke into the mike. "Papeete-Papa-One, this is Delta-Zero-Niner. Crab, we need the supplies. We can't hold out for ten days, here. Isn't there any way you can get hold of a pump? Can you borrow one from a contractor? Over."

"I'll try again tomorrow," Crabtree promised. "Call you at noon. Papeete Papa-One out."

"Things are going sour on us, Mike," said McNally, switching off. "I don't like this island."

"Why didn't you tell him about Harris?"

"After what happened to his wife? If I'd said anything about Harris, some goddam official would have overheard it. That's the way our luck's going, right now. We'd have an army of investigators all over us within twenty-four hours."

Daley nodded. "I hadn't thought of that." He rose. "Maybe Crab can find us a pump tomorrow." He picked up his torch. "It's been a lousy day. I don't want to prolong it – I'm going to bed."

"Mike?"

Daley turned at the door.

"We're going to get the stuff out, aren't we?"

"What a chickenshit question," said Daley, forcing a smile.

As he walked to his hut, he noticed a curious stillness in the air. Usually at night, there was some faint movement off the anchorage, the lightest breath of a breeze. Tonight there was none. The stillness was unpleasant. The air seemed to hang like an invisible cloud, sultry and oppressive. And the insects, the background of sound at night since he had first come to the island, were hushed. Despite the heat, Daley shivered.

In the main hut, McNally sat staring at the table top. For the first time since he'd left San Francisco, he felt depleted, as if his sources of energy and optimism were drying up. He had been able to take the news of his financial collapse in his stride. It had simply made the search more worthwhile, had given an edge to it. But the death of Harris had shaken him in a way he did not understand. It was not as if he had been particularly close to Harris. He had hired him because he was a good engineer, that was all. It came to him that he was not really close to anyone, and suddenly he began to feel afraid. He gripped the edge of the table, and pulled himself together.

"You're OK," he told himself. "You're OK."

Both men slept badly.

"Hello, Delta-Zero-Niner, this is Papeete-Papa-One. Do you read? Over." McNally grabbed the mike.

"We read you, Crab. Delta-Zero-Niner, over."

"You bastards don't appreciate me enough. I've found a pump. Picking it up tonight. I'll leave at first light tomorrow, and be with you by late afternoon, over."

"Congratulations, Crab. You've saved the enterprise. Did you steal the damn thing? Over."

White sound blurred Crabtree's reply, then his voice came through. ". . . it might incriminate me. Isn't that what you Yanks say? See you tomorrow. Papeete-Papa-One out."

"Well, some good news at last," said McNally, turning from the radio with a broad smile. "I knew our luck would have to change sooner or later."

Crabtree set his polaroid wraparounds on his nose as he flattened out and headed into the sun. Behind him in the main compartment, stowed in its improvised trunk, was the water pump he had removed from a waterfront repair shop just before midnight. He had not borrowed the pump, since he had asked no one's permission, but he had not stolen it. He intended to return it when it had served its purpose on the island. The risk of a fine was well worth taking, when the water in the shaft was all that stood between them and the massive fortune at the bottom. M. Takalu, the owner of the pump, would just have to be patient.

When he had been flying an hour, he rose from his seat, put the aircraft on George and poured himself his first cup of coffee from the huge Thermos he always carried when he made trips alone. Flying alone was a big risk, because of the danger of sleep. There was no one to wake you. George was a primitive device, and could take no evasive action should it become necessary. And this far out, no radar or radio operators checked your course and called you up if you strayed. You were, in the most sobering and chilling way, utterly on your own. The air traffic people at Papeete didn't like it. The authorities didn't like it. Crabtree had grown used to having his flight plans re-written, curtailed, refused. Now he presented flight plans that were pure fiction, giving as his co-pilot and engineer the name of a man he had invented – I. M. Maverick. Many people on the island knew of this practice. No one questioned it. Crab-tree had conformed to the bureaucratic system of form-filling. What he did in reality was his own affair.

"Good on you, Maverick, you old bastard," he said to the empty co-pilot's seat. "You're all right." He gave his snorting chuckle, and finished his coffee.

Six hours later, with the Tuamotus behind him in the west, the port engine began to vibrate. It seemed to steady after a minute or two, and he waited to see if the shuddering would come back. After fifteen minutes, he relaxed, and finished eat-ing his sandwiches. Then the shuddering came again. Anxiously he hurried up into the observation post in the wing root. Wisps of white smoke were whipping back along the port cowling.

"Bugger it!" Crabtree swore, and clattered down the ladder. He hit the extinguisher as he got to his seat, and feathered the engine. The aircraft lurched, and he could feel it losing height. Now black smoke was pouring from behind the idly turning propeller. Crabtree stabbed the extinguisher again, and the smoke turned a sickly white. He gave the button a final push, exhausting the cylinder. He stared up through the perspex. The fire seemed to be out, but he could smell the fumes in the cockpit. He turned to check the instruments.

The aircraft had been flying on automatic for some time, and

Crabtree now saw, with disbelief, that the altimeter needle hovered just below 2000 feet. It couldn't be right, unless . . . unless he had been losing height, steadily, for more than an hour. He swore again. He would never be able to regain it now. Not unless he got the port engine started again, and could he take that risk?

He glanced again at the altimeter. He was down to eighteen hundred feet. He took a deep breath, and made his decision. His thumb found the self-start button on the console to his right. He pressed it. Nothing happened.

"Come on, you old bitch," he coaxed. He jabbed the button a second time. The whine was repeated, then the engine kicked over, caught, and was running. Crabtree let out a sigh, wiped his forehead, and with great caution eased open the throttle. The engine responded. He checked the gauges. Oil pressure was down and temperature was up, but these appeared to be returning to normal. Perhaps the engine would be all right, after all. He prayed that it would, and opened the throttle wider. Gingerly he hauled back on the stick. The aircraft began to lift.

He was concentrating so hard on his instruments that he did not see the birds until it was too late. Flying in a high, massed formation, less than half of them managed to scatter before the great mechanical gull was upon them. Three hit the windscreen with sharp, concussive thuds, spattering blood and feathers. Crabtree grunted with shock, his eyes wide. Seconds later, four more birds smacked right into the starboard engine. It stopped, pouring smoke.

Crabtree throttled back on the port engine. His position was now desperate, and he knew it. If the port engine failed again, he would go down. For a moment the engine seemed to pick up well. Then the sudden extra strain told. Thick black smoke belched from the cowling. Crabtree watched in horror as flames appeared, orange and menacing, curling out of the engine's guts.

He grabbed his ear-cans and pulled them on, yelling into the crescent mike.

"This is Papeete-Papa-One. Mayday-Mayday. Heading due east of Puka Puka, bearing – '

He never finished the sentence, for at that moment the port engine exploded. Pieces of the cowling and the propeller slammed into the cockpit perspex. Burning fuel cascaded through the air. The port section of the great wing, severed just inboard of the shattered cowling, shook like a sail, lifted and tumbled away. The body of the aircraft heeled to starboard, stricken. In the smashed cockpit, Crabtree clung to the curved prongs of the stick, his body hanging awkwardly across the seats and the console. He gasped, fighting to stay conscious. The aircraft was in a dizzying spin now. He kicked at the windscreen in a desperate attempt to get out. His boots were too light. He could not kick hard enough.

"Oh, Christ, Christ . . . not this way," he sobbed.

When the aircraft hit the water, a strut smashed through the cockpit floor and caught him on the side of the head, killing him instantly. The crippled fuselage floated for a long time, until the burning fuel was spent. Then the gutted remains settled in the swell, and slipped beneath it.

At dusk, Daley switched on the anchorage landing lights. He was beginning to be worried. Crabtree was overdue, even allowing for the possibility that he had taken off late, which was unusual for him. And if he had been late to take off, he should have let them know by now.

When he had not arrived an hour after dark, Daley walked back from the anchorage beach and joined McNally at the radio in the main hut.

"Any luck?" he asked as he came in.

McNally was hunched over the transceiver in the corner. "Still can't raise him," he frowned. "Either his set is O/C, or he's still in Papeete."

"But if he's still in Papeete, why doesn't he call us from the shore transmitter?"

"I don't know," said McNally. "Maybe he got drunk. Maybe he's in jail."

"Come on, Mac. You know he isn't that stupid."

"I'll try again," said McNally. "Come in, Papeete-Papa-One. Come in Papeete-Papa-One. This is Delta-Zero-Niner, over."

The set crackled. Both men were instantly alert, straining to hear.

"Hello, Delta-Zero-Niner. This is Weather Station X-ray-Whiskey-One-Four-Two. Do you copy? Over."

"We read you, X-ray-Whiskey. Come in, over."

"Delta-Zero-Niner, we picked up a very brief transmission at around thirteen hundred today. It could have been your buddy, but we're not sure. Signal was very weak, and we had no time to get a fix on that, over."

"Hello, X-ray-Whiskey. Was this a distress call? Repeat, was it a distress call? Delta-Zero-Niner, over."

"We don't know, fellas. All we got was the call sign. It sounded like the one you've been trying. Can you give us an indication of his course? Over."

The voice faded with the last words of the message, then grew clearer just as the ship's operator switched over. McNally gave him what details he could of Crabtree's probable course. The weather ship's captain came on and promised to relay the details to other ships in the area, and to listen in case Crabtree came back on the air.

McNally and Daley took it in turns to repeat the Catalina's call-sign over and over until their voices were hoarse. By midnight, when they had heard nothing, they stopped kidding themselves. The chances of Crabtree still being in the air were so remote there was no longer any point.

McNally had called Papeete after talking to the weather ship, and received definite confirmation of Crabtree's departure that morning from the air traffic controller. Crabtree had often made clear his belief that officials only got in the way, but now McNally called Tahiti again, and reported Catalina Papeete-Papa-One missing.

"Maybe he ditched," said Daley for the fifth or sixth time. "Maybe he'll be picked up."

McNally tried the call-sign one final time, and was about to give up and switch off when the weather ship came on. For a moment their hopes soared, as they listened to the ship's call-sign, but then were dashed.

"Sorry, Delta-Zero-Niner, still no news of your buddy. We've spun the dial. Thought you ought to know there's a depression building to the east of your position, which could develop into a storm. Take care. X-ray Whiskey-One-Four-Two, out."

McNally switched off the transceiver, went to the central table and slumped in one of the canvas chairs. Daley tried not to think about Crabtree. Sleep seemed impossible, so he searched through his papers on the desk and found some weather charts he had bought in San Francisco, thinking of the weather ship's message. He puzzled over the charts for several minutes, then took them over to the table, turned up the lamp, and spread them out. McNally ignored him.

"What about this, Mac?" said Daley. "The weather ship said we're going to get a storm, right? But according to these, that's not possible."

"Mike, I'm tired," said McNally.

"This is the wrong time of year," Daley persisted. "And we're too far east for – "

"Mike," said McNally in a warning tone, "I said I'm tired."

"OK," said Daley, and shrugged. He sat down. "Maybe he ditched," he said.

"Yeah," said McNally.

Two hundred miles to the east of the island, atmospheric conditions were altering in a way they were not supposed to alter. Layers of air, warm and moist, began to rise in a long, lazy spiral many thousands of feet into the night sky. A mass of clouds was forming. On the island itself the insects were still for the second night in a row. The air did not stir. It lay over the anchorage and the beach like a presence of evil.

Daley climbed into the crate. He signalled and McNally let the winch brake off. The drum turned, and the crate descended into the shaft. McNally watched until Daley signalled again, then reached back and re-applied the brake. Daley waited until the crate steadied on the end of the rope, then climbed over the side and hung by his hands. The crate swung, and began to spin slowly. Daley waited until it was over the exact centre of the shaft, then let go and sank backwards with a splash under the water.

He righted himself, and made sure his air supply was OK, then headed down. It was dark in the shaft, and the water, trapped in the earth, was surprisingly cool, almost chill. He switched on the torch at once. It was like swimming in a flooded elevator shaft. He could not see the bottom. The water was cloudy further down, and the sides of the shaft seemed far more confining than when they were digging. Here and there, he noticed, small flakes of earth had come away. The sound of his exhaled bubbles was exaggerated, like loud eruptions in his ears. He was reminded of the diving tank in San Diego, and this gave him more confidence. He had never been scared in the tank, despite stories other pilots told of horrible accidents.

Far above, McNally watched Daley's bubbles breaking the surface. He had hoisted the crate in order to see better, and silenced the winch. He was glad Daley was doing this first dive. A tossed coin had decided it. He was glad because finding Harris would not be pleasant. Still, there would be the compensation for Daley of locating the chests – if they were there. Now McNally picked up the Underwater Personal Radio helmet – the twin of Daley's he had brought to the shaft, and put it on. He felt faintly ridiculous in the plastic orange dome in the open air, but wearing it was the only way he had of communicating with his partner.

The radio worked by bone conduction. The voice set up vibrations in the skull which passed to a tiny transceiver, and were transmitted as audio waves. These waves were picked up by the other transceiver in Daley's helmet, converted back into vibrations, and passed by his skull to his inner ear as speech.

"Mike, can you hear me? How are you doing?"

Daley was surprised by the intimate clarity of McNally's voice – louder than by telephone. He had not used UWPR equipment before.

"I hear you," he said. "It's very dark down here. I'm about halfway down the shaft, taking it nice and slow. Still can't see the bottom. There's a lot of stuff hanging in solution down there."

"Any sign of a collapse in the shaft?"

"No," reported Daley. "Just little flakes here and there. I'm going on down now."

McNally waited for perhaps half a minute. He noticed that the atmosphere seemed very oppressive. He was sweating more than usual. The helmet felt hot and unpleasant.

Below, Daley could feel the pressure of water as he went lower. He swung the beam of his torch around the walls of the shaft. The beam passed over something just below him. He swung it back, and saw the gaping hole of the flood tunnel.

"Mac, I know where this cloudy solution has come from," he said. Speaking under water sounded and felt peculiar. Again McNally's reply startled him with its clarity. It was as if he was speaking inside Daley's head.

"Don't keep me in suspense."

"It's the earth from the flood tunnel, the earth plugging. I've found the entrance. It's right where we thought it would be. I'm going on down the last fifteen feet."

There was a pause of a few seconds, then McNally, crouched

by the head of the shaft, heard Daley give an involuntary hiss.

The beam of the torch had found Harris's body. The brilliant light gave the skin of his hands and wrists a greenish pallor in the cloudy water. His head was turned away, the face sunk in the mud at the bottom of the shaft, and he was lying in a grotesque sprawl. His backpack was loose, one strap broken. The air hose had come adrift. Daley swam over the body, careful not to disturb the mud.

"I've found Harris," he said. "His air hose broke."

"Do you want to come up?" McNally asked.

"Not yet," said Daley. "I just got here."

"Any sign of where the chests might be?"

Daley directed the beam away from Harris's body, and played it round the confining walls of the shaft. Apart from the fall of earth and rocks from the flood tunnel, he could see nothing new.

McNally waited for a short time, feeling sticky and flat. He grew impatient. "Mike?"

Daley's voice came through. "Yeah, I'm here. I'll have to use the probe. It's going to stir up more mud, but I'll just have to live with that."

Daley fumbled at his belt and located the length of wire he had tucked under it. He pulled it clear, and straightened it as best he could. He was trying not to bottom out and thus stir up a blinding, silty cloud of mud. He almost dropped his precious torch, and abandoned any further attempt to straighten the wire.

"What the hell are you doing?" came McNally's impatient voice.

Daley ignored him, and began to prod the crooked wire into the sides of the shaft, keeping up a slow tread with his flippers, and directing the torch beam at the wire. He had covered most of the shaft opposite Harris's body, when the probe struck a hard surface about three feet into the wall, and about four feet above the bottom. He trod water, and manœuvred himself back to the exact spot. The wire had come out, but he could see the hole it had made. He thrust the probe deep into the wall a foot from the last hole. Again it struck something hard.

"I've got something, Mac," he said.

"What? What is it?"

"Don't know yet. Give me a couple of minutes."

"OK, but remember, we have to conserve our air supplies. You have about fifteen minutes left."

"OK," said Daley. He was well aware of that limitation. After the dive to the ship, their backpacks had been left with only twenty-five minutes' effective supply. The spares had been used in the search for Jill Harris. When these cylinders were exhausted, they would be unable to reach the bottom of the shaft again until it was pumped dry. As of yesterday, that could be a long time away.

Now he thrust the wire probe a third time into the curved shaft wall. Again, at the same depth, it struck the solid surface. The probe had served its purpose, and Daley allowed it to drop from his fingers. He switched the torch to his other hand, the beam yawing eerily. The water was already cloudier. He unclipped the small trowel he had brought, and moved again to the wall. Where the marks of the probe scarred the surface, he began to scoop away earth. A flurry of mud obscured his vision for a moment. He worked on. The wall was soft, and the earth came out easily, like ice cream. Suddenly, a great section of the wall collapsed outwards. He felt earth and rocks fall against his legs. Desperately he clung to his torch. He could no longer see the beam, and his trowel had gone. He kicked hard, and swam upwards. The beam reappeared in a boiling cloud of silt. He steadied himself, and pointed the torch down. The bottom of the shaft was a black, impenetrable mass. Harris had disappeared.

"Mike, are you OK?"

"Yeah, I think so. I was probing the wall, and it collapsed."

"What did you find?" McNally's voice was tight with expectation.

"Give me a couple more minutes, until this damn silt clears a little. I can hardly see down here."

"You have eleven minutes," said McNally.

"Don't ride me, Mac," snapped Daley. "I'm doing the best I can."

He hung above the collapsed section for a further three minutes. Gradually the boiling clouds below began to subside. He swam down. Immediately visibility was reduced to no more than a couple of feet. He held the torch up and scrabbled in the gaping cavity. Silt at once enveloped him, and now he was utterly blind. His hand brushed the sharp corner of something. He felt for it and touched it again, this time with his fingertips. He grasped, and his hand closed over metal.

"I've got hold of . . . I've got hold of . . . I don't know what it is. It feels metallic."

McNally shifted his position and stared down into the shaft. The rippling surface of the water mocked him.

"It's some kind of large . . . Jesus, Mac, I think it's one of the chests." Daley's voice had risen to an excited pitch.

"Can you try to get it open?" said McNally.

"I can't see a damn thing here. I can't even see the torch-light."

"OK, OK, Mike. Just take it easy. You have six minutes air."

"I've got hold of it, now. It's tilted on one side, I think. No, wait, I can feel the top . . . it's curved. I can feel studs on the top. Hold it, I'm going to try to pull this back."

McNally could hear Daley's laboured breathing. He was using up air very fast.

"I've got it open," came his voice. "I'm trying to get this . . . I've got hold of something metal here. I'm trying to . . ."

"Mike, if you can't get it out, don't worry. Mike, can you hear me?"

"Yeah, I hear you," grunted Daley.

"Are you OK?" McNally waited anxiously. There was no reply. He repeated his question. Still there was no response.

"Mike, for Chrissake, will you answer me? Are you OK?"

McNally had already begun to strip off his clothes, when he heard a splash in the shaft. He thrust his head over the side. Daley's helmet broke the surface, then disappeared again. McNally dashed to the winch, and started it. He let off the brake, and the crate sank out of sight. When he heard it splash into the water, he hit the brake and hurried forward again. Daley had again broken surface. He seemed to be in extreme difficulties. McNally remembered that he was still wearing the helmet.

"Mike?" he yelled. "Are you OK?"

"Yes . . . I'm OK." Daley sounded exhausted.

"I'm coming down the rope," said McNally. "Try and get into the crate."

"Don't come down," said Daley. "How the hell will we get back up again?"

McNally saw his helmet disappear below the surface yet again. Then Daley came shooting up out of the water, and with a great heave, threw something over the side of the crate. The crate tilted, Daley gripped the side, paused a moment then dragged himself inside. McNally brought the crate up as fast as he could, gripped it and swung it in to the side of the shaft. Daley pulled off his helmet and mask, and jumped out. He staggered, and fell. McNally knelt beside him. Daley looked up at him and smiled. He was covered from head to foot in black mud.

"Jesus, you had me worried," said McNally. "I thought you'd gone the same way as Harris."

Daley sucked in air, then let it out, and sat up. "Take a look in the crate," he said. "I nearly didn't make it with that. It must weigh about forty pounds."

McNally went to the crate and peered into the bottom. Lying against the beading, in a coating of black slime, was an oblong block about a foot long. He reached into the crate and grasped it. It was extremely heavy. He had to use both hands to lift it at all. He carried it clear of the shaft and laid it on the ground. He got a rag from by the winch engine, and wiped the oblong clear of mud. It gleamed. Daley grabbed the rag and spat, then rubbed until the object was shining with a rich yellow glow.

"We don't have to look any further, do we?" said McNally.

Punched into the surface of the ingot was a crest and the words: "HISP – ETID". At one end was a date stamp – 1744 – and at the other a circular mark.

"That chest is full of these," said Daley. He laughed wildly. McNally joined in and they staggered about, laughing helplessly. Daley tripped over his flippers and collapsed in a heap. McNally picked up a clod of earth and threw it into the trees with a rebel yell. All the troubles of the past few days had slipped away. They were literally drunk with joy.

"At least we can afford to get back to Papeete, now," said Daley, wiping his eyes. A fresh spasm of laughter overtook him. "I thought . . . I thought we'd be stuck here for ever," he gasped.

Neither of them had noticed the deadly calm that had fallen over the island. The birds were silent. The insects might not have existed. The hush, except for the laughter of the two men, was absolute. The first clap of thunder shocked them into instant sobriety.

"What the fuck was that?" said Daley, sitting up. A second cracking explosion answered his question. Before the reverberations had died away, lightning jagged across the sky in a blue-white flash. The thunder was almost instant. The trees shook. The ground shook. The rain that followed a few seconds later turned the ground to mud in less than half a minute. And with the rain came wind.

Daley lost McNally somewhere on the path between the shaft and the huts. He could not see the path in the streaming rain. Gusts of wind lashed the trees, and whipped fronds and branches into his face. He struck out blindly in what he thought was the right direction, and kept going. The wind began to increase.

The storm, carrying at its front the massive wave of rain clouds, was about to become a hurricane as it passed over the island. It had not yet quite reached the height of its powers, but had Daley been able to see the satellite pictures that were printing out in the weather ship's operations room several hundred miles to the west, he would have noted the classic spiral bands of cloud. The long-range radar showed the same patterns. The weather ship's captain was worried. A hurricane this far east, and at this time of year, was without precedent. He could not bring himself to believe it. Yet the barometer was still falling.

Daley reached the huts. The wind had become a tearing force that he had to fight against to stay on his feet. He opened the door of the main hut, and was thrust headlong inside by the blast. Papers swirled like feathers. The trestle table tipped over and skidded to the far wall. Daley got behind the door and pushed with all his strength. He got it closed, and leaned against it, panting.

The whole structure was shaking like an animal in terror. Daley knew the door would not hold for very long. If the wind grew stronger – and it seemed to be growing stronger every minute – the whole hut would be threatened. He re-membered something he had read about that. Fragile structures could actually implode in winds beyond a certain ferocity. He would have to leave the hut soon if he did not want to be crushed, and take his chances. He waited ten minutes, in the vain hope that the storm might pass. Instead, it grew worse. The hut was beginning to vibrate around him. Clutching up some biscuits and a canteen of water, he gathered his strength, tensed himself, and opened the door.

Daley opened his eyes. He could hear the high, echoing calls of tropical birds. Insects ticked and churred close by. For a long moment he had absolutely no idea where he was. It was dark. He could hear the dripping of water. He seemed to be dressed in rubber. He sat up, and his head hit rock. Pain shot through his head, and lights flashed behind his eyes. He lay back, and the pain subsided into a dull, throbbing ache. As he felt the dry sand beneath him, he remembered. He was in a cave.

Weeks ago, before they had found the shaft, he had come up into the hills to escape the tensions of the camp. He had found the cave then, and yesterday, when the storm had threatened to tear him bodily into the air, the cave had saved his life.

He had tried to find McNally. It had been hopeless. He could not hear himself when he shouted at the top of his voice. He could barely see. Branches, sand and even stones flew through the air in the shrieking wind. After falling and gashing his leg as he was carried twenty yards through the scrub, he had clung to the base of a palm for a time, fighting to breathe, fighting to keep his hold, fighting simply to survive. It was then that he remembered the cave. He knew that if he could follow the little stream, he would reach the hills.

Somehow he found the stream. It was now a gushing torrent, and that made it easy to follow. The cave was not more than half a mile distant, but it took him an estimated two hours to reach it. His watch had smashed when he fell. Twice more he fell, and once an uprooted tree crashed across the stream only a few feet in front of him. He had never heard anything like the wind. It was as if an old-fashioned steam locomotive was rocketing through a tunnel at full speed with its whistle held wide open, and the whole of that sound was magnified ten times on some giant stereophonic amplifier. Even when he found the cave, hidden behind dense ferns, and crawled gratefully inside, the dreadful banshee scream was hardly diminished. Later, exhaustion blotted out the din, and he slept.

He crawled out of the cave into bright sunshine. At first glance, the island looked remarkably unscathed. He stood up, and at once pain lanced through his feet. He looked down and saw with surprise that they were crusted with blood. He must have come the whole way barefoot.

He cupped his hands, and shouted. "McNally?" His voice echoed down across the anchorage. Again he shouted. "Hey, Mac, are you there?" There was no reply. Hobbling painfully, he started down the hill towards the camp.

When he reached it, it was some minutes before he could be sure he was in the right place. There was nothing left of the huts. Not one scrap of roofing or one board or one piece of equipment. Everything had vanished. He wandered around in a daze, then came on a depression in the ground. He dug with a broken branch, and found the fuel store, the pit he and Crabtree had dug. He had been puzzled by the smoothness of the ground. Now he realized that everything was covered in a thick layer of sand. A huge wave had washed the beach inland. He found a stronger branch and resumed digging.

For the next three days, Daley worked almost without pause, breaking off only when exhaustion forced him to lie down and sleep. On the first day, he located the small stove, and some cans of food. He counted this as a good omen, and ate hungrily when he woke from his first nap.

Despite the severity of the hurricane, it was remarkable what he found and was able to collect together. He did not bother to construct even a crude shelter, since he did not expect another storm. Instead, he concentrated on gathering enough materials to build a raft.

After he found the stove and the food, he discovered some plastic sheeting in a twisted pile round a stump, and a coil of rope. He kept digging and searching, and accumulated some timbers from the huts, and some empty fuel drums. From the shaft he brought the crate, and then found another crate a short distance from the hut site, caught up in the undergrowth. On the second day, he made his most important discovery. He found the tool box.

On the third day, he began to build his raft. He used the timber and the fuel drums to make the hull, binding them together with lengths of rope. The two crates furnished a rough deck, and a makeshift deckhouse. A section of the smashed radio mast served as a mast, to which he rigged more rope and some of the plastic sheeting, to act as a sail. It took him all day to assemble his materials and bind and fit them together. Then he lay down and slept for twelve hours straight.

On the morning of the fourth day, he rose, breakfasted on fruit, and dragged the raft down to the water's edge. The anchorage beach had been washed away, and the sea now lay at the edge of the trees, so that the task of hauling the heavy raft was arduous, but not long. Now he began loading up for what he knew would be a very tough trip. He did not let himself think about what could happen on that trip. Work was better therapy for loneliness than speculation.

By noon he had stacked as much fruit as he could find and gather into the deckhouse. A row of Crabtree's empty gin bottles, filled with water, stood along the aft wall – it was hardly a bulkhead – behind the fruit. The rest of the tins of food followed, then the stove and a small drum of fuel. One box of matches in a waterproof box, found with the stove, completed his stores. He stood back and looked at them; the sight was not encouraging. At best he had enough for ten days, perhaps longer if he was careful and ate sparingly. He dismissed this from his mind, grabbed the rope he had secured for'ard of the mast, and dragged the raft into the shallows. It rode the water well, buoyant and steady. He was about to jump aboard when he remembered the ingot.

"Dammit," he said to himself with a short laugh, "at least I should take that with me."

He went back and got it, knowing it would be a risky extra weight on the flimsy timbers of the decking, but determined that it would not be left behind. There had been too much struggle and disaster suffered in the cause of getting it. To abandon it now would be like giving up on everything. He heaved it into the deckhouse, amongst the paw-paws and plantains and cans of beans, pushed the raft out until he was shoulder deep in the water, and pulled himself aboard, his sunburned back streaming.

He set his makeshift rudder – a shovel secured with ends of rope – and set the plastic sail. Half an hour later, having negotiated the tricky current off the beach, and beat around the spit, he put his primitive helm down and headed into the open sea.

A mile out, he looked back at what had been his home for all those weeks, and had almost been his grave. The palms stood like sentinels against the skyline, but the beaches looked friendly and inviting. There might never have been a hurricane; there might never have been anything but peace there, thought Daley. He turned away from his last sight of land for he did not care to wonder how long, and scanned the horizon ahead.

On the island, a quarter of a mile inland, a small island dove hopped across the splintered trunk of an uprooted tree. It cocked its head on one side, its tiny eyes blinking, then hopped down on to the sand. Everything was quiet and still. The little bird hopped away, its stick feet avoiding a column of ants. Beneath the tree, the ants were eating McNally.

Epilogue

Her Majesty's Ship *Derby*, one of Britain's new Type 42 destroyers, was on her first long cruise, bound for San Francisco out of Hong Kong, via Singapore, Sydney, Suva, the Phoenix Islands and Honolulu. She had been commissioned only a few months. At 0430 hours on October 16, she was on a manœuvres detour four hundred and twenty miles north of Christmas Island, proceeding on a north-easterly course at her standard cruising speed of eighteen knots.

Lieutenant Richard Jarvis was the officer of the watch on the *Derby*'s bridge. Of the ship's complement of two hundred and eighty officers and ratings, Jarvis was the only one suffering from toothache. It had kept him awake for the past three nights, and he was tired. The gin he had drunk before dinner had not subdued it; instead he had a mild hangover. At 0400 hours, before coming on watch, he had drunk a cup of very hot sweet galley tea, in an attempt to revive himself. All he felt now was resentment at having to be on watch at all.

Jarvis knew that he should be feeling, if not elated, at least pleased. He was effectively in command of a superb fighting ship. The *Derby*, 3500 tons and 392 feet long, could knife through the water at better than thirty knots. She could alter course incredibly fast, utilizing reversible-pitch propellers, and the full thrust of her Rolls-Royce Olympus gas turbines. She could launch twin medium-range STA missiles in seconds,

Epilogue

and guide them to their target with lethal accuracy. Her three radar systems, her torpedo-equipped helicopter, and her automatic medium range 4.5 inch gun could back up this capability in defence. She could communicate with any place on earth by means of her Skymast satellite communications system. The bridge was clustered with neatly laid out instruments and read-out screens, which told him in an instant what was happening in the engine room, in the radar room, in the communications room. He could tell at a glance exactly what could, would or might happen to the ship under half a dozen differing sets of circumstances. All he had to do was push buttons, flip switches. He was – in a very real sense – in a position of power. Yet all he felt was irritation and lurking weariness.

The middle hours of the early morning were the worst of the whole day. It was not that they were eventful. It was because they were the opposite that the 0400–0800 hours watch was a bad one. Nothing happened. Even on manœuvres in the open sea like this – where the captain could, and sometimes did, call every man to battle stations without warning – nothing happened. The ship was not on an exercise. She was proving herself. Officially of course, she was in a state of readiness. But in practice, during this watch, the Derby was taking it easy. Routine conversation amongst those on watch tended to slacken to a minimum after a short time. There were times when individual members of the watch drifted into a semi-hypnotic state, in which the real world around them receded into the background, and the fantasies of the mind began to take over. It was therefore potentially a dangerous watch, and Jarvis knew it. He was fighting against this process of hypnosis even now.

Below decks, in the electronic bowels of the ship, the radar room was humming with subdued activity. Men might grow bored, or indifferent, or inattentive, in spite of all their training. Electronic equipment is subject to none of these drawbacks.

213

At 0549 hours, the radar room cut into Jarvis's blurring thoughts on the bridge far above.

"Bridge? Radar."

Jarvis started, and looked at the patterned metal grille of the amplifier. For a moment, he did not react further. He had let himself drift into a reverie about a girl he had known three years before, and his mind jammed in confusion.

"Bridge? Radar."

The second curt electrical demand pulled his attention back to the present, and he reached for the flexi-arm mike, thumbed the button and said: "Bridge."

The radar operator's voice came back clipped and efficient. "Sir, we're getting a very small signal at green three-six – could be wreckage."

"Wreckage?"

"The missing yacht, sir."

"Oh yes, the yacht." There had been a report of an ocean-going pleasure craft missing somewhere in the area. Jarvis thumbed the button again, and said: "What's the range?"

"Range: six-five-double-oh, sir."

"Thank you. I'll have a look."

"It's on the GPR, sir."

Jarvis rose from his conning chair, stretched briefly and moved to the auxiliary General Purpose Radar screen. He punched buttons and the screen came to life. He saw the blip at once. It was the only signal on the screen. He punched more buttons on the read-out TV screen beside the radar, and read the figures for range, and direction. The fact that the range was decreasing and his green (starboard) read-out was increasing indicated that the object was stationary and that they would pass to port of it. If it was the yacht, or what was left of it, they had better take a look. Jarvis resumed his chair, and pulled the mike to his mouth.

"Half ahead. Starboard ten."

His orders were repeated, and the ship slowed and came

round to the new heading. Next Jarvis informed the captain of what he was doing. Within three minutes, the captain himself was on the bridge.

Captain George Trevor was a slim, energetic man in his early forties. He was known as a stickler for efficiency. He never left details to chance in anything he did. He was conscious at all times – even fighting his way out of sleep to come up to the bridge over an unimportant radar contact – that he was in command of an expensive, complex and demanding entity, a modern warship. Many captains would have left such a radar contact to the devices of their officers, turned over and gone back to sleep. For a man like Trevor, that was impossible.

"What have we got, Number One?" he said as he came on to the bridge. Jarvis noted that he had dressed, even in that short time, before replying: "Might be the wreckage of that missing yacht, sir."

"Mmm." Trevor peered out into the night. It was still too early for even the faintest glimmerings of dawn. "What's the range?"

"One thousand, sir. I've got a man on the starboard searchlight."

"Good. What do we hear?"

"Nothing on RT, sir."

"Mmm-hmm. Fine, carry on." Trevor climbed into a chair beside Jarvis, and waited for his ship to close the object of their attention. Jarvis, his attention sharpened further by the captain's presence, had forgotten his toothache for the first time in seventy-two hours.

On its first pass, the *Derby* failed to make visual contact with the object in the water. A light wind had risen, making the surface choppy. In the brilliant arc of the searchlight, it was difficult to be sure of anything except the uneven waves. The ship passed beyond the spot, and the blip was still there on the radar screens. Jarvis reduced speed and brought the *Derby* about. He knew this was what Trevor wanted, although the captain had said nothing. Neither man wanted to resume course until the little mystery had been solved. On the second pass, they saw nothing either.

"Well, sir. Have we done our duty?" Jarvis looked across at the captain.

"Oh, we've done that, all right. But we haven't found the bloody thing," said Trevor. "Let's have one more look, Number One."

On the third pass, they found it. A low, sluggish shape in the beam of the searchlight, two hundred yards on their starboard beam. Jarvis was staring at it through his night glasses when the captain said: "That's not part of a yacht. More like a floating bedstead."

Jarvis lowered his glasses and grabbed the mike. "Stand by to lower your boat. Stop engines."

"Stop engines."

Daley did not wake up. He edged back into consciousness. He was not aware of his surroundings, or of his condition. He knew simply that there was a very bright light, and that human voices seemed in some way connected with it. He did not attempt to move. He had given up movement some time ago, during a hopeless attempt to catch a seabird, that had hovered overhead for a few minutes. His legs had not worked for days, but when he tried to reach for the bird, he had found that his arms would not work either. Later, he began to hallucinate.

The light was so bright that the cracks and holes in what was left of his deckhouse showed in strips and blotches on the rotting decking beneath his inert body. He could just move his head enough to look in the direction of the light, but he could not raise his head. He lay, slumped and helpless, listening to the voices.

"Can you see anything, Miller?"

"It's some kind of a raft, sir."

216

"Yes, I can see that. Can you see any sign of life?"

"No, sir. The cabin, or the shelter, seems to have collapsed."

"Come alongside, now."

"Yes, sir."

Daley became aware of a second light, a light that moved, independent of the blinding big light. He tried to imagine what on earth was going on. It was a pity he couldn't move, and it was no use trying to call out. His voice was lost in the harsh constrictions of his throat, and his tongue lay like a huge unchewable lozenge in his mouth, thick and dead.

"Doesn't seem to be anything in there," said one of the voices.

"No, sir. I should say the poor bastard's jumped overboard, or was washed over."

"It can't be from the yacht. It's been in the water a good while."

"No, this never came off a yacht, sir."

"All right, Miller. I think we've seen enough."

There was the sound of a small engine revving, and the second light disappeared. Daley lay staring at the cracks in the wrecked deckhouse wall just by his head. The big light was still there. What did it mean? He concentrated very hard, trying to recall some details from his memory that would help him solve the mystery. Those men had sounded as if they were looking for someone, or something. Yet they obviously had not been looking for him, Daley. Because he, Daley, was safe. He would go undetected, and float to the shore of the river. On the bank, in his tent, there was a meal waiting. And a soft inflatable bed. But he would have to wait until his raft drifted into the bank first. It might take a little time. Daley closed his eyes again. Then, quite suddenly, it came to him where he was.

"Sub-Lieutenant Garrick, sir."

Jarvis turned from peering at the half-submerged raft

through his glasses. The searchlight was still trained on it.

"Let's have your report."

"There's no sign of life, sir. It's a purpose built raft, all right, but not from our missing yacht. It's been in the water far too long – weeks, perhaps months. Obviously been knocked about by the weather, too."

"All right. Go down to the captain's cabin straight away, will you. He wants to hear."

"I'm sorry about the radio malfunction, sir."

"Yes, never mind. These things happen. You might even get a drink out of it."

Sub-Lieutenant Garrick made his way to the captain's cabin, carrying the small personal radio which had failed to work when he tried to report back from the raft itself. By the time he had explained this to the captain, and made his brief report, Trevor was anxious to get under way. He had found this little early morning diversion stimulating; it had broken routine, and given his officers and men something to do in an otherwise dreary watch. But if they were to reach Honolulu on schedule, they could not afford to waste any more time on an abandoned, waterlogged raft. He contacted the bridge that the ship should be got under way.

Jarvis gave his orders on the bridge, the turbines hummed, and *Derby* turned back on to her original course. She was already up to full cruising speed, her wake boiling behind her low, neat stern, when a rating shouted: "Look, sir! There's a fire!"

Jarvis whirled, irritated by the imprecision of the warning, and frightened also. Then he saw the rating pointing not at a part of their own ship, but away to the starboard quarter. And there, down on the waterline, was the unmistakable glowing and flickering of flames.

"They've got him into the sickbay, sir. I understand his hands are rather badly burned."

Captain Trevor finished pouring his coffee. Light was beginning to filter through the porthole above his head. He turned, and his face was set.

"Dick, how the hell did we miss him?"

"I'm sorry, sir. The search probably wasn't conducted as well as – "

"Probably!" snapped Trevor, his coffee cup poised in mid-air. He put it down. "That's not the sort of word I'd expect from you, Dick."

"I'm sorry, sir. You're right, of course. It was pure in-efficiency."

"And stupidity," said Trevor. "I'll want to see Sub-Lieutenant Garrick."

"Yes, sir." Jarvis hesitated, then spoke up. "I don't think we should be too hard on him, you know. It wasn't his fault about the radio. And conditions weren't exactly ideal."

"For God's sake, Dick, this is a warship. We don't need ideal conditions to perform our duty, and carry out operations properly. This was a plain, old-fashioned cock-up. Well, I won't have that sort of thing. Is that clear?"

"Yes, sir."

"How is he?"

"Sir?"

"The poor bugger we fished out of the water? Is he con-scious?"

"Not yet, sir," said Jarvis, relieved that the storm was past. "Apparently he's very weak. And, er . . . there are the burns, from the fuel he used to start the fire."

"Yes, that's our fault." Trevor sighed. Although his tone was still severe, a note of compassion had crept in. "Let's just hope the poor bugger doesn't die, that's all."

Daley opened his eyes. Everything around him seemed to be white. For a moment he thought he was back in the nursing home in England. Then he saw the round heavy glass of the light fixture in the ceiling, and remembered that he was at sea.

He turned, with some effort, on his side, and tried to reach for the glass of water on the locker by his bed. His hands were enormous in their bandages, and he could not manage it. A sickbay orderly appeared and held the glass for him, propping him up so that he could drink.

"Have . . . they . . . got . . . the raft?" Daley managed to husk.

"What's that, me old flower?" said the orderly, bending his head.

"Have they got my belongings . . . from the raft?"

"I think they was taken up to the captain for safe-keeping, like," said the orderly.

"Uh-huh," said Daley, and sank back on his pillow. Then he smiled.